© Alexandra Rose Scott

Philip Elliott is an award-winning author, freelance editor, and founder and editor-in-chief of award-winning literary journal and small press publisher Into the Void. Philip was a National Juror of the 2019 Scholastic Art & Writing Awards, and a winner of the 2018 Big Pond Rumours Chapbook Prize. His writing has been nominated for The Pushcart Prize and Best of the Net. A music and film obsessive, Philip lives in Toronto with his wife and their spoiled pug.

 p   pelliott__

Praise for Nobody Move

"Elliott has a real feel for comedic noir in the Elmore Leonard vein, and his debut novel screams cult classic (think Matthew McBride's *Frank Sinatra in a Blender*, 2012)"
—*Booklist*

"gritty, breathless…[female and transgender characters] have charisma, toughness, and dynamism…Elliott's descriptions of [L.A.] are impressively and effectively atmospheric…A multifaceted series opener by a promising new voice in hard-boiled crime fiction. Fans of Elmore Leonard and Jim Thompson will find much to savor"
—*Kirkus Reviews*

"a new spin on the crime thriller genre"
—*San Francisco Book Review*

"sharp, stylish and well-written. It makes reading fun again"
—*US Review of Books*

"fast-paced and chock full of interesting characters [and] chillingly delicious evil"
—*IndieReader*

"like Tarantino on the page…rushes at you from page one"
—Dietrich Kalteis, award-winning author of *Poughkeepsie Shuffle*

NOBODY MOVE

AN ANGEL CITY NOVEL

NOBODY MOVE

PHILIP ELLIOTT

Library and Archives Canada Cataloguing in Publication

Title: Nobody move / Philip Elliott.
Names: Elliott, Philip, 1993- author.
Description: "An Angel City novel."--Cover.
Identifiers: Canadiana (print) 20190093536 | Canadiana (ebook) 20190093552 | ISBN 9781775381358
  (softcover) | ISBN 9781775381365 (EPUB) | ISBN 9781775381372 (Kindle) | ISBN 9781775381389 (PDF)
Classification: LCC PR6105.L53 N63 2019 | DDC 823/.92—dc23

Published in Canada by Into the Void
Printed in the United States of America
Typeset: Adobe Caslon Pro
Designed by Into the Void
www.intothevoidmagazine.com

For my parents
who have always supported unwaveringly
all of my wild ideas

I steal from every single movie ever made.

—QUENTIN TARANTINO, *Empire*, November 1994

ELMORE LEONARD on *Charlie Rose*, 02/17/1999:

Rose: *Do you read a lot, Elmore?*

Leonard: *Not as much as I used to . . . I'd rather watch TV.*

NOBODY MOVE

1 | City of Angels

Something was off. Everything was off. Eddie could feel it. Felt it ever since he woke up this morning, in fact, that sense of something, everything, being . . . off. Not that anything had been right to begin with. Fucking season was off, that was for sure. Summer in L.A. and rained every day for the past two weeks. When Saul had called his cell right as he'd sat down with some shitty Chinese takeout for a relaxing night of shitty TV and said "Eddie, I need you to make a house call. Floyd will pick you up in thirty" and Eddie said, "What, right now? What the guy do, shit on your lawn?" and Saul didn't even answer, just hung up, Eddie knew that something was off about the whole thing and his sense of foreboding with him since breakfast had been very fucking apt indeed. Now, walking through a hallway toward the guy's condo, about to wave a gun around and threaten murder, the sensation had only increased.

"We just putting the fear into him," Floyd said. "Owes big. Boss said Bill always pays, but he late and we gotta scare his ass."

"Why such short notice?" Eddie said.

"Bill made a surprise visit to town, that's why. I watched a movie with the wife last night. *No Country for Old Men.* You seen it?"

"Nah."

"Watch that shit. There's a hitman, looks like the devil if the devil was a cowboy. Cold motherfucker. Don't even use a normal gun. Instead uses a cattle gun. A fuckin' cattle gun. Carries around a tank of gas."

They reached Bill's door and faced each other.

"Sounds inconvenient," Eddie said. "The gas tank."

"Point is, this hitman has a thing for fate. Flips a coin and makes you choose if you gonna live or die. And that's it. That's the only chance you got with this nigga. He don't care about money, and he don't care about what you have to say. He flips that coin, you live or you die."

"Sounds fair."

"Fair? What's fair about killing a motherfucker?"

"Not that part, the coin toss. Everyone gets an equal chance."

"Yeah, but you can't buy your way out of it with this man, or reason with him."

"So he's got principles," Eddie said.

"You think there's people like that?"

"Sure. Why not?"

"The man don't make sense. Who don't want money?"

"You probably wouldn't make sense to him."

"So, you think there's badass killer cowboys walking around, flipping coins and bustin' caps?"

"There's every kind of person in this world."

Floyd faced the door. "I ever meet a motherfucker like that, I got some questions. You ready?"

Eddie nodded.

Floyd pounded on the door.

It opened to a fat man in a silken dressing gown, his hairy chest exposed, a gold chain dangling over it. A thick mustache sat like a tarantula above his lips.

"You must be Bill," Floyd said.

"Who the fuck are you?"

"The Angel of Mercy." Floyd shoved Bill into the apartment, the man slipping on the tile and falling onto his ass, a pale testicle flopping out of his boxer shorts. "Or the Angel of Vengeance. Depends whose door I'm knocking on."

Eddie couldn't help smirking. The man should be on the stage.

Floyd stepped forward as Bill crawled backwards through the kitchen toward the living area. An aquarium

3

built into the wall on the right cast a shimmer across his face, a dozen neon fish swimming in circles inside it like a gang of simpletons.

"God sent us here, Bill," Floyd said. "He ain't happy with you."

"What are you talking—"

"What city we in right now, Bill?"

"Los Angeles."

"And who's God round here?"

Realization dawned on Bill's face. "I'll get the money." Pulling himself onto the sofa. "That's what I'm here for, in L.A. Collecting a payout. I just need a couple more days."

"Oh, you'll get the money? Well shit, why didn't you say so? You hear that Eddie? It's all good, man gonna get the money, our work here is done." Floyd took a step away from Bill and spun, fist raised. The blow hit hard: Bill slid off the sofa, little moans spilling out of him.

"Listen to me you redneck motherfucker and listen good," Floyd said, "'cause if I have to repeat myself, I'll fuck up the other side of your face too. You ever try take a piss with two eyes swollen up like balloons, Bill? You can't see the toilet, you're hitting the floor, the walls, the fuckin' ceiling. It ain't fun."

Floyd paused, relaxing his shoulders. "I can't leave here empty-handed, Bill."

"I don't have the money right now, but I can get it tomorrow."

"Didn't I just warn you about making me repeat myself?" Floyd sighed, and pulled his pistol out of the waist of his blue suit. Bill shivered like a canary.

That sense of foreboding came over Eddie again. He could feel himself getting paranoid, thinking what if it meant something terrible, grim reaper with a bony hand on your shoulder, all that shit. It wasn't the thought of dying that scared him—when you've been breaking into people's homes and moving product and waving guns around every day for two years the idea of death becomes about as scary as a dinner party with strangers—it was the thought of this being all he ever amounted to: *Eddie Vegas? Yeah, I remember him. Low life criminal, right? Used to work for Saul Benedict, run around pretending to be a thug? Oh, he's dead? Fuck 'im, he had it coming.*

Floyd said, "You know, Bill, it's been a long time since I killed somebody for the first time." Observing the gun in his hand, looking sad and contemplative. More theatrics. "The shit just don't bother me no more. I can shoot a nigga and walk straight into McDonald's, get some fries and a Coke, enjoy myself. But that don't mean I like killing people. It's a pain in the ass, Bill, to be straight with you, disposing of the body, cleaning the place, checking the newspapers . . ."

Eddie watched Bill. If any more blood left his cheeks the man would collapse.

"But at the same time," Floyd continued, "sometimes the best option is to get rid of the problem, remove it from your life, 'cause it just ain't worth the headache . . ."

A female voice drifted from somewhere to the right, so quiet Eddie might have imagined it. He frowned. No, there it was again; almost inaudible, but there.

"Hey, Floyd, you hear that?"

Floyd looked back at him. "Hear what?"

"Listen."

Floyd cocked his head. His eyes narrowed.

"You got someone in here with you, Bill?" he said.

Bill shook his head.

"Watch him," Floyd said. "I'll check it out."

Floyd moved toward the closed door to the right of the living area. Eddie took his pistol out of his jeans and pointed it at Bill.

Floyd opened the door and the woman's voice spilled into the room like a song. She was moaning vigorously, without a doubt being fucked in there.

"What in the hell . . ." Floyd said, staring into the room open-mouthed.

When Eddie faced Bill again the fucker was up and running at him, a wild determination in his eyes and the dressing gown flapping madly behind him.

"Fuck," Eddie said, and before he could make a decision, before he could even think about it, his finger tightened around the trigger. Bill's head flung backwards and his body followed, thumping against the floor. He lay sprawled on his back, blood dribbling out of the hole in his skull where an eye had been seconds before.

A moment of silence.

Floyd said, "You best have a good explanation for that."

Eddie just looked at him. The woman's moaning continued.

"Fuck you shoot him for?"

"I don't know, shit, he ran at me—"

"Ran at you? Why didn't you just hit him? Look at his fat ass—this ain't some Bruce Lee motherfucker."

"I didn't mean to, I just reacted—"

"Man, shut the fuck up." Floyd shook his head. "Saul gonna be pissed. Redneck owed him fifty Gs."

"Fuck."

"Yo' problem now."

"What?"

"You got to pay Saul."

"Do I look like I have that kinda dough?"

"You better start looking like it 'cause Saul ain't gonna shrug his shoulders and say 'Shit happens' over fifty Gs."

"Fuck. I'm fucked."

"No shit."

"What am I gonna do?"

Floyd tucked the pistol into his trousers. "Help me move his fat ass into that room while we figure out how to get him down the elevator."

"What was in there?"

Floyd smirked. "See for yourself."

Eddie stuck his head into the room and gasped. Four

TV screens—one on each wall—played the same porno flick in sync; the entire floor was covered in squishy foam, the kind found in a martial arts gym; shelves at the back held what must have been the largest and most colorful dildo collection ever assembled; and, in the center of the room, a sex swing hung from the ceiling like suspension lines from a parachute.

"Christ," Eddie said.

"Motherfucker got issues."

Floyd grabbed Bill under each arm. "Get his legs."

Eddie lay his gun on the coffee table, his hand shaking as the adrenaline faded and cold reality took its place. He lifted Bill's heavy legs. Floyd shimmied backwards and Eddie shuffled after him, Bill's bloody face at his crotch. This close the man reeked of sweat and smoke. Eddie couldn't look at him.

They'd made it halfway when keys jangled in the front door of the apartment. They froze, Bill swaying between them.

The door opened and a young woman entered, humming to the music blasting from her headphones. She closed the door, placed her handbag on the marble countertop, breezed over to the fridge, and withdrew a carton of orange juice.

Eddie looked at Floyd, who looked back at him.

The woman took a swig from the carton and turned. Her eyes found Eddie and doubled in size. The juice hit the floor. Nobody moved.

The woman bolted for the door. Floyd went after her, Bill's skull thumping against the tile. The woman made it into the hallway for a grand total of three seconds before Floyd dragged her back into the apartment, hand clamped over her mouth. She kicked and screamed and thrashed her arms about.

"Ow," Floyd said, retracting his hand from her face as she flung her limbs at him. He punched her in the head and she crumpled to the floor. "Bitch bit me."

The woman lay sprawled on the tile, barely conscious. They observed her for a moment.

"Now what?" Eddie said.

"You know what. Find something to keep her quiet with case she wakes up and starts screaming. I'm gonna call Sawyer."

Eddie found duct tape in a kitchen drawer. The woman came to life as he stuck it over her mouth and immediately tried to scream, her fingers clawing at him. He removed his belt and tied her hands behind her back, then pointed the gun at her and made her kneel on the floor beside Bill.

Her eyes, screaming out of her head, terrified him. She couldn't have been older than twenty.

"I don't know about this," he said. "It's not right."

"Was it right when you did him?" Floyd nodded toward Bill.

"This is different."

"You wanna live the rest of your life in a six-foot

prison cell? 'Cause I'll die before I go there again."

The woman screamed from behind her duct-taped lips.

Floyd said, "Best to use the same gun. Give it to me."

Eddie's heart hammered on his ribs. He looked at the pistol, a Smith & Wesson SD9, like an anchor in his fist.

The woman's squeals became unbearable.

"Shut up," he yelled. The gun rose and stared at her.

She went stiff as a surfboard.

Eddie could feel Floyd's gaze on his neck. A sour taste filled his mouth, his hand sliding on the coarse grip.

"Do it already," Floyd said. "Or I will."

Eddie stared into the woman's eyes. She looked familiar, the kind of young woman you'd pass on the street and think of as smart and confident and cute all at once.

"Eddie," Floyd said, stepping forward.

There was no other way. Eddie stilled his breath, said "I'm sorry," and squeezed.

2 | Angeles National Forest

Any number of bodies could be buried in Angeles National Forest. Eddie remembered a news report a few months back about a man from Glendale clubbed to death and buried in a shallow grave off Big Tujunga Canyon Road. Cadaver dogs sniffed out the corpse after a hiker spotted pools of blood. The guy had been murdered so his killers could rob him. At the time it had seemed like a lot of trouble to go through just to steal from someone, but Eddie saw it differently now. Sometimes things unravel faster than you can keep up with them.

When Floyd told Eddie that the forest was where they'd be bringing the bodies, fear scraped a cold finger down his spine. Or maybe it was that reaper again.

"You done this before?" Eddie said.

"You really wanna ask me that?"

"How we gonna get them out there?"

"Sawyer's on the way in the S.U.V. He'll wait round the corner to avoid the cameras in the parking lot. Hard part will be getting them out this building."

"Any ideas?"

Floyd glanced at the two corpses sprawled across the foam floor of the sex room. Eddie had turned the porn on the TVs off, out of respect, and now a dreadful silence choked the air out of the room whenever they stopped speaking.

"One time, on an episode of *The Americans*, they hid a dead woman inside a suitcase," Floyd said.

"Christ."

"Had to break most of her bones first, though."

"Oh fuck, I'm not doing that."

"But wasn't the biggest suitcase. Redneck over there probably got a bigger one."

"Even if he does, no way he's fitting in it."

"No, but she will."

"Okay, let's say we find a suitcase for her," Eddie said. "What do we do with him?"

He gnawed on a nail, wondering how the hell to move the fat bastard. It reminded him of the time his uncle Harvey had a stroke and fell down the stairs. Poor guy couldn't walk for two weeks—

"Call Sawyer," Eddie said. "I have an idea."

They found a large suitcase and just about managed to fit the woman inside in the fetal position. Looking at her cramped in there, still as a doll, Eddie knew he'd crossed a line that could never be uncrossed. Shit, he'd be lucky to ever sleep again.

They wiped the place down with bleach while they waited for Sawyer, then sat on the sofa and watched cartoons, the same sofa they'd scrubbed clean of blood and shards of brain.

Ten minutes later someone knocked on the door. Eddie nearly jumped.

"Who there?" Floyd said.

"Jack Nicholson. Who you fucking think?"

Floyd opened the door and Sawyer strolled inside pushing a wheelchair.

"Got your wheels," he said to Eddie in his Southern drawl.

"Where'd you get it from?"

"Stole it from some guy on the street."

"You a bad motherfucker, stealing from a cripple," Floyd said.

"Least I didn't shoot him."

They lifted Bill into the wheelchair. Eddie found a cowboy hat in the bedroom and put it on Bill's head, the front tipped down over the hole through his skull.

"Ready to do this?" Floyd said.

No one answered him.

"Sawyer, you go down first, by yourself," Floyd said. "Look suspicious we all walk out together."

"He brought the wheelchair up," Eddie said. "It would be suspicious if he leaves without it, then we come down with Bill."

"All right, we all go, fuck it," Floyd said.

"Who's pushing the wheelchair?" Eddie said.

"Don't look at me, I ain't the one shot him," Sawyer said.

Floyd didn't say anything, didn't have to.

They made it to the elevator unseen, Eddie pushing Bill in the wheelchair, his head lolling side to side, and Floyd dragging the world's heaviest suitcase. Sawyer kept in front of Eddie in an attempt at hiding how dead Bill looked.

The elevator opened to the gleaming marble of the ground floor. An old couple chatted in a corner, away from the front doors. Otherwise, the place was empty, except for the concierge who hadn't noticed them yet.

"Someone needs to distract the guy behind the counter. I'll do it if you push him," Eddie said to Sawyer, eager to be rid of the corpses.

"Do it then."

Eddie strolled toward the concierge. "Hey, how you doin'? I'm hoping you could help me find someone." At the edge of his vision Floyd and Sawyer began moving.

"Find someone?" the concierge, a clean-cut guy in his thirties, said.

"Yeah, see, I, to be totally honest with you, I met this girl at a bar last night. Smoking hot. I mean *sizzling*. She gave me her number, told me to call her today, but, wouldn't you know it, I lost my cell. All I know is her name's Abigail, she's mid-twenties with dark hair and a figure that'd make the pope sin."

The guy looked amused. "I see. That's . . . unfortunate, but, unfortunately, I can't give out information about the people who live here."

Floyd and Sawyer passed behind Eddie, halfway to the front doors. The concierge spotted them, his gaze following them now, a frown forming on his face.

"I know, man, I know," Eddie said, shuffling to the side to block his view. "I'm not gonna ask you to give out any information, I was just hoping I could leave a note with you and when you see her, you give it to her, that's all. You'd make my whole week."

"I would do that," the concierge said, looking at Eddie now, "except no one by the name of Abigail lives here."

"You know everybody's name who lives here?"

"I do," the concierge said with a whiff of pride.

"I'm impressed." Eddie glanced at the front doors. No sign of them. "I must have the wrong address then. Maybe she was bullshitting me the whole time. Either way, I drink too much. Thanks anyways." He tapped on the counter and made for the doors.

"Wait," the concierge said.

Eddie froze, heart in his ears. He turned around.

"It might be the building across the street," the concierge said. "People always confuse it with ours."

"I'll check it out. Thanks," Eddie said, and strode out the building, relief surging through his bones.

Twenty miles outside the heart of the city, Angeles National Forest was a different universe. Sawyer drove the S.U.V. through narrow windy roads flanked by rocky hills, the headlights the only source of light aside from a crooked moon hanging above them like the eye of a sleeping god.

Eddie had his window down, the warm air that smelled of citrusy pine slapping life into him.

"This place gives me the creeps," he said.

"Yeah, feels like you might run into someone burying a couple bodies," Sawyer said.

Floyd snorted a laugh.

"Where we digging?" Sawyer said, running a hand through his shoulder-length blond hair.

"I know a spot near the observatory," Eddie said. "A ditch behind some bushes. Used to hang out around here a lot when I was a kid. Never imagined I'd be doing this."

"No shit," Floyd said. "Otherwise you'd be one fucked-up kid."

They circled Mount Wilson as they climbed it, the observatory appearing out of the night like a phantom. Sawyer parked the S.U.V. off the road among a cluster of trees and killed the engine. A chirping of crickets swelled to fill the silence.

"The ditch is just ahead, through those bushes," Eddie said.

"We'll dig first and come back for the bodies," Floyd said. He exited the S.U.V. and popped the trunk, took out three shovels.

Eddie got out and grabbed one of them. He led Floyd and Sawyer to the ditch, pushing bushes out of the way and stepping over boulders.

"Down there," he said at last, standing over the ditch.

"It's deep," Floyd said. "We gonna have to throw them bodies down."

Eddie grimaced, picturing the poor girl rolling down the slope. Sooner they got this over with the better.

The soil was soft and wet from all the rain that had been drenching L.A. for two weeks. They got off to a good start. At one point, a sound like a strange laugh pierced the air.

"Fuck is that?" Sawyer said, twisting his neck to look around.

"Just a toad," Eddie said.

"Thought it was a fucking goblin," Sawyer said, causing Eddie and Floyd to double over with laughter.

After two hours they'd managed to dig four feet.

Sawyer threw his shovel down and wiped his brow, panting. "I don't know about y'all but I ain't digging one more inch."

"It's deep enough," Eddie said, sweat rolling down every part of him. "Why didn't we bring any water, fuck."

"Let's get these fools in the ground and go get a drink," Floyd said. "Shit, I'll even buy 'em."

They dropped the shovels and clambered up the slope like the undead.

Floyd poked his head through the bushes. "I don't see nobody," he said, and kept going.

Eddie followed, feeling exposed. It was unlikely they'd run into someone, but it could happen.

He helped Floyd lift the suitcase out of the trunk, ignoring Bill as best he could.

Sawyer said, "Man, something 'bout that suitcase look more conspicuous than a body."

Floyd stared at him. "Sometimes you say some really dumb shit, you know that?"

Eddie dragged the suitcase across the dirt, Floyd helping him lift it over foliage. His shoulder felt like it was popping out of the socket by the time they reached the ditch.

Floyd bent down and pulled at the zipper.

"Wait," Eddie said. Hearing the urgency in his voice, he added, "I mean, maybe we should bury the suitcase too. Easier than burning it."

"That works," Floyd said, and pushed it over the edge

of the slope. The suitcase rushed toward the grave like a sled. Eddie pictured the woman's body smacking against the sides, head cramped between her knees. Sourness oozed up his throat.

The three of them stood looking at the suitcase, a solemn silence taking hold, until Floyd said, "Shit, I think I know that bitch."

Eddie and Sawyer looked at him.

"This whole time I was thinking, how do I know her? 'Cause she looked familiar. I think she from the club."

"What club?" Eddie said.

"What club, you hear this nigga?" Floyd said to Sawyer. "Only club you ever go to. That strip joint."

Eddie felt the blood drain from his face. "No, I would have recognized her . . ." But he wasn't sure. She had looked familiar . . .

"I'm tellin' you man, she was a dancer in the club. Look." Floyd skidded down the slope to the grave and rolled the suitcase onto its back with a heave. He tugged at the zipper and opened the suitcase and grabbed the woman's hair to pull her head back.

"She stiff," he said, and gritted his teeth. He raised the woman's head until Eddie was staring into her open eyes, her mouth frozen in a scream and skin pale even beneath her make-up.

Sourness shot up Eddie's throat again. He bent over, clutching his knees, and puked a burning spray of the Chinese takeout he'd crammed down his neck before this whole debacle had begun.

"She worked at the club, right?" Floyd said.

"Yeah," Eddie said, spitting a string of yellow saliva. "Yeah, she did."

"Goddamn, that's some crazy shit," Sawyer said.

"Let's get the other one and get the hell outta here," Eddie said, and turned away, wiping vomit from his lips.

The area around the observatory was still empty when they returned to the S.U.V. An impatience was building in Eddie. They'd been in the forest for a while; their luck wouldn't last forever.

They carried Bill toward the ditch, Eddie taking his torso, Floyd and Sawyer a leg each.

At the top of the slope, Floyd said, "On three. One, two, three—"

They swung Bill over the edge and released. He bounced off the dirt and rolled into the grave, landing beside the suitcase perfectly.

The toad started up again, cackling at them over the crickets.

"This place getting under my skin," Floyd said.

They picked up the shovels and began filling the grave. Within thirty minutes the dead had vanished beneath the earth, the layer of fresh topsoil the only clue they were there.

"Nightmare's finally over," Floyd said. Eddie was pretty sure the nightmare had only begun.

"I need a beer," Sawyer said. "Blowjob wouldn't hurt

either." He glanced at Floyd and Floyd looked away.

"Beer? Shit, I need a double whiskey," Floyd said. "Nah, a triple. Fuck it, I need the whole bottle."

Eddie picked up the shovel and made for the S.U.V. All he wanted was his bed and a locked door to hide behind.

He'd made it ten steps out of the bushes when he heard a laugh from somewhere ahead. He froze. Behind him Floyd and Sawyer rustled through the bushes, Floyd blabbering about some movie as a group of kids rounded the corner on the road ahead, bottles in their hands.

The kids had almost drawn level with Eddie now as they passed, too drunk and busy joking around to notice him.

Eddie heard Floyd approaching. ". . . and that scene in the diner is the first time Bobby De Niro and Pacino shared a scene, 'cause in *The Godfather* they didn't have none together."

The kids stopped in their tracks as Sawyer burst out after Floyd, the kids noticing Eddie now too. Judging by the sudden silence, Floyd and Sawyer had noticed them back.

The kids stared at them until one of them resumed walking in the direction they'd been heading and the rest of them followed, all of them chatting again as if they hadn't just witnessed three grown men coming out of the bushes in the middle of the night with shovels.

Eddie faced the other two. "We're fucked."

"They didn't see nothin'," Floyd said. "Bunch of drunk kids won't remember shit."

"Course they'll remember," Eddie said. "Imagine you were a kid and you saw the three of us coming out the bushes like that. Fuck."

"Even if they do remember, they won't know how to find that exact spot. And who they gonna tell? 'Hey Mommy, I was shitfaced in the forest last night and I saw some men hanging round the bushes.' Ain't gonna happen."

"It's dark, they didn't see our faces," Sawyer said.

But Eddie had looked one of them in the eye, the gangly one with long hair, and by the way the kid had looked back at him Eddie knew the kid had seen his face, and he knew he'd remember it, too.

3 | A Guy & a Girl

Her coffee was cold by the time Alison had made it out of the morning city traffic and up into the hills. She swallowed a bitter gulp, grimaced, and got out of her car. She struggled with an umbrella and shuffled toward the reporters clustered behind the yellow tape that declared "POLICE LINE DO NOT CROSS." The wind blew the rain toward her at an angle, rendering the umbrella quite useless, but she kept it above her head anyway.

"Detective," said the cop watching the reporters as Alison climbed under the tape. Alison nodded at her, unsure if they'd ever met or the cop knew her by reputation.

Mike approached. "Ally, nice of you to make it. The hell took you?"

"Traffic's a nightmare with all this rain. You don't even want to know when I left the house."

Mike nodded. "Never seen anything like it. Maybe God's washing all the scumbags away."

"He has a long way to go. What we got here?"

Mike led her through the bushes toward a slope that ended in a ditch. A hole had been dug in the ditch and a large man in a dressing gown lay sprawled on his back inside it. The man appeared to have been shot in the head. Beside the hole, a suitcase lay opened on the dirt, a woman's corpse crammed inside it. A couple forensics in white jumpsuits stood looking at the bodies.

"I told them to wait for you to arrive before they start collecting," Mike said.

"Who found the bodies?"

"Cadaver dogs. Some kid called it in this morning. Said he was hanging out here last night with some friends when three guys walked out of those bushes back there carrying shovels and looking suspicious. You know, your average night in L.A."

"Seriously? Criminals are getting even dumber these days."

"Dumber or bolder."

"Both," Alison said. "Like our dipshit president and his bullshit wall."

"True enough."

"The kid see what they looked like?"

"I don't know. I got officers en route to the kid's house as we speak."

Alison nodded. "Hold that, will you?" She handed the umbrella to Mike and crouched at the edge of the slope, then lifted a leg over and jumped, her shoes driving into the wet earth. Mike came down after her and wiped his free hand on his trousers, cursing.

Alison stood over the suitcase, the woman curled into the fetal position below her. She could see now that the woman was young, as young as Jennifer had been when—

"Why the suitcase for her and not him, you think?" Mike said.

"He wouldn't fit into it for one thing."

"Yeah, but why's she in a suitcase at all?"

"Must have had something to do with when they moved her. Maybe there were people around."

"Fucking animals."

"Could be a case of wrong place wrong time for her. That might explain the suitcase—they didn't plan on moving a second body."

Alison crouched beside the suitcase and studied it. "Pretty fancy." She rubbed her finger along it. "It's leather. 'Lone Ranch Design.' You ever hear of that brand?"

Mike shook his head.

Alison stood up and took her umbrella back. "You can tell forensics they can do their thing. I want to know the time of death and who they are. A copy of forensic's photos would be great as well."

"Where you going?"

"I've got Charlie today and he's late for school. If I don't get him there soon he'll think he's got the day off."

"Give the kid a day off. Take him to the zoo."

"And be just like his father? Someone has to be a parent, unfortunately."

"Tell me about it."

Alison climbed up the slope, slipping a couple times and getting covered in mud. She reached the top and trekked through the bushes toward her car. The reporters swarmed her as she dipped under the tape.

"Can you verify that one of the bodies was buried in a luggage bag?" said one of them.

"The victims were shot, is that correct?" said another.

Alison ignored the reporters, waving them out of her path. The cop watching the reporters stepped in to help. Alison hurried past them.

"Detective Lockley," said a woman standing beside Alison's car, "one of the victims is of a similar age and appearance as the O'Malley girl, isn't that right? Do you think there's a connection?"

Alison stared at the woman. She seemed familiar. Damn reporters; they had a way of finding out all the tiny details.

The woman said, "If so, do you think these new victims might lead to finally apprehending Jennifer's killer?"

"I remember you. Frederica Lounds. You wrote that piece for the *Daily News* about how the L.A.P.D. failed Jennifer and her family. Mentioned my name a few times."

"You were the lead detective."

"And now you're, what, writing a follow-up? We both know there's nothing to suggest these cases are in any way linked."

"Is that an official opinion?" Frederica said.

"Here's your official opinion: Fuck you."

Alison unlocked her car and got inside. Music from her Spotify came on with the engine: "People Who Died" by The Jim Carroll Band.

Yeah, but what about the rest of us?

Eddie ordered another drink and watched the women writhe on the poles. He wasn't sure why he came here so often. He didn't particularly enjoy seeing women sell themselves by the inch. Maybe he was lonely.

The morning after the catastrophe in the Texan's apartment, Eddie's cell phone buzzing on the bedside table had woken him up.

"Saul," he'd said, sitting upright against the headboard.

"Eddie."

"Saul," he'd said again.

"Heard our friend is no longer with us."

"The guy ran at me."

"He was unarmed, half-naked."

"He shouldn't have run, what did he expect?"

"Probably not what you gave him."

"Probably not."

"He had deep pockets, Eddie, and he was deep in my pocket. I'm gonna need you to come see me, discuss our next steps."

"I know."

"Good. You've always been a smart guy. Let's keep it that way. You come on in and see me."

Eddie had swallowed, and rubbed his palm over his prickly shaved head.

"And Eddie," Saul had said, "don't make me have to come get you. Because I will."

Eddie had spent the day pacing around his apartment trying to summon the courage to go see Saul. The following morning he'd woken with a savage thirst and now here he was: drunk in a strip club at 4:00 p.m. with L.A.'s most notorious crime lord after him.

Red and pink and purple spotlights gyrated on the walls, cutting through the dimness. "Out of Touch" by Hall & Oates pulsed out of hidden speakers—a great song, but the combination of it all was beginning to hurt his head.

The waitress returned with Eddie's drink. "Thanks," he said, glancing at her before noticing that she wasn't the same woman as before, but one he'd never seen before. If Eddie had ever seen a more beautiful woman, he couldn't remember it.

"No problem. Just give me a wave if you want another one," she said. An earnestness to her voice told him that not only was she new to this joint, but maybe to the career. Her skin was more than tan, maybe Native American, and she was young, maybe twenty-two.

He grinned stupidly until she floated back to the bar like a dream.

He had to talk to her.

He drank in a hurry, and soon a single swallow remained of whatever the hell cocktail he'd ordered—pink and bitter and swirling it had come to him—and he felt as if he was made of air, and the music didn't seem so harsh now, actually it was pretty nice, energetic, and he was probably overreacting about Saul, he'd worked for the man for almost two years and this was his first fuck-up, Saul would understand.

But first he had to talk to that woman.

He downed the last of the cocktail and rose, steadying himself with a hand on the table, and spotted her, back leaned against the bar.

"How you doin'?" he said when he neared her.

She pushed away from the bar in a nimble movement, the few garments she wore squeezing her slender body.

"What can I do for you?" she said.

"You can tell me your name."

To the left, the man behind the bar moved closer.

"You can call me Angel," she said.

"I mean your real name, not that price tag they make you use."

She raised an eyebrow.

The barman approached.

"Hey, you buying a drink or what?" he said, his wall of bottles sparkling behind him.

"How about you buy me a drink," Eddie threw back at him. He looked at the waitress. "Goddamn, you're the most perfect creature I've ever laid eyes on, you know that?"

"All right, buddy," the barman said, hovering over him like a giant question mark, "it's time for you to leave."

"I don't recall making that decision," Eddie said, and the barman looked ready to do something about it until the waitress grabbed Eddie's arm and led him toward an empty booth.

"Let's sit down for a minute," she said.

She sat him on a squishy pink sofa. "You should be careful," she said. "They don't mess around in here."

"Yeah, well, I don't mess around either. It's fine, I come here all the time. Hey, would you sit with me?"

She glanced at the barman. "I can't. They don't like it when we—"

"Just for a minute. Please?"

She smirked, clearly a little flattered, confirming to Eddie that she was indeed new to this world.

She slid into the seat opposite him and sat with her back straight and her hands beneath the table.

"Thank you thank you thank you," he said. "You won't regret it."

"Oh yeah?"

"Oh yeah. Trust me. So how new are you to this fine establishment?"

"This is my first day."

He whistled. "I came here on the right day. I always believe in fate."

"Didn't you say you come here all the time? That's not fate, just inevitable."

"When a man finds the most beautiful woman he's ever laid eyes on, trust me, that's fate."

She smiled. He felt encouraged, and although deep down he knew it was because of the alcohol, he felt warm in his soul.

He said, "So what's your real name?"

"Dakota. But let's keep that between you and me."

"That's a beautiful name. Do you happen to be from Dakota? Either of them."

"Do I sound like I am?"

"I dunno, maybe. You don't sound like you're from L.A."

"Who is? Are you?"

"I was born here," Eddie said, "if that's what you mean."

"I don't mean anything. It's you who asked me."

"Yeah, I was born here. I'm tired of it. This place is a madhouse."

"So why not leave?"

"No good reason."

"There's always a good reason."

"Oh yeah? What's your reason then, for leaving wherever you came from?"

"Survival."

Eddie looked her over. "What you surviving from?"

"I never said *my* survival. I'm looking for someone."

"Funny you should say that. I'm hiding from someone. I shouldn't even be here, I'm on the run." The cocktail was speaking for him now but there was nothing he could do about it.

"On the run from what?"

"I fucked up and now there's some guys after me. Bad guys."

"These men are looking for you right now?"

"Probably."

Dakota leaned closer. "So, some men are looking for you, bad men, and you decided to hide in a place you come to all the time?"

"Well, I guess '*hiding*' is a strong word. I just got no place better to go."

"So what you gonna do?"

Eddie thought about it. No matter how pissed Saul was, it would look better to show up by himself than be dragged in by the guys. Much better.

"I should leave," he said. "But not until you give me your number."

Floyd hated kids, which was unfortunate because his wife wouldn't stop pestering him to give her one. Every goddamn day recently.

"Not now, baby," he said into his cell phone as Sawyer drove the S.U.V. to their destination. He couldn't catch his wife's reply over the '80s trash metal Sawyer insisted on blaring every time he drove, which was every time they went anywhere because Sawyer was unquestionably the better driver of the three of them, Eddie being the third person. One time, after a botched robbery of a San Diego jewelers, Sawyer successfully evaded an entire legion of pursuing cops, which included a helicopter. Must have been every on-duty cop in the state of California. The man could drive, no doubt, but that fucking music . . . Once, on a highway near the U.S.-Mexico border, Floyd made the mistake of switching the music off. Without so much as a modicum of warning, Sawyer swerved off the road and slammed on the brakes, the S.U.V. screeching over the dirt. The vehicle came to a halt and Sawyer looked Floyd in the eye. "I ain't driving without my Pantera," he said, casual as afternoon tea, while Floyd breathed quickly and deeply, unsure whether to punch Sawyer in the face or apologize. Before he'd come to any kind of decision, Sawyer switched the music back on, pulled onto the road, and continued the journey as if nothing had happened. Floyd was just glad he hadn't turned the music off on the freeway.

"I can't hear you, baby," he shouted into his cell phone. "I'll talk to you later, okay?" He hung up and shoved the phone into his pocket.

"Hey, Sawyer," he yelled as they passed a decrepit motel, crackheads and prostitutes spilling out of it like a sickness.

Sawyer turned the music down. "Yup?"

"I know the cat runs the bar in this place. Says Eddie's in there right now talking with some new girl. I said we'd be discrete, so we gotta get him out of there quietly, without a fuss. You got that?" He watched Sawyer's face. "I don't want security fucking our shit up."

"You know what I always found funny?" Sawyer said in that Southern drawl of his.

"What?"

"The idea of a fireman sliding down a pole like a stripper. You think they really do that?"

"Yeah, those niggas love sliding down poles."

"I don't get it. What's the advantage of sliding down a pole like a stripper? Ain't goin' put the fire out any faster."

"It does put the fire out faster, though," Floyd said. "Gets them on the ground and in the truck faster. From their TV room or whatever the fuck they got up there."

"But why don't they just put that room on the ground floor? Why they gotta slide down a pole? Seems to me the whole thing would be a lot more efficient if they didn't even have an upstairs, stayed beside them trucks the whole time."

"Well, shit. You got a point there. Maybe they always wanted to be strippers, settled for the next best thing."

"Sounds about right."

Floyd looked at him again. "Keep your cool in the club. There's a reason you the driver."

Sawyer glanced at him. "I love your serious face," he said, and winked. He steered the S.U.V. around a corner. "But you're always so goddamn serious."

Ahead of them, situated at the end of a large and near-empty parking lot like a supermarket from hell, the strip club appeared. A gigantic neon sign that would be switched on when the sun went down read "The Pink Room." On either side of the sign, holding the corners and facing each other, stood two identical faceless outlines of the female figure, complete with perky nipples and high heels.

Sawyer parked the S.U.V. near the club and switched the engine off. The music died with it.

Floyd's ears rang in the silence. "Quietly—"

"I'll behave," Sawyer said, closing his fingers around Floyd's forearm, "if you do."

"What the fuck you doing?"

"You know what I'm doing. Just like you knew in that motel—"

Floyd tore his arm free. "I told you to never bring up that shit again. Jesus fucking Christ." He punched the dashboard. "I'm serious, nigga, I'll kill you. Fuck."

"Calm down, princess."

Floyd's hands darted to the glove compartment and found his Sig Sauer. He pressed the muzzle into Sawyer's forehead.

"Say it again, motherfucker. I dare you."

For six seconds nobody said anything.

Floyd lowered his hand and tucked the pistol into the waist of his light blue suit ("baby blue," his wife had joked).

"Let's go."

Dakota peered over Eddie's shoulder. "I really should get going," she said. "Couple customers just walked in and I have a job to do."

Eddie spun to look. "Fuck. That's them."

"The men looking for you?"

Eddie nodded.

"Will they hurt you?"

"Only if I don't want to take a ride with them."

"What happens if you take a ride with them?"

"It looks bad they had to come get me, put it that way."

"Okay, stay here," Dakota said. "I have an idea."

"An idea? No, don't—"

"I've had enough of men throwing their weight around. I'll be back."

She rose and strode toward a pair of closed doors beside the bar.

Eddie watched her leave, wondering what the hell just happened.

Thirty seconds later, a hand gripped his shoulder.

"Eddie," came Floyd's voice in his ear. "Just the man we've been looking for."

Floyd brushed past him and sat in the seat Dakota had vacated. Sawyer sat on Eddie's right, so close their thighs touched.

Floyd leaned back into the seat, arms spread wide over each side.

"I got this cousin, Lamar," he said. "Total fool. And by fool I mean motherfucker wouldn't find water in a swimming pool. But, like all fools, he once spoke a sentence of true wisdom. We'd been talking about his brother, who had a certain . . . fondness for the kind of place you and I find ourselves in right now, and Lamar, in the midst of all his usual ignorant bullshit, said, 'You got to be wary of a man who spends all his time watching titties bounce.'" Floyd threw his head back and laughed. "Shit still gets me." He laughed some more, wiping his eyes, and watched Eddie, his smile fading like a Polaroid in reverse.

"You know our friend Bill used to come here?" he said. "Before you made sure he ain't goin' nowhere."

"Might have seen him here couple times, yeah."

"What you doin' in here, man?"

"It was a mistake, Floyd, what you want me to say?"

"That ain't got a god damn thing to do with it. When our employer calls for us, we come running. You know the score."

"Maybe I'm tired of doing what I'm told."

"We always doing what we told, one way or another. If it ain't someone else telling us what to do, it's our urges and impulses, the parts of us we don't even know. There ain't no freedom in this world, Eddie. Accepting that is the only way to find some sense of peace."

"What the fuck are you even saying?"

"I'm saying that I prefer my heart when it beats, and I got to bring you in. Get up."

"It's been taken care of, what's the big deal? I'll find a way to get Saul the money I cost him."

Floyd looked at him funny. "You don't know, do you?"

"Know what?"

Floyd glanced at Sawyer.

"Know what, Floyd?" Eddie said.

"You ain't been watching the news, huh? They found them, man."

Eddie hesitated. "Who?"

"Who you think? The cops."

It hit Eddie like a slap.

"No, they couldn't have, we buried them properly—"

"Don't say another word," Floyd said, glancing around. "Get up, we leaving."

Eddie looked at Sawyer.

"Boss just wants to talk," Sawyer said. "Explain it to

him."

Eddie sighed. "Like I have a choice."

Sawyer stood up as Dakota appeared carrying a tray of Champagne glasses.

"Hello boys. It's happy hour, which means a free glass of bubbly for all our customers."

"We was just leaving," Floyd said.

"Why not drink it before you leave?" she said. "Since it's free and all."

She lowered the tray toward the table and stumbled. The tray slipped out of her hands and crashed onto the wood, the drinks tumbling into Sawyer's crotch.

"Goddammit," Sawyer said, springing backwards.

"Oh my, I am so sorry," Dakota said, "let me get that for you." She already had a cloth in her hand, dabbing at Sawyer's crotch.

"What the fuck? Get off me," Sawyer said.

"I'm so, so sorry, let me dry that for you," Dakota said, rubbing the cloth vigorously.

"Stop stop, for fuck sake stop."

Eddie glanced around. The security guys at the door had noticed the commotion, as had the dancer on the stage.

"Please, just let me fix it," Dakota said, rubbing faster.

"I said stop you crazy bitch!" Sawyer said and shoved Dakota; not much of a shove from Eddie's perspective, but Dakota cried out and flew backwards, hitting the floor on her back. Eyes wide, she pointed at Sawyer.

"This asshole just attacked me!"

"Woah, I didn't attack nobody," Sawyer said, palms raised.

The security guards—two bowling balls with muscles—hurried over.

"Who's got a problem?" said one of them.

"The guy with the blond hair attacked me," Dakota said.

"He slapped her, I saw it happen," the dancer yelled from the stage.

Sawyer shook his head and stepped toward Dakota. "Hey, wait a minute—"

With shocking agility the security guard closest to Sawyer leapt at him like a panther, sweeping Sawyer's feet out from under him and pinning him to the floor, a thick arm wrapped around his neck.

"Woah woah woah," Floyd said, standing up, "there's been a misunderstanding here."

Eddie looked at Dakota, who met his gaze, a subtle smirk on her lips.

"One more step and I'll take you down too," said the other security guard.

Floyd sighed. "Can't take this motherfucker anywhere." He reached into his waist and pulled out a pistol and pointed it at the guard.

"Tell him to get his gorilla ass off my friend," he said.

Behind Floyd the barman approached with a twelve-gauge. He pumped it behind Floyd's head.

"Drop it," he said.

Floyd grimaced, but did not lower the weapon. "That you, Mark?"

"Yep," the barman said.

"How's the wife?"

"Not bad. Think she's fucking someone else."

"Shame. I always liked her."

"Me too. This what you call discreet, Floyd?"

"We fucked up here, I can see that."

"Drop the gun."

"Can't do that till my friend is on his feet."

From her position behind the guards, Dakota gestured at Eddie to follow her.

Eddie said, "Well, you all seem to have your hands full so I'll get out of your hair." He stepped out from the table.

They all looked at him, no one moving a finger.

Eddie reached Dakota and together they strode for the doors.

They broke into a jog as they neared the exit. Eddie glanced behind and grinned. He'd never seen Floyd so pissed—as if he'd lost two million in cash.

Dakota pushed the doors open and Eddie went after her. The sudden brightness blinded him. He shielded his eyes as they came to a halt in the parking lot.

"Look at that, it's not raining," he said, shirt stuck to him. "Where to?"

"Place I'm staying is ten minutes away in a cab," Dakota said. She looked silly, almost nude in the parking lot.

"You bring all the boys home with you this quick," Eddie said, "or just the ones make you laugh?"

Dakota looked at him curiously. "You're something."

He couldn't argue with that.

4 | The Long Road to L.A.

Rufus watched his cell phone ringing on the table. He should get rid of it; damn thing only ever went off when he wasn't in the mood.

He picked it up. "What?"

"Am I speaking to Rufus Kane? Brother of Bill Kane?" said a man on the other end. Rufus gritted his teeth at the whiny West Coast accent.

"Be odd if you called Rufus Kane and it weren't Rufus Kane answered the phone, don't you think."

"Well Rufus, my name's Jerry. I'm a friend of your brother's, from L.A. You might want to sit down."

"You might want to tell me why you called."

"Well . . ." The man exhaled sharply. "Bill was found dead last night. Buried in Angeles National Forest, along with a girl he liked to . . . have around."

Rufus felt the wind knocked out of him. He pulled a chair out from the table and dropped into it.

"What you just say?" he said.

The man hesitated. "Your brother, he was found dead—"

"Dead? What the fuck you mean by 'dead'? Dead don't mean shit."

"Murdered," the man said, no hesitation now. "Single bullet through his right eye."

"Who did it?"

"Not sure but definitely L.A. boys. Looks like a hit."

"I'll skin them alive," Rufus snarled and slammed the phone on the table.

He remained sitting there for a while, trying to accept this news as fact. Even called Bill's cell in case the man had been bullshitting, hoping Bill would pick up. As adults they'd never been close, but, since Ma died, there had been . . . something between them, something beyond blood. A memory came to him of Bill and him as kids, running around the trailer park, this very trailer park he lived in now that he'd returned to after Ma died. Bill, being the older by a couple years, was making up the rules for the game as they went along. They were cowboys shooting Indians and Bill warned him there was Indians up in the trees and if they got spotted the Indians would shoot 'em dead with arrows. Little Rufus told little Bill that he didn't want Bill to die and little Bill laughed, said he ain't going nowhere, they would make it out of this one alive, together.

Rufus clenched his fists and rose, made for the liquor cabinet. He grabbed the bottle of Jack, poured it into a glass, and tipped it down his neck. He did it again. The spicy fire of the whiskey ignited in his bones, his tongue wet and tingling. Like a telescope, his mind zoomed in on what he had to do.

He marched through the little kitchen and into the bedroom. A portrait of Christ, bloody palms facing outward and His face utterly expressionless despite them, hung on the wall behind the bed, almost the length of the wall itself. Rufus dropped to one knee and slid a thick arm beneath the bed. Grunting, he pulled out a dusty wooden box, black with a scarlet border. He allowed the significance of this moment to imprint in his mind, and opened the box, which creaked softly. Two daggers gleamed on the velvet, blades the length of his forearm, hilts carved from ivory, each filigreed with an elegant "R" in solid gold.

He picked up one of the daggers—slowly, gently, carefully—and savored the weight of it. He twirled the dagger in the sunlight pouring in from the window, the blade glistening like a river. He ran his finger along the tip and did not flinch when it cut him and dark blood traveled down the handle and dripped onto the floor. He nodded his approval, placed the dagger inside the box, and carried the box under one arm into the kitchen. With his free hand he poured a final drink and knocked it back. He grabbed his Stetson from the hook on the front door, placed it onto his head, and stepped out under the searing Texas sun.

"Hey, Mr. Rufus," said a young girl in a tattered and dusty pink dress, "where you goin'?"

"Far away from here, Cinderella."

"My name is Cindy, not Cinderella," she said, but smiled broadly, never tiring of this routine. "Can I come with you?"

Rufus reached his car—an immaculate teal and cream 1966 Chevrolet Impala SS Convertible—and glanced back at her. "Not this time, sweetheart." He had a fondness for the girl. He hoped she wouldn't become a whore like her mother, but the odds were against her. Already, at eleven years old, she knew how to speak to the men who visited her mother. Rufus had seen more than one of them speaking with Cindy a little too long, beyond the minimum necessary to humor a child. But Cindy was not his daughter, and if he were to be honest with himself, which he'd been trying to be lately, he didn't give much of a damn.

Rufus popped the trunk of the Chevy and placed the dagger box inside. He got into the driver's seat, switched on the local country music radio station he liked—the same dozen songs on repeat, but that was what he liked about it—and, with a quick wave to the girl, began the long drive to L.A.

The cab took Eddie and Dakota to a motel off the highway, the kind of place where the devil makes deals.

"You're staying in a motel?" Eddie said, slapping twenty bucks into the driver's hand.

"I told you, I'm just in L.A. to find someone," Dakota said.

They exited the car.

"Then why the strip club?" Eddie said.

"It's the only place I know she's been."

Dakota paused outside the door to her room. "Shit, I left my key at the club." She headed toward the reception and went inside. Eddie went in after her, greeted immediately by the unmistakable smell of cat shit. He found the source on his right: a pink litter box covered in droppings.

Dakota hit the bell on the counter and a nerdy guy in a wheelchair rolled out of a doorway.

"Yes, yes, coming," he said, and approached them. "Oh." He looked Dakota up and down, his gaze resting on her tits.

"Hi," Dakota said. "Unfortunately, I don't have my key, but I need to get into my room right now."

The receptionist pushed up his glasses. "Oh. Well—" he glanced at Eddie—"conducting business in our rooms is strictly forbidden. But, if you were to pay for another room, I might overlook—"

"Excuse me?" Dakota said. "What business is it that I am conducting, exactly?"

The guy looked at the floor and fiddled with his glasses. "Well, I mean, you're, you know, that is—"

"Just give her the key, man," Eddie said, suppressing a grin. "You don't want to make an enemy of this one. Trust me." He winked at Dakota.

The receptionist hesitated, and disappeared below the counter. He surfaced and held a key out toward Dakota, avoiding her gaze as if looks could kill.

"I'll need this key back in the morning or I'll have to charge you for it," he said.

Dakota snatched the key and strode out the door.

Eddie leaned on the counter. "Hey, it happens." He shrugged. "What's the rate for a room?"

"For you just . . ." the guy said.

"You see anyone else?"

"Singles are forty bucks a night."

"I'll take one. And, word of advice—you should clean up that shit over there. Smells like a bag of assholes in here."

Eddie knocked on Dakota's door, feeling marginally re-freshed by the shower but not so much the sweaty shirt and pants he'd had no choice but to wear again. The alcohol seeping from his system made his head hurt and limbs heavy. A couple beers would sort him out.

After a minute Dakota opened the door. Eddie found it amusing to see her dressed in tight jeans and a vintage *Pulp Fiction* shirt, as if her wearing clothes was a novelty. Her hair, wet and shining, looked even darker—as black as her jeans.

"You know, I never caught your name," she said, drying her hair with a towel.

"Name's Eddie. Eddie Vegas. Nice to make your acquaintance." He flashed his most handsome smile.

"Well, Eddie Vegas, your name sure suits you." She stepped to the side to let him in.

The place smelled fragrant—a little sweet, a little spicy. Clothes lay in a heap on the floor beside a small suitcase, including the bra and panties she'd been wearing when they met. Seeing them discarded on the floor turned him on even more than when they'd been the only things covering her body.

"I'm just gonna dry my hair," she said, and disappeared into the bathroom.

Eddie sat on the edge of the bed. He wouldn't mind lying in this bed with her. Wouldn't mind that at all.

A hair dryer started up in the bathroom.

"I guess you can't go back to wherever you live then, huh?" she yelled over it.

"I'll have to at some point. My clothes, passport and some cash are there."

"You flying somewhere?"

"No." He thought about it. "Maybe."

"Where to?"

"I don't care, just not here. I'm done with L.A."

"I read in a book once, 'You're not done with L.A. until L.A. is done with you.'"

Eddie let that one go. "What about you?" he said. "When you find who you're looking for, are you finished here?"

The hair dryer stopped. She stepped out of the bathroom, her hair sleek and soft-looking.

"Honestly, I don't know what happens after that."

Eddie stood up. "You probably can't go back to working at the club?"

"Definitely not. I can consider myself fired before my first shift even ended."

"Shit, sorry about that."

"I didn't want to work there anyway."

"That's good, I guess. You hungry?"

"I could eat."

"I know a place nearby got the best pizza you'll ever taste."

"Lead the way, Eddie Vegas."

Eddie smiled, glad she was being a little playful. The day wasn't turning out so bad after all.

The bar was one of those dives that, though dark and full

of assholes, had an inviting charisma about it once you've had a few. Photographs that could only mean something to the owner hung haphazardly on the walls, the same three guys as every other time Eddie had been here sat at the bar like fixtures, and a coin-operated jukebox in the corner cranked out the Thin Lizzy he'd queued up minutes before.

"You're really going through those," Dakota said, referring to the cocktail Eddie had tipped down his neck.

"My mom always told me to never half-do anything," he said, Dakota's perfect face swimming in front of him like a memory.

"You didn't half-do that pizza either. I've never seen anyone eat so much."

"Best pizza in the world; was I right or was I right?"

"The first one."

Eddie went to pick up the cocktail, forgetting he'd just emptied it. He withdrew his hand.

"So who is it you're looking for in L.A.?" he said.

"Someone I haven't seen in a very long time."

"You said she was at the club. She work there? Maybe I know her."

"You might have seen her. She was a dancer up until a few months ago. No one there knows where she went after, or where she lives."

"Why you looking for her?"

Dakota looked away. "That's . . . complicated."

Eddie took the hint. "Hey, you like Thin Lizzy?"

"Can't say I know what that is."

"What? That is just . . . a travesty is what that is. Thin Lizzy are the greatest rock 'n' roll band to ever walk the earth."

She raised an eyebrow. "Is that so?"

"Oh man, it is. Listen." He pointed to his ear as the next track, "Cowboy Song," began.

"Not bad," Dakota said after a few seconds, a faint smile on her lips.

"You just wait."

The drums made their entry over the finger-picked bass intro, pounding sixteenth beats building to a crescendo and exploding into a jagged guitar riff behind swooning vocals.

Eddie bobbed his head.

"I like it," Dakota said, swaying her shoulders.

"So good, right? Come dance with me."

Surprise widened her eyes. "Dance? Right now?"

"Right now," Eddie said and got up off the stool. He moved his hips, Dakota giggling at him with a hand over her mouth.

"Come on," he said. "I look like an idiot unless you dance with me."

He reached out a hand to take one of Dakota's and she let him. He pulled her out of her chair, gently, and brought her to the middle of the bar. She swayed her shoulders, still giggling at him. Her hips followed suit, and soon she was dancing like a pro, Eddie trying to keep up with her while the men at the bar leered at her like primates.

By the time the guitar solo erupted into being, Dakota had her eyes closed, her hips swaying like the breeze and Eddie lost inside a bubble with her. There was something about her all right, and it wasn't the cocktails telling him that, either.

The song faded to a close and Dakota opened her eyes. "That was fun," she said, smiling up at him. The bar behind her looked like an oil painting.

"You can really move," Eddie said.

He stumbled as he returned to his seat, brushing against one of the men at the bar.

"Watch where you're going, faggot," the guy said, a big bald head squashed onto his neck.

"Sorry, Humpty Dumpty," Eddie said. "Wouldn't want you to fall and smash that gargantuan fuckin' head."

"Mouth like that'll get you beat," Humpty Dumpty said. "You looking to get beat?"

Eddie glanced at Dakota. She was watching, it seemed to him, with great interest.

"Tell me, Humpty," Eddie said, "how many times you sat on a wall and had a great fall?"

Humpty shot out of his stool so fast it toppled to the floor. Eddie saw a fist like a slab of ham coming at him, then the oil painting swirled and the colors melted together and it all looked like a drag queen crying under a street lamp.

Floyd found a bag of frozen peas in the freezer and pressed it against his eye, wincing at the pressure on the bruise forming beneath. He dragged a chair from under the kitchen table into the living room and sat opposite Sawyer passed out on the sofa, empty pizza boxes and beer bottles scattered around him. The place smelled like the morning after a house party, except there'd been no party and only one person lived here.

After a few minutes Floyd got bored and filled a glass with water from the tap. He stood over Sawyer and poured the cold liquid onto his face.

Sawyer spluttered to life.

"What the . . ." Sawyer said, groggy, and sat up, looking around. "This my apartment."

"You one clever motherfucker. Should be on the cover of *Time* magazine."

Sawyer touched his neck. "What happened?"

"What happened? Shit, wouldn't you like to know."

"That's right, Floyd, I would."

Floyd lowered the peas. "Those gorilla motherfuckers was busy giving me this while you had a nice sleep on the floor. That's what happened."

"What you saying?"

"What's the last thing you remember?"

Sawyer frowned. "One of them jumped me . . ."

"You got jumped all right," Floyd said. "After your

outburst, pushing that bitch away."

"I barely touched her. She was rubbin' me so fast my balls would've gone up in flames."

"Another man would have been glad to have a pretty li'l thing giving them attention like that."

"I ain't that kinda man."

They met each other's gaze and held them.

"Well, you goin' tell me what happened or what?" Sawyer said.

Floyd pressed the peas against his face. "After that asshole jumped you, I had a shotgun pointed at the back my head. Had no choice but to give up my gun. Soon as I did, that other nigga gave me this—" Floyd pointed at his eye—"so I hit him back. I don't care if a twelve-gauge pointed at my head, someone hits me they getting hit back. I got him in the gut, knocked him back a step. Next thing I know feels like a sledgehammer smashing into my ribs. Surprised they ain't broken. It was the other big fucker, not choking you out anymore. I don't know at what point you passed out but when I looked at you then you was sleeping like a baby, the most peaceful fuckin' sleep I ever seen, while I got my ass beat by a couple juiceheads. That fucking bartender smirking, enjoying himself. I always knew Mark was a sly motherfucker but we got along. I even did him a favor once. He gonna pay for that.

"Anyway, the dancers got uncomfortable so they stopped beating me, told me to get out. I had to carry yo' ass to the S.U.V. You a lot heavier than you look. Brought you here 'cause my wife at home right now. I come in the door with a swollen eye and you knocked out she'd leave my ass before I could say a word explaining myself."

"You carried me home?" Sawyer said, a different expression on his face now, looking at Floyd in that way.

Floyd ignored it. "As for Eddie. Shit, I'm so pissed I can barely talk about it."

"What in the hell was he thinking? Boss only wants to talk to him."

Floyd looked at Sawyer, the dumb fuck sitting there all confused. The man could be slow picking up things.

"You not looking at all the facts," Floyd said.

"Like what? Boss said to bring Eddie in so he could talk about what happened."

"That's one fact. Here's another: Eddie ain't ever killed anyone before. That was obvious the second he pulled the trigger. Maybe he'd be easier to handle if he'd just killed some dope runner from Texas, but that young girl got nothing to do with anything, that's a different matter. Eddie's likely to unravel, lose his head and start talking. Maybe the cops track Eddie down, I ain't saying they will, I think we covered our tracks pretty good, but let's say they do. They show him one picture of that young girl, he's liable to break down right there. That means game over for all of us, the boss too."

Sawyer tossed his legs over the edge of the sofa and sat up. "So you saying the boss was gonna . . ."

"Nah, I ain't saying nothing like that. I'm just saying

the boss is aware of these facts and wants to speak with Eddie to scope him out, see how he's doing. Maybe wants to bring up the idea of Eddie laying low somewhere for a while, see how he responds. The fact Eddie ran away with that waitress—which is a whole other thing about this; I think he put that bitch up to it—it means things don't look too good for Eddie right now."

"So what's next?"

Floyd was looking at the way Sawyer's green flannel shirt was open at the neck, strands of silky blond hair rising up out of it, the hint of his firm chest below them.

Floyd said, "I go see the boss tomorrow, tell him what happened."

"*You* go?"

"Yeah, listen, boss don't know you was involved. I told him you picked me and Eddie up and drove us to the forest, but you didn't bury nobody and you wouldn't know where those bodies are even with a gun to your head. I told him those kids just saw three men 'cause you waited by the S.U.V. for us. Understand? Better for you this way."

Sawyer nodded. "And what about right now?"

"Right now?"

"Yeah. Anything you wanna do right now?"

Floyd met his gaze. There was that look again, daring Floyd to take what he wanted . . .

"Thanks for taking me home like that," Sawyer said, getting up off the sofa to stand in front of him. He stuck his thumbs inside his belt, his blue eyes drinking Floyd in.

"Don't ..." Floyd felt a heat rising in him.

"I really appreciate you carrying me home like that."

"Sawyer ..."

"I owe you . . . big." A subtle smile flickered on Sawyer's face.

The heat spread to Floyd's groin.

"How big?" he said.

Sawyer grinned. He pulled down his fly and slipped his cock out, already hard.

Floyd leaned forward and took it in his mouth, his left hand closing around the shaft.

5 | Welcome to California

The air in California has a weight to it. A stickiness. As if the sleaze on the city streets evaporates to become part of the atmosphere and drifts across the entire state, reaching even here, the mountainous desert town of Indio, two hours outside L.A. Rufus was not glad to be back.

He pulled into a roadside gas station and filled the Impala. Not much else around, just an auto body shop couple miles back and the empty promise of the desert in every direction. He retrieved his Stetson from the passenger seat (he'd drove with the roof down all morning) and placed it onto his head, a stench of gasoline wafting up with it, and made for the store.

The young man behind the counter nodded a greeting as he entered.

"Got a place I can piss?" Rufus said.

"At the back," the clerk said, "beside the cold drinks."

Rufus found the toilet and expelled a stream of yellow that took its time getting out of him. Parched and tired of driving, he craved a Coke as much as hard liquor. The first one, he could do something about.

He swiped a can from the fridge, enjoying the icy touch of it against his skin, as a beat-up pickup parked outside the station doors. A man in black jeans and a black t-shirt stepped out of it, a hard look etched into his face. He glanced at Rufus's car as he approached the station, then over each shoulder, one of his hands adjusting something behind his back. Rufus slipped his hand inside his jacket and fingered the knife holstered there. Here we fucking go.

The doors swung open and the man barged inside, taking a good look around the place. The bulge above his ass confirmed what Rufus had suspected. Asshole had to pick today.

Rufus turned back toward the fridges and watched the man in the reflection. The man went down the middle aisle and disappeared from view. He reappeared on Rufus's right and faced the fridges. Rufus watched him from the corner of his vision. The man was eyeballing Rufus now, looking him up and down. Rufus stood up straight, all six feet seven inches of him, and looked down at the man.

"Where'd you escape from, a circus?" the man said.

"Hell," Rufus said.

The man's smug expression faltered. He reached behind his back and withdrew a revolver, the barrel glinting in the fluorescent light.

"Stay back here if you wanna die another day," he said, and moved toward the front of the store where he pointed the gun at the clerk's head. "Open the register," he said. "Now."

The clerk opened his mouth but otherwise could have been a mannequin.

The man smashed the butt of the gun into the clerk's face. "I said open it."

The clerk stumbled backwards with a cry, his fingers pressed against his nose and blood oozing between them. He didn't need to be told a third time.

"Move back," the man said, and bent over the counter, grabbing fistfuls of dollars and shoving them into his pocket. "Is this it? Bullshit." He looked out the window for a moment and turned around. "Hey, freak," he said, looking at Rufus. "That your Chevy outside?"

Rufus gritted his teeth. Fucking California. Asshole had to get greedy. Anyone with half a brain knows you don't rip off a classic car without a plan. They're too hot; you won't get five miles before the cops spot you.

The man aimed the revolver at Rufus's chest. "Sweet ride you got there. Give me the keys."

Rufus clenched his fists and judged the distance

between them: about twelve feet. "They're inside my jacket pocket. I got to reach inside to take 'em out."

"Do it. Slowly. Then slide them to me."

Rufus raised a hand and placed it inside his jacket. His fingers closed around the handle of the dagger. He stared into the man's eyes, committing his face to memory, as he had always done before taking a life.

Rufus glanced outside the window.

"Cops," he lied, nodding toward the doors.

"What?" the man said, following Rufus's gaze.

It was all the opening Rufus needed. His hand shot out of his jacket in a blur and flung the knife. The blade buried into the man's sternum. He dropped the gun and staggered backwards, staring at his chest.

"Oh," he said, tragically, and looked around the building as if seeing it for the first time.

Rufus removed his other dagger from the opposite holster. He marched toward the man, grabbed him by the hair, and slashed the blade across his throat. The man spluttered, hands darting to his neck. He fell to his knees, gasping like a goldfish, and crumpled onto the floor.

"Oh my god," the clerk said, mouth hanging open again. "I don't even . . . oh my god."

Rufus pulled a handkerchief out of his jeans and wiped the blade. He returned the knife to its holster and bent down to retrieve the knife he'd thrown. With a firm tug it came free of the man's chest, dark blood rushing from the wound like lava from a volcano.

The clerk appeared about to vomit. Rufus studied his face. He couldn't have the cops hearing about this mysterious savior who had slit a man's throat and hopped into his classic Impala to drive west onto I-10. That wouldn't do at all.

"I . . . I better notify the police," the clerk said, reaching for the phone on the wall behind him.

"You better not," Rufus said.

"No? Don't you think we should—"

"Out of the question."

Anxiety replaced the shock on the clerk's face. "I don't understand."

"Do you believe in God?" Rufus said.

The clerk frowned. "Why are you asking me that?"

"Because you're about to meet Him," Rufus replied, and stepped toward the clerk, his knife dripping blood onto the linoleum.

They'd identified the man as William Kane, the wealthy owner of the largest trucking company in Texas and suspected of involvement in the drug trade, a couple of his drivers having been caught transporting Mexican cocaine across the U.S. Kane had dodged conviction both times, claimed he had nothing to do with it, his drivers made that decision by themselves. Word up the ladder was that Kane was a D.E.A. informant being used to build cases against the organized crime rings he supplied the cocaine to, and this fact may have been leaked from a mole inside the D.E.A., making it likely that Kane's murder was a sanctioned hit. The girl, on the other hand, no one knew anything about other than she'd never been convicted of a crime and nobody was looking for her. Another innocent made to pay the price for someone else's sins.

Alison stood in the kitchen of Kane's condo and looked around. It was modern and clean. Too clean. A couple of expensive-looking paintings hung on the wall in the living area opposite an aquarium built into the wall.

"The suitcase was his," she said.

"How you know that?" Mike said, combing through the kitchen drawers.

"I looked up the company, Lone Ranch Designs. It's a high-end boutique store in San Antonio where Kane's company is based. Plus, look at this place. The suitcase was made of leather for Christ sake, course it was his."

"So, you're saying . . ."

"They were murdered in here."

"We shouldn't touch anything then. I'll get forensics out."

"I want to have a look around."

Alison opened a door to the right of the kitchen and found herself in Kane's bedroom. It looked like something out of a palace: a full-bodied lion skin rug lay in the the center of the floor, the poor creature's limbs spread apart and head perched on the floor, mouth open, eyes staring up at her, and behind it a four-poster king-sized bed, more valuable paintings on the walls. The room smelled faintly of whiskey and cigars.

Alison looked through the chest of drawers beside the bed: socks and underwear, rolls of cash, a forty-bag of coke, jewelry. A gold-rimmed card caught her eye: the outline of a woman was printed onto the black background beneath the words "THE PINK ROOM," and in the center, "VIP Access — William J. Kane." Alison knew the place. Jane Doe might have worked there. Jennifer had been a dancer. Too many times Alison had questioned girls like that, mixed up in things they knew little about, or worse, she'd find them already dead, caught in the crosshairs.

She pocketed the card and left the room.

Mike said, "I'm just thinking, when the killers moved those bodies out of here the girl was in the suitcase, but what about Kane? Maybe somebody saw something."

"Yeah, someone probably did. We should check the cameras, speak to the staff. Maybe run an article in the *Times*, ask if anyone saw anything."

Alison noticed a door to the right of the living area, a couple yards from Mike.

"What's in there?" she said.

Mike opened the door.

"Jesus H. Christ," he said, a grin forming on his face. "You need to see this."

On the way out of the building, Alison stopped to speak with the concierge, a well-groomed, thirty-something man.

"I'm Detective Lockley with L.A.P.D.," she said, flashing her badge. "I'd like to ask you a few questions."

"What's this in relation to?"

"A double murder that took place in one of these condos."

The man's eyes opened up.

"Double . . . I should get my supervisor." He reached for a phone.

"You'll do just fine. Can you tell me what hours you work here?"

"Every weekday five p.m. until two."

"So you were here Tuesday night?"

"I was here."

"You know all the people who live in here?"

"It's my job to know them."

"And you need to activate those elevators for people who don't have a fob, right?"

"Yes, and they need permission."

"Permission?" Alison said.

"From the owner of the condo they're visiting."

"How does that work?"

"Which?"

"The permission."

"Well, if the owner is expecting them, most times I'll already know, and have it written down. But if not, I phone up and ask."

"And then?"

"Then, if the owner tells me to let them up, I get them to sign in, and then I activate the elevator."

"Have you got Tuesday night's sign-ins with you?"

The concierge seemed to think about it. "I can't just give them out, even to a detective."

Alison nodded. "You're right. That's okay, I can have a warrant within the hour, and then you'll come into the station with me and make a statement, okay? To be official about it."

He bit his lip. "Well, I guess I could let you have a look at them. They have to stay here, though."

"A look is all I need."

"Which condo?"

"Two three seven."

The concierge looked up at her. "That's Mister Kane's room. Is he . . ."

"Afraid so."

The concierge nodded. "This might be a terrible thing to say, but that's somewhat of a relief. Mister Kane is far from the nicest person who lives here. Was, I mean . . ."

He flicked through a couple pages of the large binder opened on his desk and lifted it onto the counter, rotating it.

"There," he said, pointing at the top left corner of the page, "Tuesday night."

A section for each day of the current week, just one

signature on the page. It looked like "Kayla," no surname.

Footsteps clattering against the marble floor grew louder as a man walking by said, "Hey Dave, how's it going?"

"Not bad, Mister Baldwin," the concierge said back, "nice to see the rain's giving us a break."

"Damn right it is. I got a friend coming up to see me later, name of Mandy."

"Duly noted."

"Have a nice night," the man said.

"You too, Mister Baldwin."

Alison looked at Dave. "You know this person?" she said, pointing at the signature in the binder.

"Oh yeah, that's Kaya, she comes here all the—" Alarm took hold of his face. "You said 'double' . . . Don't tell me she's—"

"We don't know who the other person is yet. This Kaya, what's she like?"

"Kaya's the coolest. Always has an interesting story to tell me, and she's really generous and thoughtful. She brings me coffee all the time, even though I always tell her I don't want any." His face fell again. "Please tell me she's not the one—"

"What does Kaya look like?"

"A little short, not tiny. Slim, dark hair, brown eyes. Very young."

"She's white?"

"Yes, white. Her skin is a little tan, though. In the

right kind of light she looks a little . . . exotic."

"You have a thing for her." Not a question.

"Well, no, I don't have, we're just friends, she's nice to me, and—"

Alison waved his words away. "When was the first time she came here?"

"Must be about nine months ago. Maybe a little less."

"No one else went up to Kane's room Tuesday night? You remember anything suspicious, anyone that stands out?"

Dave screwed up his face thinking about it.

"No, I just remember Kaya going up. She had a donut for me." He smiled.

Alison nodded. She'd expected as much; professional criminals would have no trouble getting up that elevator. Probably had their own fob.

"One last thing," she said. "There's no security cameras in here, right?"

"No cameras. Management had some installed but enough of the residents opposed it they had to take them down."

"Why would the residents oppose it?"

Dave smirked. "A lot of rich, famous and otherwise influential people own condos here, and they don't want any record of their . . . private lives finding its way into the wrong hands. You know, married musicians taking fans to their rooms, football stars hanging out with drug dealers, that kind of thing. The privacy is what they pay for."

"Sounds exhausting," Alison said, and, upon hearing herself, laughed. She was the one following in the footsteps of the dead, and followed everywhere she went by their faces. What could be more exhausting than that?

6 | The Boss

"**A** hardened and shameless tea-drinker, who has, for twenty years, diluted his meals with only the infusion of this fascinating plant; whose kettle has scarcely time to cool; who with tea amuses the evening, with tea solaces the midnight, and with tea welcomes the morning.'"

Saul planted his hands on the table and stared down at Floyd. "Who said that?"

Floyd waited.

"Doctor Samuel Johnson," Saul said, "the renowned English scholar who among many other things single-handedly created the first great dictionary of the

English language. It took him nine years."

Floyd nodded, unsure how to respond. "Sounds like the man had a lot of time on his hands."

Saul sat in the chair opposite Floyd. A painting of a white whale in a stormy green ocean hung on the wall behind Saul, the tail arcing up out of the water above a tiny rowing boat and the few men inside it about to be flattened. Saul had told him once that the whale was Moby Dick. "Believe it or not, not all of those men in that boat will die. Just one of them will live to tell the tale," Saul had said. Floyd had always found the painting a little out of place in Saul's otherwise extremely modern Michelin-star restaurant filled each evening with the rich and famous.

"And look at what he achieved with that time," Saul said. "He made sure he would be remembered forever. What about you, Floyd? What have you done with the time given to you?"

Floyd knew better than to respond to the man's philosophical questions.

Marcel, the waiter, arrived with a tray carrying five teabags and a steaming pot. He set the tray and pot on the table.

Saul pointed at the first bag. "This is Yame Gyokuro. Grown under the shade rather than the sun, this green tea is harvested only two weeks each year in Japan, making it one of the more valuable and treasured of teas. With a full, lingering mouthfeel, the aroma is of sea salt and vegetation, and the flavor is sweetly complex, hints of baked pear giving way to a buttery aftertaste. The tea next to it is the most prized of all white teas, Baihao Yinzhen, also known as Silver Needle, with only the top buds of the plant used to produce the tea. It leaves a lingering sweetness in the mouth, tasting of maples and peaches and smelling of cacao and pine. An exquisite tea. Third, we have Tieguan-yin, an oolong tea named after the Chinese Goddess of Mercy, Guanyin. This tea becomes a creamy amber liquid and smells of fresh flowers. Fourth is Darjeeling black tea, named after the area in India in which it is grown. It's known as the Champagne of teas for its nutty muscatel notes unlike any other tea. And, finally, we come to top-grade Irish breakfast tea, a misleading name as in Ireland this tea is drunk morning until night. A true classic black tea, rich and strong, it is taken with milk and sugar in that country, which, while a strange practice for traditional tea-drinkers, is one I have become quite fond of."

Saul looked at Floyd, Marcel beside him, waiting. "The tea you choose will depend on how you feel, what you're looking to get out of the experience. Which tea will you choose, Floyd?"

Floyd looked at the tray, already forgetting which tea was which and most of what Saul had said about them.

"I'm feeling a little Irish today," he said.

Saul smiled. "Good choice. Marcel, return with some milk and sugar, would you?"

Marcel nodded and took the fifth teabag off the tray and ripped the packet open. He withdrew the teabag, placed it inside the empty cup on the table, poured in the steaming water from the pot, and drifted away.

Saul watched Floyd for a moment, neither of them saying anything.

"You know what I dislike even more than curious pigs?" Saul said.

"What's that?"

"Pigs curious about murder. When it's drugs, they can be paid off, or they lose interest, move onto the next case. But when it's murder they won't stop until they've caught their killer. It's political. You can get away with a lot being vaguely associated with most crimes, but when that crime is murder, anyone that so much as smells like they're involved is going down for it. You understand what I'm saying?"

"I think so."

"Why is Eddie not sitting in front of me right now?"

Floyd scratched his chin. "There was . . . complications."

Marcel returned with the milk and sugar.

"Thank you, Marcel. I'll have the lobster now," Saul said.

Floyd watched Marcel nod again and float away. The man was like an apparition.

Floyd went to take the teabag out of the cup.

Saul raised a hand. "Not yet. This tea steeps for five minutes."

Floyd sat back.

"What do you mean by complications?" Saul said.

"Eddie didn't wanna come with us. We had him in the club, sitting there about to walk out with him when this waitress appears outta nowhere and spills some drinks all over Sawyer. Next thing I know she's screaming 'bout Sawyer hitting her and the security get on our ass. One of them grabs Sawyer, pins him to the floor. Then the fuckin' barman points a shotgun at my head. While all this is going on Eddie slips out the front doors with the waitress. I think he told her to cause a distraction."

Saul rubbed the tablecloth, frowning. "I like Eddie. He's been a good worker. Smart enough to not get greedy, dumb enough to not ask questions. But, lately, his heart hasn't been in it. He's been restless, hungering for something else. And he's been drinking too much, talking too much . . . and now you're telling me that he split with some slut. Apart from the money he cost me, which I consider owed to me, him on the loose like that is dangerous. Even if the cops don't track him down, he's likely to get arrested for being a drunken fool. The thought of Eddie and his big mouth sitting in a police station, paranoid and caught off guard—that thought makes me nervous."

"What you saying, Boss?"

"I'm saying Eddie's a stray dog, riddled with rabies. Dangerous. There's only one thing to do with a dog like that."

Floyd nodded. He'd been hoping Saul wouldn't say that. He looked around. A cream grand piano gleamed in the center of the oval-shaped dining area. Later, as every evening, it would be played by a world-class pianist as people paid hundreds of dollars to eat tiny portions of food at the tables spread out around it. Mirrors along each wall created the illusion that the tables continued forever in each direction.

Floyd was about to ask Saul what he planned to do about Eddie when Marcel arrived with the biggest, reddest lobster Floyd had ever seen. He placed the lobster on the table and left, Floyd nearly drooling at the tangy smell of the lemon-garlic butter wafting up from it.

Saul picked up his napkin and tucked it into his collar. He grabbed the lobster with both hands and ripped off the tail, then peeled the shell loose until the meat slipped out. He picked up the meat with his fingers, steam rising from it, dipped it into olive oil, and shoved it into his mouth.

"My chef makes the best lobster in the world," Saul said, glistening butter sliding down his chin. "People come from all over the world to taste it."

But you won't offer me any, will you, asshole?

Saul picked up the lobster and twisted off a claw.

"I have a plan that will sort out both problems," he said. "The other problem being the money we need for expansion." He pressed the claw into his plate and pulled out the meat. "Have you ever heard of Diego de Dios, otherwise known as the Puerto Rican?"

"The hitman? I've heard some stories."

Saul looked interested. "Tell me one of those stories." He pushed more lobster into his mouth.

"Well, I heard he ice cold. If looks could kill this nigga couldn't leave his house without people dropping dead. I heard one time some mob guys in New Jersey hired him to take out a judge who was gonna put one of the higher-ups away. They told him to make it obvious the judge was taken out, send a message. The Puerto Rican, never one to disappoint a client, had no trouble with that. The judge was found naked on the floor of his kitchen, his kidney missing from a bleeding hole in his side and a puke-filled plastic bag tied around his head. Later, they found the kidney. Was in a hundred little pieces floating around the vomit. The Puerto Rican had made the man eat it before he smothered him."

Saul clapped a hand on the table and laughed heartily. "I love it. The man's got style."

Floyd grimaced as Saul continued shoveling lobster into his face. 'Style' wasn't the word he'd had in mind.

"Why we talking 'bout a crazy motherfucker like the Puerto Rican?"

"Because that crazy motherfucker is going to sort out our Eddie problem, and you are going to be there to sort out our money problem."

Floyd looked at the whale in the painting, then the tiny men in the boat. He didn't like the sound of that. Didn't like the sound of it at all.

Jerry Boylan sounded even more whiny in person than when he'd called to say that Bill had been murdered. Rufus sat across from him, the man behind a big desk in his private fourth-floor office. A photo on the desk faced Jerry, probably of a wife and kids. Behind him, a wall of glass overlooked the ordered gray and green of Pershing Square in L.A.'s financial district.

"Mister Kane, once again I'd like to offer my condolences for your loss. I got to know Bill quite well over the years and we always got along. He seemed a decent man."

Fucking lawyers. Bullshit coming out their ears.

"My brother was the furthest thing from a decent man a man can get. Let's cut the bullshit and get to it. I don't want to be in this city any longer'n I have to."

The lawyer shifted in his seat. "You're not happy to be back then?"

Rufus narrowed his eyes at the man.

"Bill talked about you every now and again," Jerry said. "Told me you were quite the player around here a decade or so ago. What was it he said? 'My brother's name used to strike fear into the hearts of every no good sonofabitch in this town.'" Jerry smiled. "You were a contractor, right? Killer-for-hire?"

Rufus couldn't believe what he was hearing. "I've killed men for saying less than that."

"Well, Mister Kane, the reason I ask is I might have

need of your services, should you be willing to provide them."

The man seemed pretty dumb for a lawyer.

"I don't do that no more."

"I'm talking big money."

"I said I don't do that no more."

Jerry nodded. "All right, no problem, just thought I'd ask. I've got a case I don't think I can win, and, well, never mind." He fiddled with something on his desk. "Is it true you're a Christian now? Bill was worried you'd found God in that trailer park you went back to."

"No man finds God. God finds the man."

Jerry looked at him thoughtfully. "How does that work, being Christian and coming here to take care of your brother's killers?"

"'For the Lord loves the just and will not forsake His faithful ones. Wrongdoers will be completely destroyed; the offspring of the wicked will perish.' Psalm thirty-seven twenty-eight."

"So God's cool with it?"

"'When justice is done, it brings joy to the righteous but terror to evildoers.' Proverbs twenty-one fifteen. 'Learn to do right; seek justice. Defend the oppressed. Take up the cause of the fatherless; plead the case of the widow.' Isaiah one seventeen.' I'm just God's hand."

Jerry appeared irritated. "Sounds like you found more than God out there."

"No man—"

"No man finds God, yeah yeah. Well then, let's get down to it. As I mentioned on the phone, someone seems to have wanted Bill dead. I don't know who. There's only one person I can think of that maybe would, you might know him, Saul Benedict, came up in the years since you've been gone. Owns the drug trade in this city, among other things. Practically runs the place."

Rufus said nothing.

Jerry continued: "Bill was the middle-man between Benedict and the Mexicans that supplied the coke. But Bill carried more of the stuff than Benedict could sell, so Bill delivered the rest to other buyers in other states. For the privilege, Bill had to make regular payments to Benedict. This arrangement worked for a while, until Benedict started expanding his business. Then things got . . . murky, because Bill was selling to the competition. Thing is, I can't see why Benedict would want Bill dead. Bill was just the middle-man. If he had a problem with the Mexicans selling it to everybody, that's something Benedict would have to straighten out with them. I imagine that he *has* straightened it out with them, in fact. Bill just transported the stuff where the Mexicans told him to. In a way, it was unfair for Bill to ever have to pay Benedict for the privilege of selling to other buyers in the first place when it was really the Mexicans selling it to them and Bill just moving the stuff. But 'fair' and 'Benedict' are two words you'll never hear in the same sentence. And to be honest, I think Bill just found it easier to keep the man happy. I mean, Bill was making a fortune."

"Where can I find Benedict?"

"He owns a restaurant in Beverly Hills called The Long Goodbye. Pretty famous place, has two Michelin stars, I believe. Benedict is there most of the time, specially during the day before the place opens. Or so I hear."

Rufus nodded and went to get up out of the chair.

"Easy cowboy," Jerry said, raising a hand. "I got a little more for you than that."

Rufus sat down.

"Bill liked to frequent a certain strip club. Well, he didn't call it that, he called it a gentleman's club, and the place refers to itself as a gentleman's club, but, trust me, I've been to gentleman's clubs and I've been to strip clubs, and this place is a strip club. Anyway, this club is where Bill met the girl who was with him the night he was killed. The cops haven't identified her, but I know it's her; Bill had her around all the time the last few months. Her name's Kaya. So, today, on my lunch break, since I had nowhere else to look, I paid a visit to the place, spoke to some of the girls, asked them if they knew Bill. General consensus was that they knew who he was, and that last they heard he'd stopped going there around the time one of the girls stopped working there, a girl he had a particular fancy for, the same girl I just told you about. Apparently it's not uncommon for the more rich clients to find a girl they like, you know, one they *really* like, and pay for her to be their own private dancer, if you know what I mean. But then they tell me something else, something that really piques my interest. Yesterday, a new girl started working at the place and spent the whole time asking about the girl, Kaya, saying that she was worried about Kaya, that they used to be close until they fell out of touch and the last place she knew Kaya worked was this club. Then, to make matters even more interesting, that same day some guys come in and cause some trouble with this new girl, one of them shoves her or something, and the way the whole thing looked to one of the other girls working there she was sure that they were trying to kidnap this new girl asking about Kaya."

Jerry leaned forward, getting excited. "So, I'm thinking, what if we're looking at this the wrong way around? What if it's the girl that was into some shit and Bill was the one caught in the middle? It's a leap, I know, specially 'cause why would they kill her in Bill's home and not hers, but maybe that's to throw the cops off the scent. And, to be honest with you, anything is better than trying to go after Saul Benedict. I don't care who you are, Hand of God or the grim reaper, going after a man like that is suicide. And this girl asking about Kaya like that two days after Kaya was killed and then maybe getting kidnapped right after? That smells like something to me."

Rufus digested this information.

"How do I find the girl?"

Jerry smiled, his eyes with a glint in them now. "That's the best part about this whole thing. This new girl was being pretty cagey to these other girls, asking lots of questions but not giving much away. She told them she was new in town and when they asked her where she was staying she just said it was some shithole motel nearby run by a creep in a wheelchair who doesn't clean up his cat's shit."

Jerry licked his lips. "Thing is, I happen to know the exact place she's talking about. I represented the person who turned that guy in the wheelchair into a guy-in-a-wheelchair. My client hit the guy and run but was seen on camera speeding from the scene. A messy case; I got him off with a settlement 'cause the guy he hit had been in the wrong too, sprinting across the street like a fuckin' lunatic. Like all my clients, that client was a rich one and the settlement was nothing to him. So, to arrange this settlement, I visited the wheelchair guy at the motel he ran and, my god, the stench. I can still smell it. There was a litter tray on the floor full of shit. I mean *full* of it. Couldn't even see the stuff the cat was supposed to shit on. I felt sorry for the cat. And the place is a shithole if ever I saw one. Not far from the club either. That's our guy, no doubt, which means that's the place. It's called the Starlight, just off the one thirty-four outside Eagle Rock. It would be a good idea to check that girl out before you go kicking down Benedict's door."

The lawyer was a fool but Rufus saw his point. He stood up, had learned all he could from this man who knew his intentions, his name, and what he looked like.

"I take it you don't believe in God," Rufus said, one

7 | Showdown at the Starlight

Eddie woke alone in his motel room with a head like a bowling ball. Damn hangovers. Almost enough to make him quit drinking. He staggered into the shower, so thirsty he stuck out his tongue and let the hot water collect on it. Memory of the night was slippery. There was the pizza place, he remembered that clearly 'cause he'd been sober then. After that came the bar. He danced with Dakota, her looking gorgeous, and pretty sober too if he remembered correctly. Then there was Humpty Dumpty at the bar, mouthing at him. Shit, did he get in a fight with the guy? Dakota won't be impressed with that. Explains waking up alone.

Eddie went to put clothes on and remembered he didn't have any, just the smelly jeans and shirt he'd worn the entire day and night before. Then he remembered that he didn't have anything at all, not even cash, just those smelly clothes.

He put the clothes on and called for a cab, his cell nearly dead, and left the motel room to knock on the door of Dakota's.

It opened.

"You're still alive then," Dakota said. She looked like she'd been up and dressed for a while.

"I'll take your word for it."

"That hungover, huh?"

"Nothing a beer won't fix."

She raised an eyebrow.

"Just kidding," Eddie said, not sure if that was true.

They were silent for a moment.

"So . . ." Dakota said, looking cute with her hands in her back pockets. Eddie hoped the bar fight had been the worst of it.

"Yeah, so, I'm going to head back to my apartment, grab a few things. Just thought I'd let you know."

"Is it safe? You know, for you to go there?"

Eddie scratched his head. "Yeah, it'll be fine. They probably think I skipped town already, or they got bored looking."

"Okay."

The way she was looking at him made him nervous.

"So, yeah, I'll see you later, I guess?" he said. "You wanna go grab some food?"

She glanced away. "Yeah, maybe. I was going to look some more for my friend today. She liked art, was always drawing stuff. I was thinking I could ask around art galleries, see if people recognize her, maybe know where she lives. At least she liked it when I knew her . . ." A shadow of sadness swept across her face.

"Yeah, yeah, that sounds like a good idea. I could help you if you want? Or, maybe you wanna do that by yourself. I'm easy." Christ, he could hear himself.

Dakota smiled. "Yeah, I'd like that. I'll wait here for you. I guess you won't be long?"

It surprised him. "I'll be as fast as an L.A. cabbie can be persuaded to drive. It's not far."

He waved goodbye, that gorgeous smile imprinted in his mind, and stood by the road to wait for the cab.

In his Chevy, parked in the parking lot of the motel, Rufus watched a man knock on the door of the woman, named Dakota he reminded himself, who had been asking around about the girl killed with Bill. The man was slim with a shaved head and the walk of a two-bit thug used to looking over his shoulder. Rufus watched the woman, Dakota, smile at him. She had a look about her, at least half a nigger. Now she was shutting the door as the man walked away.

Rufus waited until the man got into a cab, then waited some more. Twenty minutes passed and no one else entered or left the woman's motel room.

Rufus placed his Stetson on his head and exited the car. He walked toward the motel room and tried the door. Locked. He glanced behind and, seeing no one, knocked on the door.

"That was quick—" Dakota said as the door opened. She looked up at him, surprise cutting her off. Up close he saw she wasn't half anything, but full Indian. Not very dark, though.

"Good morning, lady. I got some questions that need answering. I suggest you step aside and let me in so I don't got to hurt that pretty li'l face o' yours."

She moved her mouth wordlessly.

"I won't ask you again."

Dakota blinked and stepped back into the room, looking dazed. Rufus went inside and shut the door.

"Sit down," he said, extending an arm toward the bed, the duvet on top in a messy heap. The air was a little thick in here, and smelled of perfume.

The woman stood there, looking unsure. He saw now that she was young.

"I got no reason to hurt you if you answer my questions. I ain't got many."

"Okay," Dakota said, talking now, easing herself into obedience.

"Sit down."

She sat.

Rufus removed his hat and placed it on the little table at the end of the room. He pulled a chair out from under the table and fell into it with a sigh.

"I'm goin' be straight with you. I don't think you got the answers I'm looking for, but I may 's'well ask."

"I don't think so either."

"What you think I'm here to ask you 'bout?"

"I think you have the wrong person."

"Is your name Dakota?"

Her eyes widened a little.

"You was at a strip club called the Pink Room yesterday, asking questions 'bout a girl worked there?"

Her eyes widened a little more.

"Now that we're on the same page, I'm goin' ask you why you was asking 'bout that girl, and you goin' tell me. Ready?"

Dakota nodded.

"Why you asking 'bout that girl?"

"I'm trying to find her. I came here, to Los Angeles, to repair our relationship. I hoped she'd still be working there, at the club, but she's not."

"You know where she is?" He threw it out there and watched her face. Nothing.

"No, and I have no idea where to look."

He saw she meant it.

"Is she . . . in trouble?" Dakota said.

She'll never be in trouble again, he thought of saying. "Not with me."

He could see she didn't know what to make of that.

He said, "Three men came to the club, tried to take you out of there. That correct?"

"Take *me* out of there?"

"That's what I said."

"*Two* men came into the club. The third was already in there. They tried to take *him* out of there."

"What you do, get in the way?"

"I made it difficult for them."

"Why?"

She looked down at her feet. "Honestly, I don't know."

Rufus watched her. Was she lying to him?

"I need more than that," he said.

"The guy was charming, I felt sorry for him. I don't know what to tell you."

"You didn't know who he was?"

"I don't know anyone here."

Rufus thought about it. Whole thing was getting complicated. He remembered the man knocking on her door. "He the same man you spoke to outside that door twenty-five minutes ago?"

Dakota narrowed her eyes. "What the hell do you want with me?" Giving him attitude now.

"Answer the question."

"Yeah, it's him."

That's who he needed to speak to.

"You know why you Indians lost your land?" he said.

The shock in her eyes. She'd kept her face blank, but the eyes gave it all away. The eyes always gave it all away.

"It's 'cause you're dumb. Weak. We shoulda killed all of you when we had the chance. Now you people linger like the last remnants of a disease in your li'l corners of this great country."

Rufus shook his head. "Look at me, gettin' all political with a redskin. He say when he was coming back?"

Dakota said nothing, giving him a hard stare now.

He lifted his jacket, let her see one of the daggers. "I could get this into one of your nipples from here. Easy."

"Soon. He said he'll be back soon." Her gaze fixed on the knife.

Rufus nodded and let go of his jacket. "That's what I thought. Got any whiskey?"

Dakota frowned. "Why?"

"I like to drink while I wait," Rufus said, and settled back into the chair.

Floyd had been sitting in his wife's Toyota—the S.U.V. Eddie would have recognized—outside Eddie's apartment all morning, thinking that only an idiot would be dumb enough to show up at their own apartment after running out on Saul Benedict, but, lo and behold, that idiot shows up. He watched Eddie shut the door of the cab he'd just popped out of and enter the apartment block, glancing over his shoulder. But the cab didn't leave. Eddie must've told the driver to wait. Floyd would have to follow the cab.

Eddie came out soon after with a backpack over one shoulder, looking pretty pleased with himself. Yeah, probably feeling like James Bond right now. Not for long.

Eddie got in the cab and it pulled away. Floyd turned the key in the ignition and followed.

They'd been driving for about ten minutes when the cab took an exit off the 134 and soon after pulled into an ugly motel, a faded sign announcing it as the "Starlight." Eddie got out and the cab took off, Eddie heading for one of the motel rooms. He knocked on the door and a woman opened it. Floyd couldn't see her clearly but he'd bet his balls it was that bitch from the club. Eddie disappeared inside. The door remained open.

Floyd drove slowly into the lot and parked beside an attractive classic Impala. He picked up his cell and dialed Sawyer, the man probably at home already having given up on asking around hotels for his "mentally disturbed brother-in-law" named Eddie who may have just checked in and who he needed to find right now thank you very much, there's a man's life at stake here.

"Yeah?" Sawyer said.

"I found him."

"Where?"

"A motel called the Starlight, off the one thirty-four."

"Knew he'd be too cheap for one these hotels."

"You a genius."

"So my mom tells me."

"City's quiet tonight, huh?"

"What you mean?"

"I ain't hearing a damn thing in the background. City must be a fuckin' ghost town tonight."

A pause.

"Yeah, pretty quiet," Sawyer said.

"Cut the shit and get out here."

Floyd hung up.

He waited in the car for sixty seconds and grabbed his gun from the glove compartment. Fuck it, it's just Eddie and some woman in there. How difficult could it be?

When Dakota let him into the room the very last thing Eddie had expected to see, perched on a chair at the back of the room like a laborer at rest, was a gigantic cowboy with cold eyes and a hard stare. He did a double take, glancing between Dakota and the cowboy. His first, irrational thought was that this man was Dakota's lover and that Dakota had slowly been reeling Eddie in to some long con, but that didn't make a shred of sense, so he said, "Am I missing something here?"

The cowboy laughed—a deep, humorless laugh. "Tell him why I'm here."

Eddie looked at Dakota. She seemed resigned. "He wants to ask you some questions."

Eddie looked at the cowboy, totally lost. The strap of his backpack pressed into his shoulder.

"Tell him what about," the cowboy said.

Eddie kept looking at the cowboy this time.

"He wants to ask you about his brother," Dakota said.

"Tell him why," the cowboy said.

"He was murdered."

Eddie's heart nearly came up his neck. The man was the embodiment of Texas; he should have connected that right away. Eddie kept his gaze on the cowboy, hoping his expression hadn't given much away.

"I don't know anything about any murder," he said, and eyed the small TV on the table. Could he smash it over the guy's head faster than the guy could stop him? He couldn't see any gun on him.

The cowboy looked about to say something but instead gazed at something behind Eddie, a look of surprise coming over him.

Eddie turned to find Floyd standing there staring back at him, looking more confused than any of them.

"Y'all 'bout to fuck or what?" Floyd said.

"I'm still trying to figure that out," Eddie said.

"Swingin' party's over," Floyd said to Eddie. "You need to come with me 'fore this whole thing gets outta control."

"Who's the nigger?" the cowboy said.

"Who you callin' nigger you redneck motherfucker?"

"I'm callin' you nigger, nigger."

Floyd paused for a moment, his angered expression morphing into one of deep thought.

"My wife, she likes to read," he said. "Got a subscription to *National Geographic*. Keeps them on the coffee table, right next to the remote. I don't know what she likes about them 'cause they bore me to tears, but sometimes, when I'm flicking through the TV and there ain't nothing on but ads and bullshit, I'll pick one those magazines up, flick through it. Mostly I just look at the pictures."

Floyd took a couple steps toward the cowboy, drawing level with Dakota, looking down at the man sitting in the chair.

"One time the new issue sitting on top of the pile was a special issue about the concept of race. Two li'l girls in white dresses looked up at me on the cover, one white and one, like you say, a nigger. Under the photo it said those two li'l girls was twin sisters. I had to open that shit up, find out how something like that could happen. 'Cause if I ever have a kid—and believe me, I don't wanna, but I can't hold the wife off forever—I need to know if a little white baby might pop out. 'Cause if that can happen then lemme tell you this ain't no country to be a black man walking around holding a li'l white girl's hand. Shit, cops would shoot my ass before I got both legs out the door."

Floyd took another step toward the cowboy, four feet from him now.

"Well, I did find out how those twins had different

skin, but I found out something else, something that made me laugh. Really laugh. 'Cause I was thinking of all the dumb fuck rednecks like you with your white pride and your shiny heads and your fuckin' rage. What I learned was that all human beings are, in fact, Africans."

He glanced behind, grinning like a shark, and faced the cowboy again. "Sounds crazy, I know. But it's true, it's written. It's history. Human beings came into existence in Africa three hundred thousand years ago, and they remained there, in Africa, for over two hundred thousand years. In fact, the D.N.A. of every human being alive today, which includes you, motherfucker, can be traced back to one person who lived in Africa sixty thousand years ago."

Eddie looked at the cowboy. The man had a mean look in his eyes, sitting tense in the seat.

"You know what that means," Floyd said. "But I'll spell it out for you 'cause I know you dumb as shit. It means that you are, in fact, a nigger." He let the word hang there. "You a nigger just like me. You got my nigger blood running through your veins. You got my nigger eyes and my nigger hands. And when you disrespect a nigger, my nigga, you disrespect yourself."

The cowboy sat still, his Rottweiler gaze fixed on Floyd, the man no doubt aware that Floyd could shoot him before he'd get to him but mad enough to risk it.

Neither of them moved, the silence of the room like a presence.

Faster than Eddie's eyes could follow, Dakota grabbed the glass vase from the dresser beside her and brought it down over Floyd. It smashed against his skull, the sudden noise of it startling. Floyd hit the floor and next thing Eddie knew Dakota was rushing toward him.

"Run," she said.

He didn't need to be told twice.

They sprinted until they reached the road, Eddie's lungs burning.

"He's not coming," Eddie said, panting.

He watched as the cowboy appeared in the doorway of the motel room, a black shape in the shade of the building, the large hat on his head looking almost absurd. The cowboy looked back at them for a moment before shutting the door and vanishing behind it.

"The hell?" Eddie said.

"Come on," Dakota said, and continued down the road.

Eddie put the second strap of the backpack over his other shoulder and jogged after her, the sun a frying pan on his neck.

8 | The Pink Room

Strippers, as a rule, don't like talking to cops, but seven years in vice before her three in homicide had taught Alison that they open up pretty quick when the cop asking them questions is a woman.

Alison sat at a table near the back of the club, a place called the Pink Room that seemed unsure of whether to present itself as seedy or classy. She sipped an over-salty margarita and observed the clientele: a mixture of chubby, middle-aged men, some of them with the aura of wealth about them; small groups of younger men, drunk and grinning; a few loners, spread about in pockets with their shoulders hunched and gazes glued to the dancers;

and a man and woman in their mid-twenties at a table in the center of the room, watching the dancer closest to them. Bass synthesizers thumped out of the walls, a kaleidoscope of colors drifting across them. 8:00 p.m. and the place was heating up.

Alison had almost finished her drink by the time one of the dancers finished her set and approached the door to the dressing rooms, which Alison had intentionally sat beside.

"Can you help me with something?" Alison said as the dancer drew level with her.

"I'm not a server, honey," the dancer said.

"And I'm not here for the tits," Alison said, flashing her badge.

"I should have guessed. Whatever it is I don't know anything about it."

"A girl was murdered. Around your age."

Uncertainty softened the dancer's face.

"I'll buy you a drink," Alison said.

The dancer hesitated, and sat down. Alison got the server's attention.

"You got five minutes," the dancer said.

The server arrived. "What can I get for you?" she said.

"I'll have another margarita," Alison said.

"The usual, thanks honey," the dancer said.

The server left.

"What's your name?" Alison said.

"I don't wanna go on record."

"No record, just a few questions."

The dancer looking at her, upright in the chair. Probably wasn't even twenty-one, which was illegal with the place serving alcohol. Life had seemed so innocent to Alison at twenty-one, getting cheated on by assholes the equivalent to an apocalypse. But then she hadn't grown up in Los Angeles, or fled here from somewhere else. Transferred from the small city of San Marcos ninety miles south, L.A. had come as a shock to the vice squad newbie—and the only female. Speaking with young women in places like this reminded her of that.

"My name's Alison. I'm a homicide detective."

"Mandy."

"You work here a lot, Mandy?"

"Most evenings, six to eleven."

"You like it?"

Mandy shrugged. "It's a job. I've had worse. I make decent money."

Alison nodded.

Mandy said, "The girl who was murdered . . . did she work here?"

"Why do you say that?"

"Girls leave suddenly sometimes and never come back. Some of them hang around with shitty guys."

"Will you look at a picture of her for me, tell me if you recognize her?"

"I guess."

"I have to warn you, this picture was taken after she

was killed."

"Oh."

Alison reached into her bag and took out the case file. She found the photograph and placed it facedown onto the table.

The server returned with their drinks. Mandy swallowed half her whiskey in a gulp and relaxed into her chair. She looked at the photograph on the table.

"Go ahead," Alison said.

Mandy exhaled sharply and picked up the photograph.

She gasped and placed it back onto the table and pushed it away from her, looking off to the side.

"I know her," she said weakly.

Alison's pulse quickened. "You do?"

Mandy nodded, still looking away. "That's Kaya. She worked here until, like, February."

Alison tried to contain her eagerness, not push the girl too hard. "Do you know her surname?"

Mandy was gazing into some other world.

"Mandy."

Mandy faced her, suddenly looking even younger.

"Do you know Kaya's surname?" Alison said.

"Yeah, it's ..." She screwed up her face. "White. Kaya White. It's strange—you're the third person to ask about her recently. I figured something might have happened to her, but this ..."

"Who asked about her?"

"Some guy came in here only a few hours ago asking about her. I'd just started my shift, but I heard him talking to a couple of the girls. When I asked them who he was, they said they didn't know, just that he said he was a lawyer. But they got the feeling he knew something about Kaya he wasn't saying."

"Do you know what he asked them?"

"First he asked about this rich guy that liked Kaya, and then asked a few questions about her. Nothing much. Like I said, it felt to the girls like he already knew the answers."

"This rich guy, is he from Texas?"

"Yeah, and he looks like it too."

Alison nodded. William Kane.

"Those girls the lawyer talked to, are they still here?" she said.

"No, they worked the day shift."

"And what about the other person?"

Mandy looked puzzled. "Other person?"

"You said I'm the third person to ask about Kaya. Who's the first?"

"Oh, yeah, so, day before yesterday a new girl started working here as a waitress—we all have to start as servers first, so they see we're comfortable walking around in underwear and serving drinks, and sometimes we pick up extra waitressing shifts even when we're dancers. This new girl, she was . . ." Mandy thought about it, crossing one fishnet leg over the other. "Different. That's the word.

I can't be any more specific than that 'cause she was different in a very general kind of way. Beautiful, though. I've never given much thought to sleeping with a woman but damn, I'd let that girl take me home. She was Indian, I think."

"Indian? As in the country?"

Mandy giggled. "Sorry, no, I mean Native American or whatever you're supposed to say. Said her name was Dakota. She didn't sound Native American or anything but she had that look about her, you know? And her accent wasn't from around here. Hard to say where."

Alison nodded. "Go on."

"Anyway, I was working that day, which is unusual 'cause normally I work evenings, but there I was and this new girl starts talking to me. Nothing strange, just small talk, but then she starts asking about Kaya. When's the last time I saw her, do I know where she lives, do I know why she stopped working here. I told her what I told you, that she stopped working here a bit after Christmas and that's all I know. Me and Kaya were friendly but we never hung out, and I don't know where she lived. No one here knows that kind of stuff about each other, it's just not how it works. It seemed to upset this girl, Dakota, when I said that. I asked her why she wanted to know so bad and she said that her and Kaya used to be real close but they drifted apart, stopped talking. She said she was worried about Kaya and this is the last place she knew Kaya worked. For what it's worth, I believed her."

Alison sipped her margarita, wondering what this all meant. This Dakota girl probably had nothing to do with anything, just looking for her friend. But that lawyer . . .

"This is where it gets strange," Mandy said, and Alison felt like saying, We're long past that, honey. "A few hours into Dakota's shift these three guys show up. Well, one at first, and she sits at a table with him. Then two more arrive. I didn't see the whole thing, I was busy working, but I saw one of the men smack her, hard, and I think they were trying to take her some place before the security guards stopped them and she got away."

"Take her some place?"

"I don't know for sure, but something wasn't right about the whole thing. And I guess why else would there be three of them if they weren't there to kidnap someone?"

Mandy had a point.

"Thanks for telling me all that, Mandy. I appreciate it."

Mandy downed the remaining whiskey and hopped to her feet in that energetic way of the young. "No problem, just catch whoever did it. Kaya was a sweet girl."

She turned and strode through the dressing room doors without looking back.

When Floyd opened his eyes, he was looking down at his legs straight ahead of him on the floor while something wet and warm hit the back of his neck. He lifted his head to see the gigantic redneck with a hand around his dick poking out through his jeans, piss streaming out of it. He tried to lunge at the man but something tightened around his arms, which he now realized were behind his back. Lowering his head again he spat and closed his eyes while the hot piss that reeked of alcohol and ammonia splashed over him.

"Yeah, I figured that'd wake you up," the cowboy said.

The piss trickled to its completion and the cowboy zipped himself back up.

"Now, what was that you was saying 'bout my nigger blood?"

Floyd glanced behind and saw that his hands were tied to one of the legs of the bed with what looked like a cable, becoming aware now of the ache in his biceps. He summoned all of his strength and pulled as hard as he could. His arms barely budged.

"Fuck you want with me?" he said, panic swelling inside him as possibilities vanished by the second.

The cowboy slipped a hand into his jacket and took out the longest knife Floyd had ever seen. It gleamed under the light as the cowboy moved his hand, the tip looking sharp as a spear. Floyd felt vibrations down his spine.

"Well, all your talk 'bout niggers got me thinking. What if niggers're black all the way through? What if niggers got black hearts pumping black blood through their black nigger bodies? I think it's worth finding out."

"Hold up, hold up, you don't need to lose your fuckin' mind here man, Jesus."

"Don't say the Lord's name, you ain't one of His. In the Bible it's written 'So God created mankind in His own image.' It ain't talking 'bout niggers."

Who the fuck was this nut and what was Eddie doing with him? Floyd pulled his arms again, gritting his teeth, his head about to burst.

The cowboy stood over him, one leg on either side of Floyd's.

"Could be there's a way you can keep your skin. But it depends on you."

"What you want?"

"Answers. If they're good enough, maybe I'll go get me a whore 'stead of spending my evening cutting up a nigger."

Floyd looked up at him, the man's face a mile away. "What you wanna know?"

The cowboy took a wallet out of his pocket and tossed it on Floyd's lap. It was Floyd's wallet.

"Floyd Hibiscus. That's a strange name, even for a nigger. What's your part in all this?"

"I was wondering the same about you."

"What you want with Eddie?"

"Boss wants to talk to him."

"Who's your boss?"

"Someone, trust me on this, you don't wanna fuck with."

"Answer the question."

"Saul Benedict. Runs this city and everyone in it."

Floyd watched the cowboy's face, hoping for hesitation, but instead the man grinned horribly, yellow teeth baring down at Floyd.

"'We can make our plans, but the Lord determines our steps.' Proverbs sixteen nine. You've been delivered to me, Floyd Hibiscus."

Motherfucker was crazy. Floyd straightened his fingers and wrists and tried to push them through the knot. Too tight.

The cowboy got on his hunkers and held the knife under Floyd's face, the blade swaying like a cobra.

"It was you killed my brother."

His brother . . . Jesus Christ, he meant Bill Kane. Floyd froze, the words ringing through his head, all of it clicking into place.

The cowboy looked into his eyes. "And that Eddie, he did it with you. That's the truth, ain't it?"

Floyd shook his head, his mind racing. "I don't know what in the hell you talking 'bout. Eddie owes the boss money, that's all I know."

The cowboy looked at the blade, waving it under Floyd's chin, the tip nicking his skin.

"That's the truth," Floyd said, pressing his head against the bed. "I don't know anything 'bout no—"

The cowboy pulled his hand back and thrust it forward. A burning pain erupted in Floyd's chest. He screamed and looked down to see the knife sticking out under his right shoulder, a golden "R" glistening on the hilt.

The cowboy stood up and let Floyd ride it out.

"I'm gettin' horny for some whore pussy," he said eventually. "Lie to me again and the next one goes in your black heart. You shot my brother, correct?"

Floyd shook his head, gasping. The blade in his chest was blocking his breath.

"It was . . . Eddie . . . we was just . . . collecting . . . Eddie fucked up . . . got scared . . . an accident."

Floyd could sense the man above him, his head too heavy to lift.

The cowboy said, "I know a thing or two 'bout killing and there ain't no way to kill someone by accident. You got to work at killing. You brought your guns to my brother's home. You threatened his life with those guns. You took his life with those guns. All that after stealing from him for years. There ain't no lies before God."

Floyd said nothing, just hung there, his body getting weak. There was no talking to a man like this. He closed his eyes and waited for the redneck to finish him off. In his mind he saw his wife with the baby he'd never given her, and right after it he saw Sawyer and his flannel shirt open at the neck, his blond hairs sticking up out of it, and he felt confused by this pairing of images but didn't have the energy to care, beginning to drift now, a warm darkness replacing his pain.

He'd just about passed out completely when he heard

a splintering of wood to his left, then the harsh pop of a pistol going off somewhere above him.

They checked into a fancy hotel downtown for no reason other than it was where the cab driver stopped and asked if here was okay and Eddie said it was as good as anywhere else. He and Dakota walked up the steps and through the rotating doors into a reception area that was small but elegant, dark wood panels for walls and a waterfall streaming gracefully behind the woman at reception. Eddie asked the woman if they could get a couple rooms and when the woman told him the cost he could hardly believe it and asked the woman could she repeat that when Dakota said to her, "We'll just take one room," and Eddie looked at Dakota and she looked back at him, giving nothing away until she smirked and placed a hand on his chest and said, "You're funny," and he was left wondering what, exactly, she had meant by it.

They had a look at the hotel room, which was as nice as Eddie had expected. Dakota showered and changed her clothes, Eddie trying not to glance at her when she came out of the bathroom in her bra and panties and put on tight black jeans and a short leather jacket over a black top.

"Feeling colorful I see," Eddie said.

"Dark times, Mr. Vegas." She raised an eyebrow

jokingly, her hair and skin appearing a shade darker.

They hadn't been alone until now, so they hadn't talked about what had happened at the motel, but Eddie expected Dakota to ask him about it any minute now and he wasn't sure what he'd say. How do you explain why you're being pursued by not just a couple thugs but also a seven-feet-tall cowboy from hell, one talking about his murdered brother and the others waving guns around trying to kidnap him? He could barely make sense of it himself.

At Eddie's suggestion they wandered down to the windowless hotel bar and drank overpriced drinks under the gentle glow of blue neon. They sat on the same long cushioned seat, and after a couple drinks Dakota's face shimmered before him like a spirit.

Eddie knew what she was going to say before she said it: "Who'd you piss off so badly and how'd you do it?" No beating around the bush with this woman.

"A terrible man called Saul Benedict. He thinks I owe him money."

"Thinks?"

"He's wrong."

"How does a man like him get something like that wrong?"

"That's the thing, a man like him is *never* wrong. Men like him do whatever the hell they want with no one to stop them. He says I owe him fifty large and that makes it a fact. But not to me."

"How'd you get mixed up with someone like that?"

Someone like that. Assuming he was any different.

"I worked for him."

She frowned. "Doing?"

"Intimidating people and moving product, mostly."

"By product you mean . . ."

"Cocaine."

She let it settle.

"Moving it where?" she said.

"To meeting points with the dealers who sell it on the street. I'd collect their earnings, count it before giving them more product."

"Did that man today do it with you?"

"Floyd, yeah, we did most jobs together. Also, another guy, called Sawyer, the guy you spilled the drinks on in the club—which was genius, by the way—he was the driver in case we ever needed to make a quick getaway. Man, you should see Sawyer drive. He can do things with a vehicle that I thought only happened in the movies."

He glanced at Dakota and saw he had her full attention, kept going. "Yeah, this one time—see, before I ran with Saul and the guys, I was self-employed—"

"Oh, you were?"

"Professional thief."

"Ah." Amusement in her eyes.

"Hotel rooms mostly, but I did some jewelry stores now and again. Did a bank once."

Surprise in her eyes now. "You robbed a bank?"

Eddie smiled, couldn't help himself. "It's not as glamorous as you'd think. It was just me so I wasn't going for the safe or anything like it. I needed quick cash. If you wanna rob a bank, and you're okay with a small return, just slip a note to the teller that says you've got a gun and will start shooting up the place if the teller doesn't put as many bills as will fit in the envelope you've got with you. Then when she grabs the cash from the drawer—the tellers are always female from what I've noticed—tell her no marked bills, none of the cash from the bottom of the drawer. The tellers are told to give up the money and offer no resistance—they have to give it to you. She was a nice girl, my teller, didn't seem to mind. I even said to her, 'First time being robbed?' She nodded, then giggled a little. I couldn't believe it."

"She didn't push the button under the desk?"

"They're instructed not the push it unless the situation has become potentially violent. Takeover kind of thing. The last thing anyone wants is a shootout."

Dakota looked at him intently. "Would you have started shooting?"

He smiled. "Honey, I didn't even have a gun."

"You're a piece of work." But she was smiling.

"So anyway, how I met the guys—"

"Wait, you said hotel rooms?"

"Yeah?"

"What's there to steal in a hotel room?"

"Oh, baby." He slapped his hands together. "Everything. Hotel rooms are the only places you need to rob if you do it right. You do the expensive hotels with the rich guests, get a room for yourself, and in the middle of the night you sneak into other guests' rooms and take their cash and jewelry while they're sleeping right there. They're loaded, it doesn't mean anything to them, and they don't even have to wake up. A victimless crime. I used to travel around the country staying in all these fancy hotels. Made quite a bit."

"Why'd you stop?"

"I met the guys, started working for Saul. But I think really I stopped 'cause I was lonely. I liked the thought of being a part of something. I'd watched too many fuckin' gangster movies, tell you the truth. Plus all that traveling. Anyway, when you're a thief, it's only a matter of time before you get caught. Every pro knows that. It's just most of them are addicted to the thrill of it."

"But not you."

"Not me. I'd grown tired of it, actually. And now I'm sick to death of all this gangster shit too, the hostility, the confrontation, all the dumb fucks getting so worked up over what they perceive as disrespect. Honestly, after a while feels like a bunch of kids in the schoolyard who never grew up. And, sometimes things go too far, bad things happen . . ."

Dakota was staring at him.

"Anyway, so, when I met Floyd—actually it's a pretty funny story. He was in one of the hotel rooms I was fleecing—"

"He was in one of the rooms?" Surprise in her voice, loving it.

Eddie chuckled. "Yeah, with his wife. She kept telling Floyd she wanted a weekend away, so, eventually, Floyd booked a five-star here in L.A. The wife goes, 'What? You booked a hotel in L.A.?' and Floyd says, 'You said you wanted to get out of the house.' Floyd's a funny guy.

"I snuck into Floyd's room that night, late, nearly four a.m. When I shut the door behind me there wasn't a sound except for the breathing of someone asleep. I should have spotted that right away—that I heard just one person breathing. Two people sleeping has a rhythm to it. Next thing I know a deep voice says, 'Don't move, motherfucker, 'less you want twelve holes through you.' A bedside lamp came on and there he was, sitting on the edge of the bed in a white vest and boxer shorts with little watermelons all over them. A gift from his wife he told me later. I said, 'I knew you people had a thing for watermelon, but that's taking it pretty far,' messing with him. He said, 'Try telling the wife that.'"

"Were you scared?" Dakota said.

"Oh yeah. When someone points a gun at you, don't matter who you are, you look the grim reaper in the eye. In this case I figured the guy was either gonna shoot me or, more likely, call the cops and make me wait for my own arrest."

Dakota shook her head, eyes alive. "I can't even

imagine it."

"Yeah, but it worked out. We got to talking and Floyd was impressed with my process. He asked me if anyone had ever caught me before. I said no, first time. Turns out Floyd's pretty much an insomniac. He was in prison once, long time ago, for dealing dope, when his cellmate tried to strangle him in his sleep. Nearly succeeded, too. Floyd woke up to the fucker, two hundred pounds, with his hands around Floyd's throat, a crazed look in his eyes. Floyd was just lucky a guard walked by needing a piss."

Dakota grimaced. "That's terrifying. It's no wonder he can't sleep."

Eddie nodded. "It was a wake-up call for me too. At some point someone else was gonna wake up and catch me, see my face. Or shoot me. So when Floyd said he had a job going, needed a guy could keep his cool, I jumped on it."

Dakota sipped her drink and slid a little closer to him on the seat. "What was the job?"

"A jewelry store. My first. Which would mean armed robbery. I was graduating. We did a few more jewelry stores after that, Floyd and Sawyer doing it as a side thing, Saul not knowing about it. I wasn't working for him yet. Which brings me to what I was originally trying to say: Sawyer's driving. The last place we robbed the shit hit the fan. Up until then all the robberies had been easy, not a hitch, and we got cocky, sloppy. We had previously agreed not to rob a place if there was more than a couple customers inside, or if the street outside was busy, so we did the robberies early in the morning, just after the places opened. But this time we got held up because of an accident on I-5. Bumper to bumper for hours. We should've called it off, done it another day, but like I said, we'd gotten cocky. A couple cops were in the area when someone on the street who'd seen it happen ran into them. The cops caught us coming out, started shooting at us. I felt a bullet go past my ear. Eventually we made it into the car and Sawyer did his thing. You have to understand that, until then, we'd never had much need for Sawyer. We cruised away slowly from the robberies before then. So, in a way, I guess he was proving his worth. And prove it he did. By the time we got away from the jewelry store we had half the fuckin' police force after us. Even a helicopter. But Sawyer got us away from them all without breaking a sweat. After that I swore no more armed robberies, or any kind of robberies. I don't want to be shot at by cops. And I don't want to shoot some poor cop either, his family at home. Didn't fire a single shot that day."

Dakota was still staring at him, a glimmer in her gaze. "Eddie Vegas, there's a lot more to you than meets the eye."

He smiled, enjoying the way she was looking at him. "It's like anything, you get used to it pretty quick."

She inched closer to him. "Have you ever had to shoot somebody?" The scent of sweet cherry vodka on her breath.

He looked at the floor. "Yeah."

He felt her hand on his thigh and glanced up, saw the hunger in her eyes. But the face of the dead girl popped up in front of him, her eyes frozen open, mouth a gaping hole. Now the dead girl's face became Dakota's face, swimming in his vision with those eyes open wide, dead but forever afraid. He felt the drinks coming back up.

"You feeling okay?" Dakota said.

"Yeah, yeah, just need some water." He picked up the glass of water on the table he'd not yet touched and sipped from it.

"Want to lie down? We can go up the room?" Her hand inched toward his crotch.

He felt better. "That sounds perfect."

Her face was close to his, lips red and glistening. He moved his mouth toward hers and kissed her, gently at first, then putting more into it, his hand sliding up her leg.

Actually, he felt pretty fucking great.

9 | Dakota's Tale

Floyd returned to consciousness as the cowboy flung a knife toward the door of the motel room. Floyd tried to twist to see but he was tied too tightly to the bedpost and had little strength left. The sound of a struggle ensued, and of a body thumping against the floor.

The cowboy returned and bent over Floyd and wrenched the knife from his chest. Blinding agony screamed through Floyd's bones and erupted out his mouth. The shooter charged the cowboy but the cowboy had expected it and swung an elbow behind him. The shooter dropped onto the floor before Floyd recognized him as Sawyer, who was squinting up at him now, bright blood streaming from his nostrils while the cowboy strolled toward the door, one hand casually adjusting his hat, and disappeared into the parking lot.

Sawyer crawled toward his gun five feet away and grabbed it and pulled himself to his feet. He staggered toward the doorway as a vehicle screeched in the parking lot. He raised the gun in the doorway but soon lowered it again, the sound of the vehicle fading.

Sawyer shoved the pistol into his pants and crouched before Floyd.

"You okay?" he said.

"Do I look okay to you? The hell took you? Mother-fucker was two seconds from killing me."

Sawyer worked at the knot. "Who is he? He's faster than the devil. Knocked the gun outta my hand before I could get a clean shot."

Floyd shook his head. "Later. Just get me to a hospital, I'm bleeding like a bitch."

Sawyer undid the knot and Floyd's shoulders slumped forward and Sawyer had to catch him before he hit the floor. Sawyer pushed Floyd upright and recoiled, then quickly attempted to hide this reaction.

"It's not my piss you fuckin' idiot," Floyd said. "That redneck, he ..." Floyd looked away.

"Hey, it's okay, you were tied up, there was nothing you could do ..."

Floyd felt his eyes well up and couldn't stop it. "I thought I was dead, man. I thought I was fuckin' dead ..."

"I know." Sawyer gripped Floyd's shoulder. "But you're not, you're alive."

Floyd gazed into Sawyer's eyes, thoughts of pulling him in close swarming his mind. Sawyer touched Floyd's cheek.

Floyd remembered the tears on his face and felt ashamed.

"Get me the fuck outta here, will you?" he said. "I'mma 'bout to pass out."

Sawyer helped Floyd to his feet, Floyd draping a throbbing arm over his neck, and together they shuffled toward the S.U.V.

"And don't say a word 'bout that later," Floyd said.

"About what?"

"Exactly."

At last Eddie understood why they called it "making love." Until now he'd only been having sex, and, my oh my, what he had been missing.

Dakota lay nude across him, her small breasts pressing into his chest, warm and firm, a look in her eyes he hadn't seen before: peaceful, relaxed—maybe even content. Why not? He felt pretty damn content himself.

"I don't know how people can hurt each other after doing something like that," she said. "But we do."

"I'd never hurt you."

"I believe you, Eddie Vegas."

They lay there in the serenity of the hotel room for a minute.

"Dakota, it occurs to me that while you know a lot about me, I know nothing about you."

"What do you want to know?"

"Jesus, where to begin."

"The first question that pops into your head."

"Are you Native American?"

"Funny that would be the first thing you'd ask."

"Why's that?"

"Because what does it matter? It's so superficial. But of course it matters. It always matters."

Eddie slid backwards and sat up against the headboard. "I didn't mean it like that."

"It's okay. Yes, I am Native American, of the Oglala Tribe of South Dakota."

"Your name . . ."

"It's just a name. It reminds me of where I'm from."

"So what's your real name?"

"What does it matter? It's just another name." Holding back on him now.

"Okay. Who, exactly, are you looking for here in L.A.?"

She leaned a hand on his chest and sat up.

"My sister."

"Oh."

"But we were never close. We're half-sisters, technically, sharing our mother. Until a few months ago, I hadn't heard from Kaya in over two years. Since she left the reservation."

Eddie watched her gazing deeply into her memories and waited for her to continue.

"For you to understand why I came here, now, to find her, you need to know more about her life. Our life."

"I'm listening."

Dakota sighed with a weariness far beyond her years and sat upright next to Eddie. "I don't know . . ."

"Come on, I want to know. Please." He held her hand.

"Okay." She appeared to concentrate for a moment.

"Kaya and I grew up in Pine Ridge Reservation. She's younger than me. My father, Oglala like my mother, killed himself shortly after Kaya was born. He didn't leave a note but everyone knew it was because he couldn't live with the shame of my mother giving birth to a *wasicu* child—a white child. You see, my mother was raped by a *wasicu*. I never knew for sure who but I have reason to believe it was one of the F.B.I. agents investigating the murder of a white girl from Rapid City. Kaya, although half Oglala, is white. We look alike in subtle ways if you look closely enough, but to the reservation she was *wasicu*, and they never let her forget it. Kaya was born with the curse of the half-blood: two halves that can't make a whole."

Dakota let go of his hand and made a fist with it, her gaze on something far away.

"I didn't treat her any better. I was Oglala like the other kids, trying to survive in that terrible place, and being accepted is a large part of how you do it. More than that, though, as I grew older I came more and more to blame Kaya for my father's death. My father, like many of us, lived a life of abuse and neglect from his first breath. But he was a soft, gentle man, full of love, and one of the few who had managed to avoid the bottle. He made me feel safe. I think his presence in my life, even for what little I had of it, is a big part of the reason I coped better than most of the other kids. Better than Kaya. By the time I began to understand the complexities of trauma through generations, as well as the powerlessness an Oglala man would feel by his wife being raped by a *wasicu*, and then having to rear that man's child—because he would have loved that child like his own, and he knew that—well, by then it was too late and the damage had been done to Kaya, to our relationship. I—"

Dakota's voice broke and she lowered her head, one hand wiping at her eye.

"I could have been there for her, like a big sister should be. Kaya had no one. Our mother had been losing her mind steadily ever since my father died, and Kaya was picked on by everybody her whole life. She had the most difficult life of anyone I've ever known. Then one day, at seventeen years old, she left the reservation and I never heard from her again—until six months ago."

Eddie squeezed her shoulder. "Shit, I don't know what to say."

Dakota wiped her eyes. "It gets worse. When she left,

Kaya left a note on my pillow. In the note she made a list of all the times she'd ever been raped. Beside each was a name and a date. There were four names, but over a hundred entries."

"Jesus Christ."

"The first was dated November seven, two thousand and six."

Dakota looked at Eddie. Her expression was of the most haunting sadness he'd ever seen.

"Eddie, that would make her seven years old."

"Oh my god." He felt sick.

Dakota slipped her hand around his. "She signed the note, 'Your sister, the *wasicu* of the Oglala Tribe,' and when I read that I cried and cried and cried. For days I cried. All the trauma I had repressed, hers and mine, came out in a torrent of tears. She wrote nothing of where she was going, just that she would never return. I had lost my sister, the only family I had, our mother long dead by then."

"But then she contacted you."

"Out of the blue, yeah. I had thought about trying to find her but I had no idea how. Where to even begin? She could have been anywhere. I walked the four miles to the nearest post office every day, hoping for a letter. Then, one day, almost two years later, it came. Kaya wrote that she was living in Los Angeles and doing well. She worked as a dancer at a club called the Pink Room and made good money, had even met a man there who treated her well and wanted her to live with him whenever he was in town.

I sensed something not quite right with that part but I was just so glad to hear from her. She even wrote that she missed me and hoped that, in time, we could learn to be sisters. There was no mention of me coming to see her, and no return address, but for the first time in a long time, maybe my whole life, I felt hope.

"So, I bided my time and waited for the letter that would ask me to come see her, all the while thinking about how I could raise enough cash to get to L.A. But no more letters came. Eventually I couldn't wait any longer. I arrived in L.A. five days ago to discover that Kaya had quit working at that place over four months ago. I had no money and wanted to talk to the staff about her, so I asked for a job. They gave me one and I started working there the next day. Then you showed up."

Eddie let her story settle.

"So you lived on a reservation your whole life?" he said.

"I'd make trips into nearby cities with friends some-times when we got older, but yes."

He thought about the wording of what he wanted to ask her. "Then how come you don't seem like you're from a reservation?" Still fucked it up.

She let it go. "I think that's because, in my mind, I never was. I always wanted to get away, live a different life. Some of my friends left, the ones who didn't become slaves to drugs. Even if Kaya hadn't left first, I probably would have, one day. At least that's what I told myself."

"But you don't sound Native American. You don't even sound like you're from South Dakota. You have an accent but it's . . . kind of weird, to be honest, hard to place. And the way you speak is—"

"Like I'm from here?"

"Exactly."

She smiled. "When I was fourteen, one of the older boys stole electronics from Rapid City. Cell phones, TVs, computers. We had a little TV at home but the coverage was awful and we got nothing good. He said he'd give me a D.V.D. player he stole in return for letting him see me naked. So I did."

"You *let* him?"

"It was a good deal, and he was one of the nicer, gentler boys. I felt I could handle him. I mean, I was fourteen and grew up watching the women around me being exploited. I felt like a grown woman doing some smart business for herself."

"And was it . . . okay?"

"Yeah, he just sat and jerked off, then left without saying a word. An hour later the D.V.D. player was on our doorstep."

"Okay . . ."

Dakota pinched his cheek. "I know you find that confusing. The first night I came here I looked up lots of articles on Native Americans, Pine Ridge, other reservations. One article said that ninety-four percent of Native American women living in Seattle that they had surveyed claimed they had been raped or coerced into sex. Native American women are two and a half times more likely to be raped than any other ethnic minority in the United States. I once overheard a family friend ask my mother for advice. She said, 'What do I tell my daughter when she is raped?' *When*. Not if. Trust me, I got away lightly. Not like Kaya ..."

"That's totally fucked-up. I had no idea."

"This terrible legacy of colonization and genocide and inherited trauma has devalued us even to ourselves, destroyed our communities. Sometimes I think beyond saving ..." She gazed at the floor, seeing something else.

Eddie became aware again of her incredible beauty and felt an urge to kiss her, and did. She still tasted of cherry.

"So you got a D.V.D. player," he said, prompting her.

"Yeah, and that's when my whole world changed. I started borrowing D.V.D.s from Oglala Lakota College, a small tribal college on the reservation. They had a little library. The D.V.D. collection was small, mostly donations, but I didn't care. I loved every single one I got my hands on. I would watch the movies over and over, knowing every word. I'd repeat the lines the characters would say and try to say it like them. When I was a bit older I got a membership at the library in Rapid City and borrowed as many D.V.D.s as they'd let me every few weeks, hitching a ride there with someone who had a car and was making a trip up anyway. One of my favorites was *Thelma & Louise*.

I'd stand in front of the mirror pretending I was Louise rescuing Thelma from the man trying to rape her and say, 'You let her go you fuckin' asshole or I'm gonna splatter your ugly face all over this nice car.'"

Dakota had put on a Southern accent when she said it, giggling now into her hands. "I liked to pretend to be the badass women I saw in some of the movies, women who don't let anybody mess them around or tell them what to do. When I saw *Kill Bill* I jumped around the room with an imaginary sword in my hands while Uma Thurman sliced up a million bad guys. I'd been a huge fan of hers since I saw *Pulp Fiction*, which was my favorite movie until then, but after *Kill Bill*, I was in love."

"*Pulp Fiction*, you have that shirt—"

"Yes, although—" she shot Eddie an exaggerated look of guilt—"I stole that shirt, plus pretty much all my other clothes, from stores here in L.A. I had to, I didn't have much else, and I wanted to look like I fit in, especially for when I see Kaya."

"You're pretty badass, Dakota."

"I'm glad something rubbed off. I watched all those movies for years and tried to talk the way they talked. Not just that, I wanted to think like them, move like them—I wanted to *be* them. And when I arrived here, the home of all these movies and actors and that whole world, I think a part of me *did* become them. I'm not the same person who left Pine Ridge a week ago, Eddie."

"I bet." He felt tingles in his groin at the way she was

speaking about herself, so full of energy, full of power.

Dakota looked at him with an expression of utmost sincerity. "You have to understand, it's not that I don't appreciate my culture and heritage, my people—because I do, I really do, and I wish there was some way I could help them—it's just that I never had the opportunity to appreciate something else."

Eddie nodded. "I understand. If I help you find your sister, would you leave L.A. and go somewhere with me?"

She looked at him thoughtfully. "You want me to be with you?" Not feigning the surprise, meaning it.

"Dakota, even in all the crazy situations I've been in, some of them straight from your Hollywood movies, nothing has ever made me feel as alive as I feel when I'm with you."

It hit her in the heart; he could tell by her expression.

"Yes, Eddie Vegas, I'll come with you."

She kissed him and he cupped her breast, eager to make love for the second time in his life.

A thought entered his mind. "One last thing: What happened to the men who . . . did that to your sister?"

Dakota narrowed her eyes and looked past him, a hard look on her face. "They got what they deserved, put it that way."

Eddie knew better than to ask. He lay Dakota on her back and kissed her slender belly, the cool evening air from the open window washing over his back.

10 | Heavy Rain

Alison kissed Charlie on his soft cheek and pulled him closer, the two of them wrapped in a blanket with a bowl of salty popcorn between them. On the TV *Toy Story 3* was drawing to its close, Alison surprised to find herself tearing up at the incessant hardships these children's toys endured. Charlie's little face looked up at her, content with this rare opportunity to watch his favorite movie with his mom. He was a quiet boy, and that made her love him even more, the love sometimes a painful thing in her chest. So when her cell phone beeped as a text message came through, she cursed it silently, knowing exactly what it meant. She knew Charlie knew it, too.

He watched her with resigned eyes as she leaned forward to pick up the phone.

Homicide: 4th Fl., 543 S. Olive St., 90013.

She sighed. That address was beside Pershing Square, twenty-five minutes away. The problem with being on call in this city: you always get fucking called.

"Sweetie, I'm really sorry but I got called into work."

Charlie turned back to the TV without a word.

"I'll get Sarah to come and sit with you while I'm away."

No response.

"I'll make it up to you, sweetheart, I promise. How about we go to the movies tomorrow, after school? We can see anything you like. We can even get pizza."

Nothing; she may as well have left already.

Alison kissed Charlie's cheek and stood looking at him for a moment, stroking his head. There it was, that pain again, like a shard of glass lodged between her ribs.

"I love you," she said, and went upstairs to change into something less comfortable, dialing Sarah on the way.

The address turned out to be the office of a hotshot lawyer known to represent some of the city's richest criminals. Alison remembered the lawyer, named Jerry Boylan, had gotten a top banker off the hook during a rape trial in what the media painted as a fluke win but one which, in reality,

L.A.P.D. had been expecting, the D.N.A. evidence found at the scene having proved inconclusive. But everybody and their mother knew they'd caught the right guy, everything pointing the finger at him, including the victim, but nothing irrefutable. That snake lawyer twisted the whole thing, made the victim look like a jilted ex-lover and got the jury—mostly older conservatives—sympathetic to the banker: What's a poor guy to do when a spurned woman cries rape, after all? So Alison didn't much care that the lawyer had been murdered until she saw the wound in his sternum: deep and narrow and identical to one she'd read about in the paper just that morning. The article (written by Frederica Lounds, no less) claimed that two men had been murdered three days ago in a gas station in Indio, just off I-10. But what had caught Alison's attention was the method: an approximately three-inch deep, half-inch wide penetration in the sternum of one of the victims, and both of the victims with their throats cut. The lawyer had the same wound in his sternum. His throat had been cut, too.

Something shiny beneath the desk caught her eye. She bent down and picked it up. A Zippo lighter of solid gold with a silver "R" engraved into it. R? Probably not the lawyer's.

As Alison stood looking at the lawyer dead in his chair behind his desk, and then looked out the wall of glass behind him at Pershing Square four floors below, she remembered something else: Mandy, the dancer in the strip club, had said that a lawyer had come into the place that same day asking about Kaya. Was it you, Jerry? Were you involved in the murders? Certainly you had the clientele for it.

"You all done here, Detective?" said a voice behind Alison.

She spun to find a forensic standing there, a case in her hand.

"Jeez. Creep around much?"

"Sorry."

The young woman could have been doing jumping jacks behind her and Alison wouldn't have noticed, lost to her thoughts.

"It's okay, I was ten miles away," Alison said. "All these bodies, they ever get to you?"

The woman hesitated, probably shocked a detective had given her the time of day.

Alison said, "I guess not. Would make it pretty difficult to do your job if they did."

"Sometimes. It's not the fact they're dead that bothers me. It's that they were murdered."

"I hear you. Nobody in this city realizes how many murderers share it with them. Eat the same food, walk the same streets, vote for the same politicians." She looked at the forensic, the woman waiting patiently for whatever this was to end. "You know what I've learned in my over three years now in homicide?"

"What's that, Detective?"

"Not a goddamn thing. People kill people. Period."

"Know what I've learned in my two analyzing crime scenes?"

"That detectives are jaded assholes?"

The forensic smiled. "That murderers make as many mistakes as the rest of us."

Alison nodded. "Except when they don't," she said, thinking of Jennifer O'Malley cut into twelve pieces and scattered across twelve locations, not a single clue left behind.

The forensic said, "Sometimes, to make it easier, I pretend they're dummies. Like I'm back in uni, learning how to do it."

"That might work for you here, collecting evidence. But when I'm out there speaking with distraught families, interviewing suspects, and when the months keeping rolling by and the killer's still out there, getting away with it, the only chance these people have at justice means I can never forget that they are people."

Alison shook her head, hearing herself. She needed a vacation, just her and Charlie and hot sand between their toes.

"Yeah, I'm done here, go ahead," she said.

She took one last glance at the lawyer, his sliced throat aimed at the ceiling, terrible shock in his eyes, and left the office.

10:45 p.m. Mandy should be out soon, if she was working tonight. Sitting in her car parked across the street from the alleyway at the back of the Pink Room, Alison took a bite out of the veggie burger she'd got at a drive-through and chugged her coffee. The rain had returned, pummeling the roof like a thousand tiny fists while the car's speakers sang her music library to her, currently "Spark in the Dark" by Alice Cooper. Sometimes it was better to live in the '80s.

Alison spotted the shape of a man almost entirely hidden within the darkness of the alleyway, the slow burn of a cigarette giving him away. He faced the back door of the club, waiting for someone, it seemed, his back leaned against the wall.

Alison put her hand into her pocket and was surprised to feel something there. She pulled it out: the lighter. Shit, she'd totally forgotten about it. It should have been checked for prints. By now, any prints it might have had would have been totally destroyed by her own. It was unlike her to make such a mistake. The lack of sleep was getting to her. She flicked open the cap and thumbed the wheel. A flame crackled into life. Was it the same lighter her killer had used to light his cigarettes? She had a feeling it was.

Ten minutes later the back door of the club opened and white light beamed out of the crack as a woman came out into the alleyway. The woman opened an umbrella above her head as the door swung shut behind her. For a moment, everything went black. When Alison's eyes adjusted she saw that the man had approached the woman, saying something to her now. The woman pivoted away from him, shaking her head vigorously, and marched toward the street. The glow of a streetlight illuminated the woman's face: Mandy.

The man ran after Mandy and grabbed her shoulder, spinning her, then grabbed her throat with one arm, slamming her into the wall. Mandy dropped the umbrella, her hands clutching at her neck.

Alison was out of the car and running before she felt the emptiness of her holster and remembered that she'd set her Glock onto the passenger seat. Too late to go back; she'd have to attack the guy, the element of surprise her only advantage. *Always assume the perp is packing*, one of her trainers in the academy had said. She never forgot it.

She sprinted up behind the man, the heavy rain drowning out her footsteps, and jammed a heel into the back of his knee. He cried out as his leg buckled, and released Mandy, who gulped at the air. Alison swung her fist as the man dropped, hitting him firmly in the jaw, sharp pain shooting up her wrist. The man collapsed onto the pavement on his back.

Alison glanced at Mandy and went to check the man for a weapon. He lashed out a leg and caught her in the stomach, knocking the wind out of her. She doubled over, gasping, a hand on her belly, and heard the click of a revolver being cocked.

"Lewis stop!" Mandy said. "She's a cop!"

Alison looked up to see what would or wouldn't be the last thing she'd ever see. Lewis hesitated, the revolver in his hand staring at her hungrily. A huge tattoo on his neck gave it a stretched look.

"Damn it," he said. He got to his feet and backed away slowly, still pointing the gun at her, until he turned and fled into the darkness.

Alison struggled to an upright stance, sucking in deep breaths. Her knuckles throbbed.

"What the fuck were you thinking, lady?" Mandy said, rubbing her throat, red now with a handprint. "He's gonna make me pay for that."

"Make you pay? Why don't you have him arrested?"

Mandy shot her a look that said, *You for real?* "You fucking cops, you're all the same."

"I don't get it. The guy was choking you."

"Yeah, Lewis is a problem. But he's my problem. And he was just trying to scare me. But now . . ."

Mandy picked up her umbrella, held it above her head, and fished a cigarette out of her purse.

"Where'd you meet a piece of shit like him?" Alison said.

"You're looking at it."

"The club?"

"Where else?"

Mandy lit the cigarette and sucked deep. She exhaled a plume of smoke and her body relaxed, a calmness settling over her.

She said, "He was nice at first. They always are. We went on a couple dates. I wouldn't usually date a customer, it's, like, an unspoken law of stripping, but, I dunno, he was charming I guess. Then we slept together and everything changed. Lewis started freaking out about me being a dancer, jealous of other men watching me. I said it's my fucking job, asshole, and he said 'No, your job is to be my woman.' Me being a dancer is how we met in the first place, so . . ." She shrugged her shoulders. "Fuck if I know how men think. All I know is they're all broken in some important way. Fucking assholes."

Mandy took another drag and looked at Alison curiously. "What you doing here anyway?"

Alison had almost forgot. "I have another picture for you to look at."

"Lucky me."

"Nothing gruesome this time."

"Come on then, give it here."

Alison took her phone out of her pocket and found the photograph of Jerry Boylan she'd downloaded from his website, the slimeball smirking up at her, smug even in death. She handed the phone to Mandy without saying anything.

Mandy looked at it for two seconds and handed the phone back to her.

"Look at you, Clarence Starling. Catching killers and kicking ass."

"You recognize him?"

"It's the lawyer who came by yesterday asking about Kaya, as I'm sure you've figured. I'd ask how you found him but you probably can't tell me, can you?"

Alison pocketed the phone, aware now of how soaked she was from the rain. "No, I'll tell you. He was murdered."

Mandy blew smoke at her. "Sounds like you got your hands full."

"In this city, always. Thanks again for your help, Mandy. See you around. And get yourself some pepper spray. Next time that asshole tries anything, blind him."

Alison made for her car, beginning to shiver now. If it was because of the rain or having stared down a barrel, she couldn't say.

"Hey, Detective," Mandy called from behind.

Alison looked back.

"Can you give me a ride home?"

11 | Gay Larry

Right as Eddie was about to fall asleep, his eyes snapped open. He squinted into the darkness of the hotel room and listened. Just the sound of Dakota breathing beside him.

He slipped out of the bed and crept silently toward the opened window, peered out. The street below was dark and empty except for a group of young women dressed to the nines, flailing their handbags about and laughing. He looked at the clock beside the bed: 12:31 a.m.

Eddie stood over Dakota and shook her shoulder, whispering her name. She stirred but didn't wake. He shook her harder.

She squinted up at him. "Kaya?"

"Dakota, get up, we have to leave here. Now."

"What? What time is—"

"Get up, come on, we have to go."

She sat up, switching the bedside lamp on. In the light her hair was messy, half of it coming up over one side of her head, her eyes so squinted they could have been glued shut. But, fuck, she was still gorgeous.

"What's going on?" she said.

He forced himself to remain calm. "What's going on is Saul's men are going to bust in that door any second and shoot both of us in the head. We need to leave right fucking now." He failed.

It opened her eyes. "Shit, okay. Why?"

"Why what?"

"Why do you think they're coming all of a sudden? You seemed pretty relaxed when you were fucking me last—"

"I know I know, but, look—" He thought about it. "Just as I was falling asleep, I had this image of that big cowboy sitting there in your motel room when I arrived, and then I thought of how Floyd walked in right behind me, and then I thought, how did they find the room?"

Dakota stared at the bedsheets for a moment. "Floyd probably waited outside your apartment and followed you there. But the cowboy . . . I have no idea how he knew all he knew . . . You're right, it's not safe here. Why do you think they'll shoot us? Don't they want to take you somewhere?"

Eddie shook his head. "That was then. I've slipped away twice now, and lemme tell you, Saul is not a patient man. I once saw him shoot a man in the kneecap for being five minutes late to a meeting. He'll be so pissed by now he'll just want me out of the way. And that means you too, you're part of this whole thing now. And I can tell you another thing: we won't get away a third time. Not even Jesus Christ himself would get away from these guys a third time. And that fucking cowboy, I don't want to see him again." He thought about Floyd and Sawyer as he said it. They'd been through a lot together, the three of them; could they really kill him in cold blood? A second later, the answer arrived: Yes, they could. These men were of a different breed, he'd always known that. And if they were coming to execute him, there'd be more than just the two of them . . .

Dakota said it as he thought it: "Where will we go?"

He looked at her. "What if we left the city right now, didn't look back? We'd get away—"

"Not without my sister."

It was an argument he had no hope of winning. He nodded. "There is someone they don't know about. I was going to bring you to him tomorrow anyway. He might be able to help us find your sister. But I don't know if he'll go for it. It's been years."

"Who?"

"Gay Larry."

"Gay Larry?"

"Gay Larry."

"Right."

"Trust me, you've never met a man like Gay Larry."

"Actually, there was a Gay Larry in the reservation."

"Really?"

"No."

"You're funny. Now get changed, we gotta go."

"We're just gonna show up?"

"I'd call him but I don't remember his number. Last I heard he was doing well for himself, living up in the hills. I remember the house because I drove by it last summer. Well, I'm pretty sure it was his place."

What if Gay Larry had moved since then (if it was even the right place)? Shit, what choice did they have?

Gay Larry lived on Mulholland Drive in one of those extremely modern and expensive houses that hang out of the Hollywood Hills like tumors. When Dakota saw a street sign in the cab, she said, "Mulholland Drive! Like the movie!" Then, "Well, I hope not like the movie . . ."

Eddie said, "Honestly, sometimes I feel like I'm living in a movie. No, not just one movie, but different parts of lots of movies."

The cabbie said, "Sometimes I feel like I'm Robert De Niro in *Taxi Driver*, but the L.A. version."

That shut them all up.

The cab vomited them out at the gate at the bottom of Gay Larry's driveway.

"Here goes," Eddie said, and pushed the intercom.

Nothing happened so he pushed it again.

"Who is it?" said a deep male voice.

"Is that you, Larry? It's Eddie Vegas."

"Eddie fucking Vegas. To what do I owe the headache?"

"Larry, fuck am I glad to hear your voice. Can we come up?"

"Who's we, honey?"

"Oh, my . . . wife, Dakota, and me. We could use your help."

A pause. "Come on up, handsome."

A motor hummed and the gates came apart. Eddie slipped through the crack, Dakota behind him.

"So I'm your wife now," she said.

"Sorry about that, I panicked. Should have said girlfriend."

"You don't make much sense sometimes."

"You only figuring that out now?"

"Fair point."

"Listen, don't say a word about why we're here to Gay Larry. And whatever you do, don't call him Gay Larry."

"I wasn't going to."

They passed a red Lamborghini Huracán Spyder as the front door opened to reveal a tall, broad-shouldered woman, a scarlet dress wrapped tight around her body.

"Eddie fucking Vegas," the woman said in Gay Larry's deep voice. Eddie nearly jumped. Christ—the woman was him.

"You've changed I see," Eddie said.

"Only on the outside, honey."

Then again, not that much, Eddie thought, glancing at the bulge pushing through the crotch of Gay Larry's dress.

"This is my wife, Dakota. Dakota, meet my old friend, Gay Larry." Fuck.

Gay Larry ignored it. "It's a pleasure, Dakota." He took hold of her hand by the fingertips, placing his other hand gently on top. "After you two." He extended an arm toward the house.

Eddie followed Dakota inside.

Eddie said, "You just leave that Lamborghini out there, huh? You don't lock it up in the garage?"

"Oh, I keep my nineteen seventy-one Pontiac G.T.O. Judge in the garage," Gay Larry said behind him. "It's much more precious to me. There's only seventeen of them in the world."

"Wow."

"And Eddie, I'm not gay. I've told you that before."

"Old habits, Larry. I don't mean anything by it."

"I know, honey. But my name isn't Larry, either."

The doorway opened up into a huge foyer, everything made of marble. A gigantic chandelier sparkled above them. Dakota stopped walking and Eddie did the same.

"It's not?" he said.

"No, Eddie, it's not. My name is Lois now."

"Ah. Okay." Just when he thought the week couldn't get any weirder.

"Follow me, lovelies," said Gay Larry—no, Lois; he'd have to remember that.

Lois led them into a room that contained a cream, leather, L-shaped sofa and a massive flatscreen attached to the wall in front of it. A cream rug on the floor absorbed their footfalls as they sat on the sofa. The entire right wall was made of glass and Lois told them to look out through it. It was too dark to see anything out there until a light blinked on outside and the view opened up: a green swimming pool glinted under the brightness and beyond it a million city lights twinkled up at them.

"Wow, that's the most beautiful thing I've ever seen," Dakota said.

"Unbelievable, Larry," Eddie said.

Gay Larry stared blankly back at him.

Shit, he'd called him Larry again. "Fuck, sorry Larry—Lois." He felt Dakota sniggering beside him.

"This is difficult for you, isn't it?" Lois said.

"It's certainly different."

Dakota said, "Oh for fuck sake, her name used to be Larry, now it's Lois. Simple." Enjoying herself. "It's lovely to meet you, Lois. Your home is breathtaking."

Lois beamed. "How did you convince this gorgeous

woman to marry you, Eddie?"

"With a gun."

Lois let loose a laugh. "I'd believe it. I'll fix us some drinks and then I want to hear all about that story. Have you grown up yet, Eddie, or are you still drinking beer? And what about you, darling, what do you fancy?"

"Surprise me," Dakota said.

"Oh, I like this one already. And you, Eddie?"

"I'll have what she's having."

"Back in a flash," Lois said, and swept elegantly out of the room, long blond hair (a wig, Eddie assumed) swishing behind her.

Eddie looked sideways at Dakota. "I haven't a fucking clue what's going on anymore."

"What's going on is we're sitting inside the most gorgeous house I've ever seen, looking out at the most beautiful view."

"Yeah, it's something." He reached for the remote control and slapped his thumb at it until the gigantic TV came alive. A news reporter started telling him about terrible things. He set the remote down and watched the woman speak.

"How did Lois make her money?" Dakota said.

"Porn."

"For real?"

"Yeah, owns a company that produces it. Although he—" Eddie made bunny ears with his fingers—"'acted' in hundreds of them before that. That was all gay porn, hence the nickname, but his company produces all kinds of stuff."

"Her. You should respect Lois's wish to be called 'her.' Did you come up with that nickname?"

"Nah, of course not, it's just all I ever knew to call him. Her. She didn't mind so much back then. Did say she wasn't gay every now and then but I don't know who she thought she was fooling with that, sucking off guys every day."

Lois returned with three neon blue cocktails on a shiny gold tray, tiny pink flamingos bobbing up out of them.

"Here you go, lovelies. This is my own recipe. I call it 'Blue Velvet.' Have a try."

Eddie and Dakota reached forward and grabbed a cocktail each. The scent of it wafted up Eddie's nose: A touch of citrus but also something else . . . soap?

Dakota was sniffing beside him.

"There's cilantro in this," she said.

"Very good," Lois said. "Essence of cilantro. Are you two going to smell it all night or drink the damn thing?"

Eddie sipped. The initial taste was extremely sour, then deliciously sweet, a touch of lime and ginger coming through, and after that, a refreshing leafy flavor rested on his tongue beneath an alcoholic warmth.

"Holy crap, that's the nicest cocktail I've ever had," he said.

"Absolutely delicious," Dakota said.

Lois sat back into the sofa beside Dakota, her cocktail in one hand. As she crossed one leg over the other, Eddie caught a glimpse of her balls and nearly choked on the straw.

"You okay there, Eddie?" Lois said.

He nodded, coughing. "Just went down the wrong way."

On the TV, the news reporter said something about how unnatural and bizarre the rain in Los Angeles had been while wildfires decimated Northern California.

Lois turned in the seat to face Dakota. "So, I simply must know, what on Earth do you see in a man like him?"

Dakota hesitated, and Lois said, "Because, this guy—I know you married him, but let me tell you, Eddie is a slippery one, aren't you, Eddie?"

Eddie said, "What we talking about here?"

"You know exactly what we're talking about."

"For Christ sake, Larry, that was years ago."

"Lois."

"Lois, Alhambra was years ago."

"That doesn't mean it didn't happen. To be honest, I never thought I'd see you again."

"Yeah, well, me too."

"What happened in Alhambra?" Dakota said.

Eddie and Lois looked at each other.

"Eddie, why don't you tell your wife what you did in Alhambra. I'm interested to hear how you describe it."

"I don't want to talk about that right now, Lois. For

what it's worth, I am truly sorry. Really, I am. You didn't deserve it. I was young and reckless and totally fuckin' petrified. I hoped the years would have, you know, fixed it between us. I mean, look at you, look at this house. Shit, you got the better deal in the end. I have nothing."

Lois stared at him with narrowed eyes for a moment, then looked away, her face softening. "You're right. Let bygones be bygones. I am grateful for what I have, no doubt. But you have nothing? What about your wife?"

"Oh, well, of course, I'm very grateful for my wife." Eddie looked at Dakota and forced a smile of a man over-whelmed with appreciation. "Dakota is the light of my life."

"Cut the shit, Eddie, I know you're not married. I know you. You don't even have rings for God's sake."

"We couldn't afford them, got married on an impulse."

"Are you capable of saying something that isn't bull-shit?"

"All right, you got me. I don't have a wife."

"Are you going to tell me why you're really here or will that be bullshit too?"

Eddie glanced at his feet, thinking about it. Lois would know if he was lying, but could she be trust-ed? Then again, maybe some trust was necessary if he expected Lois to help them find Kaya.

"All right, Lois, I'll give it to you straight. There's some men trying to find me, find us—" he glanced at Dakota—"and when I say 'find,' I mean they want to bury us in the desert. They're watching the hotels, I think, so we had to come stay somewhere they wouldn't be able to link me to. You're the only person I know that they don't know about. We plan on leaving the city, maybe even the country, but there's someone we have to find first. And, well, to be honest, I was hoping you could help us out with that last part."

Lois sipped through her straw, uncrossed her legs, placed the cocktail on the coffee table, recrossed her legs, and said, "So you're telling me that some men want to kill you, and you've decided to put my life in danger by hiding here, in my home. Do I have that right, Eddie?"

"There's no way they could know we're here. I know you don't owe me anything, that it's me who owes you, but we were friends once La—Lois. We just need to lay low for a while, until we find Dakota's sister, and then, I swear, you'll never see us again."

Lois seemed to think about it. "Who wants to kill you?"

"Saul Benedict."

Lois's eyes popped. "Saul Benedict? Oh, Eddie, you silly little man. What have you done?"

"I fucked up a job and now Saul wants me to pay him the fifty grand I cost him. Like I have it. So I bailed."

"How did you get involved with Saul Benedict?"

"Started working for him a couple years ago. Long story."

Lois sighed dramatically. "Okay, Eddie, for old time's

sake, you and your friend—whose role in this you have not at all explained, by the way—can stay here for tonight. But as soon as that sun rises I want you out, and I'm not helping you find anybody. I've got a good thing going now and I don't ever want to see you again after tonight."

"Thank you thank you thank you. You won't regret it."

"I hope not, Eddie. Now if you'll both excuse me, I need to use the little girl's room. Back in a flash."

Lois left the room and Dakota scooted across the sofa toward Eddie.

"So much for not saying a word about why we're here," she said.

"I didn't have a choice. It's just a few hours, then we're gone."

"Then we find Kaya."

"Yeah. Then we get the fuck out of L.A., whether she wants to come or not."

"How are we going to find her?"

"Fuck you asking me for? She's your sister. I figured you had some kind of plan."

"I was hoping you did. I don't know anything about this city."

Eddie slapped his knee. "Well, isn't that fantastic. Asking someone rich with connections like Gay Larry was the extent of my plan. Why don't we just go knocking on doors? Who knows, your sister might open one of them. Better yet, we'll shout her name on the street. She might hear us and come running." He shook his head.

"We haven't a hope of finding her."

Dakota's lip trembled and she gazed at her feet. Eddie felt it in his chest like a wound.

"I'm sorry. That was a stupid thing to say. I'm an idiot, don't listen to me. We'll find your sister, she's around here somewhere. You said she was a stripper. We'll visit every strip club in the city, ask around. I bet we find someone who knows her, if we don't find Kaya herself. Okay?"

Dakota nodded like a child being scolded. "I'm all she has, Eddie. And she's all I have. My little sister. I miss her."

"We'll find her, I promise."

Dakota rested her head on his shoulder and he rubbed her side gently. Once again he was reminded of how much he cared about this woman who'd drifted into his life like a dream. Who he barely fucking knew. It was a nice feeling, warm and serene, but with a pain attached to it, a pain that could grow if he let it.

The news reporter on the TV returned after an ad break and informed them of a robbery downtown that had turned into a shootout with police, the gunman injuring two officers before they put him down.

Eddie said, "Hey, you want a glass of water? I'm dying here. I'll be right back with some water, okay?"

He came out into the massive foyer, the air colder in here. Light spilled out of an open door opposite him. He moved toward it and heard Lois's voice: "Does this mean we're even? My debts are paid?"

Eddie peered his head inside and Lois spotted him.

Lois said, "Listen, I must be off, I have an old friend over tonight, but we'll figure this out tomorrow, 'kay?"

Lois put the cell phone down. "Bastard. I owe him some money and he won't stop letting me know about it."

"I know the feeling."

"You looking for something?"

"Just water."

"Glasses are in that cupboard there."

Eddie grabbed two and set them down beside the sink and filled them with water.

"Lois, I've always taken you to be pretty upfront. What's with all this 'I'm not gay' shit? You're wearing a fuckin' dress."

"Not just any dress, honey. This is a Jean Paul Gaultier."

"I don't know what the fuck that means, Lois."

"It means I've been enslaved by vanity and capitalism."

"Okay."

"I'm not gay, Eddie, because I'm not a man. I am a straight woman."

"Lois, I don't mean to be rude when I say this, but I can see your fuckin' cock pushing through your dress."

Lois glanced at it. "Yes, that's unfortunate. I've made a down payment on the surgery but it'll be a while until I'm that far into the journey. You're a little behind the times, Eddie. There are many women walking around with male genitalia, just as there are men with female genitalia. And everything in between. Gender and sex are not the same thing."

"I know that, I mean, shit, I just thought you were gay."

"No, I'm a beautiful, heterosexual woman trapped in this, let's be honest, gorgeous man's body."

"So that surgery—they're gonna make you into a woman?"

"They're going to make the outside match the inside, yes."

"Must cost a lot."

"Oh, Eddie, an arm and a leg. Or in this case a cock and a pair of balls. The estimate for all the surgeries is one hundred and twenty thousand dollars. I imagine it will magically grow as the time approaches."

"Shit, that's a lot. Not to you though, right? You're loaded."

"Not quite. I'm going broke, the business is going down the toilet. All this free porn is killing the industry, and the big companies driving it are forcing producers like me into bad deals. I'll have to sell my beautiful cars, which kills me to say, but it's more important I become my true self."

"That's tough, I didn't realize."

"Before I can begin the surgeries I have to go on hormone treatment for one year and prove I can live as a woman during that time. A 'real-life experience' they call it. Hence the dress. I feel a little silly in it, to be honest with you, still having the body of a man and all, but, in another way, it feels quite freeing not having to pretend anymore."

"I had no idea, Lois. I'm sorry for being, you know . . . insensitive."

Lois smiled. "I never thought I'd hear Eddie Vegas say the word 'insensitive.' You must be getting soft. Come on, your beautiful wife is all by herself."

Lois left the kitchen. Eddie picked up the glasses of water and followed her.

When he entered the room after Lois, Dakota smiled at him. It surprised him for a second. He smiled back at her and her gaze moved onto the TV. Her face changed then, the smile faltering at first, then dropping away completely, replaced with a look of surprise, followed by one of horror, her bottom lip coming away from the top.

Eddie faced the TV and his blood ran cold. The glasses slipped out of his fingers and smashed at his feet. On the screen three women posed in matching black bras, underwear and fishnet tights, all smiling at the camera. Text beneath the image read "(L-R) Colleague of victim, Tiffany Johnson; Victim, Kaya White; and colleague of victim, Mandy Leibowitz at the Pink Room in Los Angeles." The reporter's voice spoke over the photograph: " . . . of this, the only known photograph of one of the murder victims, Kaya White, whose last known whereabouts is her previous place of work, a gentleman's club called the Pink Room in Los Angeles where White worked as a dancer. L.A.P.D. requests family, friends and associates of White, as well as anyone who has any information, to please come forward . . ."

Eddie felt his legs buckle and stuck a hand out to guide him onto the sofa beside him, his gaze never leaving the screen. It was the woman in the middle Eddie couldn't take his eyes off. He'd shot her and buried her in the dirt and now here she was, staring back at him.

Jesus Christ. He'd murdered Dakota's sister.

The full weight of it didn't hit until a scream tore free of Dakota's throat—a guttural, violent, agonized scream that ripped its way out of her body like a demon from hell. He couldn't bring himself to look at her until she collapsed onto her hands and knees, that awful scream still going through her.

"I'm so sorry, I'm so sorry," he heard himself repeating uselessly in her ear, somehow on the floor beside her, but he saw that she couldn't hear him, couldn't hear anything but her own terrible scream rebounding off the cold marble floor and coming back to her.

12 | Indio

They walked hand in hand among the tombstones, Charlie asking what they were for.

Alison said, "When people die, their bodies are buried under the ground and these tombstones go on top so that people know where to find them."

"Why aren't they pretty colors?" Charlie said.

She had no answer to that.

They arrived at the reason for their visit: a cream granite tombstone larger than all the rest with the image of Jennifer O'Malley etched into it. Beneath her smiling face cursive script read "Cherished Daughter."

"Who's that girl?" Charlie said, pointing at her.

"Her name is Jennifer. Mommy was supposed to help her once, but couldn't."

His little face looking up at her. "Help her with what?"

"Help her to find somebody."

"How come she's dead?"

"Sometimes people just die, sweetie. There's no reason."

"How did she die?"

An image of Jennifer's severed arm inside a white plastic bag flashed in Alison's mind and she smelled the putrid rotting flesh and was right there at those garbage bins all over again.

She rubbed Charlie's head. How to answer that without lying to him?

"Somebody hurt her, Charlie. Some people are not nice like Mommy and Sarah and your dad. Some people, not many, but some people want to hurt other people. That's why you don't talk to strangers or go anywhere with someone unless Mommy said you can."

Too many words; she saw it by his faltering expression.

"Do you want to put the pretty flowers on Jennifer's grave?" she said. "They can be a gift from you."

Charlie nodded and stretched out his arms. Alison bent down and handed him the bouquet of orange marigolds and guided him as he shuffled to the tombstone.

"Put them right here," she said, tapping on the base of the stone.

Charlie set the flowers down and looked up at her.

"Good boy. Jennifer will be really pleased with them. I bet she's watching over us right now and saying thank you."

"You're welcome, Jennifer," Charlie said, and giggled, his little hands up at his chin as if surprised by himself.

Alison chuckled, and as she watched Charlie giggling back at her, her chuckling became a fit of laughter. They stood giggling at each other for a minute and the day seemed to brighten around them, the gray clouds moving on.

"Detective Lockley, it's nice to see you here," said a woman's voice.

Mrs. O'Malley watched them from the path.

"And who is this handsome young man?" Mrs. O'Malley said.

"This is my son, Charlie. We came to give Jennifer some flowers, didn't we, Charlie?"

Charlie nodded shyly, one hand on Alison's leg.

"That's very kind of you, Charlie. Jennifer loved flowers." To Alison: "Three years, can you believe it?"

"Three long, fast years. How have you and Mr. O'Malley been doing?"

Mrs. O'Malley gazed down at her daughter's grave. "I'd like to say it gets easier but that simply isn't the case. You just get more numb. Frank couldn't even come here today. He comes a couple times per week, usually, but today he got up and went straight to the bar."

"I can't even imagine . . ."

"Any new murder cases, Detective?"

"A young woman was murdered recently. The same age as Jennifer was."

Mrs. O'Malley scowled and shook her head. "The poor girl. Find whoever did it, Detective. Find them for Jennifer."

"I'll do my best. We'll leave you in peace. Say bye bye, Charlie."

"Bye bye," Charlie said, and waved.

"Goodbye Charlie, it was lovely to meet you. It was nice seeing you again, Detective."

"You too, Mrs. O'Malley. Take care."

Alison took Charlie's hand and together they walked around Jennifer's grave and onto the path.

"Detective," Mrs. O'Malley said.

Alison glanced behind.

"Jennifer thanks you for everything you did for her. And so do we."

Alison smiled and continued through the cemetery with Charlie, the dead watching them from every side.

Alison dropped Charlie off at his father's condo so his father could bring him to school later (it didn't start until 11.00 a.m. today for some reason she hadn't bothered to discover, glad of the sleep-in), not staying to receive another lecture from her ex-husband on the toll the job must be taking on her (this coming from a man who forclosed on people's homes for a living and couldn't give a shit), or, worse, be smugly gawked at by the perky-titted twenty-two-year-old he was fucking.

She made it to Indio just under two hours later and found the police station—a small, flat building located inconspicuously beside a wide and empty road—almost without realizing it. She parked her car in the near-empty parking lot and stepped out into the sunlight. It seemed brighter this far east of Los Angeles, the temperature a little higher. More than anything it was the silence that struck her. She could hear the softness of the breeze and nothing else. It felt peaceful, allowing her mind to slow down. She remembered something British horror author Susan Hill had said about it being difficult to write a ghost story set in a big city on a sunny day. Susan Hill had obviously never worked homicide in L.A. But out here, far from the city, surrounded by all this space—there were no ghosts out here.

Inside the station she flashed her badge and asked for Detective Holland.

A minute later a tall man with a mustache out of *Magnum P.I.* invited her into his office. It smelled like dust and coffee and appeared left behind by the twenty-first century.

"Detective Lockley," he said, looking her up and down, "it's nice to see you in person. Have a seat." He flashed her a smile and extended a hand.

She sat down as Holland perched his ass on the corner of his desk, looking down at her, his crotch level with her head.

He said, "I must say, you're even cuter in person than you sounded on the phone."

She blinked at him. "What the fuck did you just say?"

"Hey, I'm just offering a compliment, no need to get hysterical." Grinning stupidly at her.

"Offer me one more compliment and I'll write you up for sexual harassment, how about that? And get your prick out of my face."

The grin fell off him. He stood up and got behind the desk, sat down.

"On the phone you mentioned having some information about the gas station murders," he said, looking pissed now. Men.

"I might have. Yesterday a lawyer was murdered in Los Angeles. Nothing new there, except that his wounds matched the wounds of your gas station victims."

"So our killer moved on up to the city. I figured as much, given the fact the gas station's off the interstate. How do you know it's the same killer?"

"A three-inch-deep wound in the sternum from an uncommon, extremely sharp double-edged knife, his throat slit, and no witnesses? Come on, don't insult me."

"So, what, the guy's on a spree?"

Alison almost rolled her eyes. "Think about it. The

lawyer was killed in his private office on his private floor. It's locked from the outside, so the lawyer would have had to let the killer in. That's very different than killing a gas station attendant and an ex-con who did three for armed robbery. Was there a gun at the crime scene? It wasn't in the paper but I figure that's why he was at that gas station, the ex-con, because he lived nowhere near it."

Holland crossed his arms, looking distrustfully at her. "Yeah, there was a gun. We linked it to two murders in the Inland Empire. Also robberies."

"Then the gas station murders were self-defense. Well, not the clerk, obviously; he must have killed the clerk to preserve anonymity. The lawyer was always the only target."

"Look at you, Detective, got it all figured out. You drive all the way out here from the big city just to show me how clever you are?"

"I drove all the way out here so you can show me around your nice little town and help me ask if anyone remembers a man from Texas passing through the day of the murders."

Holland screwed up his face. "Listen, lately my wife snores worse than the goddamn bulldog she keeps at the end of the bed. I didn't get a wink of sleep last night and I haven't had my lunch yet. Stop fucking around and tell me where you're going with this."

Alison crossed her legs and sat back into the chair. "Six days ago a Texan named William Kane was murdered in his condo in downtown L.A. Kane owned the largest trucking company in Texas which doubled as transportation for Mexican cocaine all over the country. Apparently Kane was a D.E.A. informant, so could be that someone found out and had him executed. Maybe he was killed for another reason. Maybe someone intimidated him and, afraid he'd been found out as a rat, he was jumpy, tried to fight back or escape. A young woman was with him that night. She was killed too. She used to work at a strip club in the city.

"Here's where it gets interesting. A girl working at that club told me that a few days after those murders, a lawyer shows up asking questions about the murdered girl. A couple days after that a lawyer called Jerry Boylan is murdered in his office. I know what you're thinking—there's not necessarily a connection there. I thought so too, so I looked through the lawyer's files, and what do I find? The contact details of his clients, one in particular jumping out to me. A Mr. William Kane of San Antonio, Texas. So then I'm thinking, what if Boylan sold out his client and leaked that Kane was an informant? Or, maybe whoever had Kane killed had Boylan killed too, cleaning house. That would make sense except for one thing: those gas station murders."

Alison uncrossed her legs and leaned forward. "The interstate beside the gas station passes through Texas. Whoever killed Boylan worked for Kane and killed Boylan in retaliation. Our killer came from Texas."

Holland whistled and placed his hands behind his head, leaning back into his chair.

"I'll give you thirty minutes of my time," he said. "Then I'm getting surf and turf."

Holland took Alison around some businesses in the town. It was a strangely sparse place, Indio, all the buildings spread out across wide roads, distant mountains on every horizon.

At one point in Holland's car (some masculine-looking Ford that came as no surpise), Holland said, "Listen, sorry for talking to you that way in the station. You've done some good police work here, and, in retrospect, that was a little rude of me."

"Okay."

"Okay? Is that it?"

"I don't forgive you, if that's what you're looking for."

"You're a real hard-ass, aren't you?"

"I'm sick to death of my male colleagues, that's what I am. What do you want, me to be impressed by you? I'll tell you what, from now on treat your female colleagues exactly like you treat your male colleagues. View them as cops, not *female* cops. When a detective from another department comes into your office, a detective who *happens* to be female, say 'What can I do for you, Detective?' and sit down behind your desk instead of waving your balls in the detective's face, and don't for a second even *think* of commenting on any aspect of the detective's appearance or femininity. Do all that and maybe I'll have some respect for you."

Holland stopped trying to make conversation with her after that.

The workers in the businesses they visited—small restaurants and cafés, mostly, places someone might stop to refresh after a long drive—had no memory of any Southerners on the day in question.

After several fruitless visits, they pulled up outside a liquor store.

"This is the last place. Then I'm having lunch," Holland said.

They entered the liquor store—a small, dim place with an old man behind the counter squinting at them.

"How you doing, Marty?" Holland said.

"I'd feel better if I didn't have piles in my ass. Doctor says I got to put the cream on three times a day. Rubbing cream on my ass three times a day ain't my idea of a good time. Other than that, I'm doing all right. You here for a bottle of red for Martha?"

"No, not today. I'm here on police business. This is Detective Lockley from Los Angeles. She wants to ask you a couple questions."

The old man peered at Alison as if trying to see through fog.

He said, "I don't know where you got your information but I didn't do nothing wrong, officers."

"I'm glad to hear that," Alison said. "Actually, I'm here to ask if you remember serving a customer with a Southern accent on Thursday. This man came from Texas and is wanted for murder, so we're doing what we can to track him down. Maybe he doesn't have an accent, but maybe he does. Maybe he mentioned where he was coming from."

Marty scratched his chin. "Thursday, eh? No, no, I don't think so."

The man probably couldn't remember what he ate for breakfast.

"Nothing at all? You're sure?"

Marty nodded slowly, looking very confused about the whole thing.

"Well, thank you anyway." Alison began to turn around.

"Wait now," Marty said. "Now that you mention it there was a feller came in here and bought a bottle of Jack. A very big man. But he didn't say a word, not even when I asked him about his car. That's why I remember him—his car. Nineteen sixty-six Chevrolet Impala. Beautiful. She had a teal paint job with a cream roof and hub caps. I know she were a sixty-six 'cause I had one myself in the early seventies."

Marty gazed into the distance. "Those were the days. Cruising along the West Coast with the top down, the wind blowing back my hair. I had long hair back then, believe it or not. Dark and shiny like a horse's mane. The women loved it. There was this one young lady I met in Eureka and let me tell you, she could do things with her mouth that I'd never experienced—"

"Did you get a look at the license plate?" Alison said.

He appeared confused for a moment. "Oh, the license plate. No, no I didn't."

"Why do you think the man might be from Texas?"

"Texas? What about Texas?"

Alison sighed. The man hadn't a clue what he was talking about.

"This was Thursday?" Holland asked him.

"Yes, Thursday. No, wait now, it could've been Wednesday."

"All right, thanks Marty, you've been a big help," Holland said.

"You want a bottle of red for Martha?"

"Not today, Marty."

Outside the store, Holland said, "Well, Detective, that's all I got for you. Hopefully you get lucky back in the big city."

"In my experience luck doesn't much come into it."

He looked beyond her. "Maybe you haven't gambled enough then. Come on, let's get you back to your car."

It took fifteen minutes for Dakota to calm down. When her screaming finally ceased she got to her feet and paced around the room wailing like a banshee and resting her head against the walls. It was an awful sight to see, and when Dakota finally slumped to the floor in silence, her gaze vacant and far away, Eddie could no longer bear to be in the room with her. He asked Lois if she had a few cigarettes and a lighter, which she did, and said he was going for a walk, keep an eye on Dakota, and keep her away from anything pointy while you're at it.

The night air was thick and warm, the moon sharp like a scythe. A gentle breeze raised the hairs on Eddie's arms. He walked the road down the hill, passing rich people's homes and looking out at the twinkling city spread out below him. He hadn't intended to go so far but the further he went from Dakota's pain and his responsibility for it, the more air he could suck into his lungs. He found some boulders to the side of the road at the edge of the hill and sat on one of them. He lit a cigarette and filled himself with smoke and gazed down at the city of Los Angeles, wondering if he'd ever make it out. The place had a way of keeping hold of you. What was that Dakota had said? *You won't be finished with L.A. till L.A.'s finished with you.* Something like that. How'd she know so goddamn much about everything? She could never find out about what he'd done to her sister. He'd carry that one to the grave.

An owl screeched from somewhere above and Eddie flinched. A few seconds later a car passed, the white headlights dazzling him for a moment. What little calm he'd managed to find was well and truly gone now, but he should head back to the house anyway, tend to Dakota. He finished the cigarette and stamped on it, holding the smoke in his lungs until he craved oxygen, and made his way up the hill.

He knew something was wrong when he'd pressed the intercom four times and nobody had answered. He eyed the gate and noticed for the first time the points like arrowheads on top. One of those up his ass and he'd be shitting blood the rest of his life.

He gripped one of the cold iron bars and pulled but it didn't budge. Wedging his foot above a curve in the design, he pulled himself up, his fingers straining on the lip below the arrowheads. He released his foot, raising his other foot off the ground at the same time, and wrapped his hand around one of the spikes. Pulling hard, he swung his leg over the top, his second hand coming up to support him, and balanced over the top of the gate, his crotch inches above the arrowheads and his forearms trembling, a burning pain shooting through them. With seconds left before they buckled and he lost his balls forever, he drew in a deep breath and swung his other leg over. The momentum threw him over the side as he let go of the gate. He hit the ground with a grunt, scraping his hands on the concrete.

The front door of the house hung open. He ran inside and heard the TV going but nothing else and rushed into the living room to find only Lois inside, slumped on the floor with her back against the sofa and a hand clamped over a bloody wound on her belly.

"Where is she?" Eddie said, kneeling in front of Lois. He shook her shoulders. "Where's Dakota?"

"Eddie, I'm sorry. I made a mistake." Her voice raspy. "My god this hurts."

"You told them you fuck, didn't you? On the phone in the kitchen. You fucking told them."

"I owed Saul money. Like you. And I had no way to pay him back, either. When you said he wanted to kill you for it, I panicked. Made a deal. Gave them you in exchange for clearing my debt. But they shot me anyway, the bastards."

"Jesus Christ, they're going to kill her, Larry."

"Lois—"

"Oh fuck off you piece of shit. You can really hold a grudge."

"It wasn't about that. Well, maybe a little." Lois looked at her bloody belly. "Eddie, this really hurts."

"No shit, you got shot."

"I'm sorry."

"You're sorry you got shot. This is why I bailed on you in Alhambra—because you would have done it to me in a heartbeat."

"You know what, Eddie, you're right. I admit it. Will you please call an ambulance?"

"You've got some nerve."

"Please, Eddie. I don't want to die in a man's body."

Eddie stood up. "How the hell did you get involved with Saul?"

Lois grimaced and groaned. "You remember Snake-eye Ricky?"

"Of course I remember that crazy asshole."

"I needed money, for the down payment on my surgery plus other expenses. He said he knew a big-time gangster who loaned money at a good rate. The way he described the whole thing he made it sound attractive. You know how Snake-eye can talk. It was a mistake."

"Man, Saul has a hand in everything, the greedy fuck."

"Eddie, I'm really in a lot of pain here. I think I'm dying."

"If you were dying you wouldn't feel so much pain. Now shut the fuck up for a minute let me think."

Eddie stood there trying to think of what to do next.

A phone rang in the foyer.

"For you," Lois said.

Eddie marched out of the room and picked up the receiver.

"Where is she?" he said.

"Eddie," came Saul's slick voice. "Nice to hear from you."

"Cut the bullshit, Saul. Where is she?"

"You know, Eddie, I'm sorry it's come to this. All I wanted was to talk with you, find a way to sort this out, peacefully, together. But you escalated it and escalated it and now here we are."

"When you want to talk with someone you don't send two guys with guns. You couldn't have just called my cell, you fuckin' asshole?"

"Your problem, Eddie, you got no respect. You think the whole world's against you."

"Nah, just you, you fat fuck."

"You want the girl to live through the next ten minutes you better shut up real quick."

Eddie kept his mouth closed.

Saul said, "That's better, can't hear myself think here. Where were we? The girl. You want her to make it out of this alive, you got a job to do for me."

"Don't you have enough guys to do your jobs?"

"This job's specially for you, Eddie."

"What is it?"

"You'll love this. It's a bank."

"Course it is. What's the take?"

"Two million."

Eddie's breath caught in his throat. "What? There's no way we could get cash like that without opening the safe."

"Correct."

"Jesus Christ, Saul. How'd you get to be so fuckin' greedy?"

"I was deprived of breast milk as a baby. Now listen, smartass—I'll sweeten the deal. Pull this off and not only will I let the girl live, but your debt will be cleared and you'll be out of the business, which I know is what you really want. You can walk hand in hand into the sunset with that slut and live out the rest of your days in peace, as long as you stay out of California."

Eddie scratched his neck and thought about it. There was no way Saul would let them live, but maybe he could form a plan to save Dakota.

"All right, I'll do it."

"I know you will, Eddie. I wasn't asking. Twelve p.m. tomorrow at your apartment. Be there."

"Wait. It's after midnight. Do you mean tomorrow today or tomorrow tomorrow?"

"Today. Monday."

"How do I know she's alive?"

"Because what fun is a dead bitch?"

Saul hung up.

Eddie cursed and slammed the phone down. He went to leave the house, hesitated, and turned back to dial for an ambulance.

13 | The Plan

Since Floyd tried the Irish breakfast tea in Saul's restaurant, he'd been having it at home, his wife thinking he'd had a stroke when she saw him carrying three cartons of teabags through the door. He needed it very sweet, dropping three heaping spoonfuls of sugar on top, and, now that he thought about it, that was probably what had him hooked. So, sitting now at Saul's table in The Long Goodbye, Floyd asked for some Irish breakfast tea before Marcel had even brought out the platter, much to Saul's delight.

"It left an impression on you, I see," Saul said.

"It's, I dunno . . . comforting."

"Comforting is exactly the word."

The restaurant was quiet, it not even 10:00 a.m. yet. Marcel the waiter was the only staff member Floyd had seen, and, as far as he could tell, Saul was otherwise alone.

"How's your shoulder?" Saul said.

"Not as sore as it should be, considering."

"We'll find him and make him pay soon as this job's done, mark my words on it. A man like him can't stay hidden in this city very long."

"He ain't tryna hide."

"Even better then."

"Listen, boss, this nigga, the Puerto Rican—"

"You have your reservations."

"I looked into him. Man is serious business. Does big contracts, you know—multiple targets, high-profile shit. Why you bringing in someone like that for something simple we could do ourself?"

"Would you do it yourself, Floyd?"

That stopped Floyd for a moment.

Saul said, "I'm simply sparing you the decision by bringing in the Puerto Rican. And the man can keep his cool, we might need that."

"Why we even doing this? Eddie fucked up, sure, but the man was a good worker, loyal—"

Saul raised a hand, three fat rings shining on his fat fucking fingers.

"I'll stop you right there, Floyd. It almost sounded like you were questioning me for a second."

"With all due respect, Boss, from where I'm sitting, none of this makes any fuckin' sense. My ass might be dumb, but I ain't no dumbass."

"Your fondness for Eddie is making it all seem more complicated than it is. I'll simplify it for you. Right now Eddie is a walking bag of evidence ready to put you in prison again, this time for the rest of your life. I'm sure your loyal wife will remain faithful as ever when she's visiting you for twenty minutes a week and talking with you through plexiglass. The other thing is, we need money to expand our operations. I've spoken with the Mexicans. They're installing somebody to take over Bill's company to keep distribution flowing, and they're increasing production. Either we buy the extra product or someone else does. And, Floyd, we can't afford to let those pieces of shit in San Fran get their hands on it. We can push them out if we do it now, but it's our last chance. We're not just fighting for control of California here, we're fighting to survive."

"I know."

"Remember, this is your business now too. After this, you and I are partners."

"You wasn't bullshitting me 'bout that, huh?"

"You've been a loyal worker for many years now. You're the only one I can trust, and you're smart, dedicated. As we expand, I need a partner to help me manage operations. Pull this job off, and that's you. You'll make more money than you've ever dreamed."

"All right, but if I'm to be your partner then you can get used to me questioning you. Now, I understand why you want Eddie out of the way. I understand 'cause I want him out of the way too, I ain't going to prison again, but I think Eddie would leave town if we let him. He ain't totally fuckin' stupid. But fine, Eddie gets taken out, I get it and I ain't got a problem with it. One thing I don't get is why we using him for this job. Why not treat them as separate issues? I do the bank with some pros, and the Puerto Rican does Eddie, separate."

Saul signaled to Marcel and the man hurried over. "Bring out two glasses and the Springbank, and don't spill a drop."

Floyd went to speak and Saul raised a hand, looking back as Marcel left, clearly going to make Floyd wait until his lapdog returned.

Marcel came back with two glasses of an amber liquid and set one down before Floyd. A smell of whiskey wafted up to him.

Marcel drifted away and Saul picked up his glass and swirled it, sniffing.

"Taste it," Saul said.

Floyd picked up the glass, heavier than he'd expected, and swallowed some of the whiskey. It was thick but silky with a smoky, leathery taste and a fiery afterburn.

"What do you think?" Saul said.

"Scotch ain't my kind of whiskey but this is pretty good."

Saul took a sip of his. "I bought this bottle six years ago. It's one of the most expensive whiskeys in the world. Seventy thousand dollars it cost."

Floyd was sure he'd heard him wrong. "You say seven thousand?"

"Seventy. The price of a C-Class Mercedes-Benz. Taste it again."

Floyd swallowed some more.

"It tastes better now, doesn't it?" Saul said.

"You know what, it does."

Saul nodded. "I kept the bottle sealed for almost two years. Then one day, after one of his movie premieres, Tom Cruise came in here with half the cast. This was before I was in the drug business and everything else. We'd just been awarded the second Michelin star and there was a buzz about the place. We used to try get celebrities photographed here, good for business. Now I couldn't give a shit, bunch of assholes. Anyway, me being the hungry fool I was back then, I bring out the Springbank saying 'Mr. Cruise, this bottle of scotch was distilled in the year nineteen nineteen and cost seventy thousand dollars and I'm giving you a glass on the house.' The little shit watches me open it, waits until I've finished pouring, then says, 'Thank you, but I don't drink.' Some slut next to him says, 'I'll have it.' 'Not a fucking chance' I say and take it back, drink it myself. I've been drinking it a couple times a year since then, and you know what I've learned? Three things: Nothing is as good as it seems; you can always be more rich; and I fucking hate Tom Cruise."

Floyd smirked, the whiskey warm in his chest.

"Point is, Floyd, when we're partners you can buy seventy-thousand-dollar bottles of whiskey. You can buy the wife a house in the Bahamas and ship her there when you need a break from her. You can buy a truck full of whores and fuck them one by one while pouring liquid gold on their tits, if that's what you want. But before that can happen, we need that two million. You want to know why I'm using Eddie and the Puerto Rican, I'll tell you why. Firstly, we didn't have near enough time to find two competent guys I can trust. I got tipped off about this job three days ago, and it has to be done today. And before you say it, I said 'two' guys because I'm not using that fuckhead Sawyer. Yeah, he can drive, but this is the kind of job that goes so smooth you drive slowly away, invisible. I want someone who keeps their cool waiting in the car, someone who won't lose their mind or bail at the the first sign of trouble. The Puerto Rican matches that description, and offers the added bonus of taking care of Eddie afterwards. The Puerto Rican is the rare kind of man not in this business for the money. He has his own principles. I don't know what they are but I do know that his reputation is immaculate, more valuable to him than a couple million bucks. He wants only what I agreed to pay him, nothing more. Finally, Eddie is no stranger to armed robbery, and you and him have worked together many times. What's better? You and two guys you've never met and can't trust, or you and Eddie, and the Puerto Rican cool as a cucumber in the car? Plus, Eddie has the motivation not to fuck us over on this, or bail. We both know he freaked out after killing that girl. He won't want another on his conscience, and that faggot who gave him up said Eddie has feelings for her. When you put all the pieces together, it's not just a good plan, it's the best damn plan you've ever heard."

Floyd frowned, sure he was missing something here. "What faggot who gave him up?"

Saul grinned. "Now we get to the fun part. I have something to show you. Come on."

Saul stood up, not much taller than when he'd been seated, and shuffled on his little legs toward the kitchen, which was empty. It was just Marcel in here with him after all.

Saul cut through the kitchen and stopped outside the closed door to the manager's office. He opened the door and stepped to the side to reveal a woman kneeling on the floor looking up at Floyd, her hands and ankles tied together, duct tape over her lips.

"I believe you two know each other," Saul said.

Sitting in his Chevrolet in the heart of Beverly Hills across the street from a restaurant called The Long Goodbye, Rufus watched the nigger he'd stuck his knife through go inside. It pleased him to see the man wincing and rubbing his chest as he opened the restaurant door. Rufus almost went in after him—he'd been sitting outside since before 9:00 a.m. and had seen only a short, fat man with the swagger of someone used to giving orders (who must have been Benedict) and one other man go inside—but he wanted the one called Eddie, too, and the one with the long blond hair who had stopped him finishing off the nigger. No harm waiting a while longer, see who else turns up. He could wait all day.

A skinny woman with hair so bleached it looked white walked out in front of his car, a fluffy white dog on a leash trotting behind her. She crossed the street and waited under the palm trees that divided it until the coast was clear to make it to the other side. The sky was blue and clear and the sun burned hot above the car.

Rufus fingered a cigarette from the packet in his jacket and reached for his lighter before remembering he'd lost it somewhere, possibly that lawyer's office. It was unusual for him to lose something and this irritated him. What if the cops had found it? So what? A lighter won't tell them shit.

Rufus turned up the radio as Johnny Cash crooned "The Man Comes Around."

Yes, He does. But now The Man has arrived, He has been taking names, and His judgment will be swift and terrible.

"This one slippery bitch. How'd you find her?"

Saul said, "Eddie's got a faggot friend likes to wear dresses and pretend to be a woman. He shows up at this friend's house on Mulholland Drive, looking for somewhere to lay low. Not leaving town like you said, Floyd, but staying right here to help this one find her sister." Saul looked at the woman on the floor. "We had a nice talk about what you got to do with all this, didn't we, beautiful?"

Being gagged, the woman couldn't answer, just stared at the tile, looking distant and defeated.

Saul said, "Yeah, this one has Eddie wrapped around her little finger. But it didn't work out very well, did it, Dakota? Floyd, you won't believe this, you'll think I'm bullshitting you. Guess who her sister is."

"Oprah Winfrey. Fuck am I supposed to know that?"

"I'll give you a hint: You and Eddie murdered her."

Floyd blinked, a dizziness coming over him. "What you saying?" He glanced at the woman who was looking up at him now with raw hatred in her eyes. No one had ever looked at him like that before. If she didn't have duct tape over her mouth, she'd no doubt be screaming at him. Shit, she was probably putting an Indian curse on him right now. The thought of it made his skin crawl.

Saul grinned like a fish. "What are the chances? I know. Dakota here had no idea till I told her. I asked her what she had to do with all this. She said she was looking for her sister but was too late because someone killed her. I said, 'Who's your sister?' 'Kaya White' she tells me. I could hardly fucking believe it. The girl you and Eddie buried with Bill—her fucking sister. The sister worked at that strip joint which is why Dakota started working there, trying to find her. Dakota meets Eddie there and the two of them help each other out. Little does she know she's helping the man who killed her little sister. It's like poetry."

Floyd's head was spinning. He avoided the woman's gaze but felt it burning into him.

Saul said, "But Eddie's luck ran out. His faggot friend owed me twenty large. Called me up last night and said, 'Mr. Benedict, I thought you'd like to know that Eddie Vegas is in my home right this minute and has a woman with him and I'm hoping giving you this information will clear my debt.' I said, 'Yeah, sure' and sent a few of the guys around to grab the girl and shoot the fucking faggot while they're at it for ever giving me a headache in the first place."

Floyd couldn't help looking irritated. The fat motherfucker was losing it.

"You killed the man did you a favor?" he said.

"I didn't say I killed him. I told them to shoot him somewhere it'll hurt. If he dies, that's his problem."

"And you told Eddie if he wants to save the girl, he gotta do this job."

"Plus I'll consider his debts paid and let him leave the business freely so long as he never returns to California."

"But really the Puerto Rican gonna kill Eddie soon as the job's done, and her too—" he nodded at Dakota. "So you get your money and your problems solved all at the same time."

"Now you're thinking like my partner."

"This some crazy shit, Saul."

"It's certainly a unique arrangement of circumstance."

Sudden pain shot through Floyd's wounded chest. He winced. "One thing I don't get, though—what if Eddie's friend never gave him up and you didn't find him? Who'd be doing the bank?"

"I got a dozen guys can do the bank, a couple of them on standby since I got the tip. But I want you and Eddie to do it for the reasons I explained."

Floyd eyed Saul warily. Didn't the man say only a few minutes ago that he ain't had no time to find guys for this job? Something smells like salmon up in here, and it ain't coming from the kitchen.

Floyd said, "And you want the Puerto Rican there 'cause you don't trust me and Sawyer to do Eddie after."

"I want the Puerto Rican there because the man is a consummate professional who will get the job done at all costs and will not be swayed by panic or emotion. I'm curious about the guy, might like to use him again in future. As for Sawyer, this job is beyond his temperament and professionalism, or lack thereof."

Floyd nodded, his mind racing trying to keep up with the facts. "All right. What's the plan?"

Waiting for the Puerto Rican to arrive, Floyd left the restaurant and walked to the nearest convenience store and bought a pack of cigarettes and a lighter despite the fact he didn't smoke. The oppressive heat of a Los Angeles summer had finally returned and beads of sweat slid down his neck. He clamped a cigarette between his lips and set it on fire. Saul's plan was madness but there was an elegance to it all the same. But he was becoming arrogant, harder to deal with. Working for him was becoming dangerous and uncomfortable, and the idea of being partners with the man wasn't much better.

Floyd sucked at the cigarette until only the filter remained and took his cell phone out of his pocket, dialed Sawyer.

"Floyd," Sawyer drawled. "Feeling better?"

"I'll live."

"Damn right. You get the cowboy?"

"No, I got something even better."

"Yeah? What's that?"

Floyd glanced over his shoulder. "How's two million dollars sound?"

14 | The Puerto Rican

Floyd wasn't sure what he'd expected the Puerto Rican to look like but it wasn't the man sitting in the passenger seat of the Honda Civic Saul had acquired for the job because it was, according to Saul, the most popular car in L.A. and therefore the least likely to stand out. The Puerto Rican, or Diego as he told Floyd to call him, was short and thin with narrow shoulders and skinny wrists. He had his hair tied behind his head in a ponytail and wore a white short-sleeved Cuban shirt over beige linen pants. The man looked like an extra in *Miami Vice*.

Diego wasn't much of a talker, either. All he'd said so far was "Call me Diego" after Floyd asked him if he was the Puerto Rican, and "I drive" as they walked toward the car. "Not yet you don't," Floyd had replied, and got into the driver's seat. He needed to be behind the wheel if he and Sawyer were to get rid of Diego the way they'd planned.

Driving in silence with a glorified serial killer beside him unnerved Floyd, so he opened his mouth. "You really from Puerto Rico or is that one of those funny names don't make sense?" Stupid question; of course the man was from Puerto Rico—look at him.

"Yes, I born in Puerto Rico." His accent was strong, his voice nasal and a little high-pitched.

"But you live here?"

"Yes, I live in U.S.A."

"Where in the U.S.A.?"

"I live everywhere and nowhere."

Floyd didn't know what to say to that so he shut up for a minute and watched the road. They passed a group of kids on skateboards. Floyd glanced at Diego. The man's eyes were opened wide, as if he was surprised, except that they'd been open like that since the moment Floyd met him. Diego was either always surprised, or never.

"You like L.A., Diego?"

"Yes, I like the weather and the many thing to do." Looking straight ahead as he spoke.

"Yeah, most people like the weather. Except that it's been raining like crazy most of the past few weeks."

"Yes, I hear about this."

"No one knows what to make of it. It's like L.A.'s in some strange bubble, its own little universe. That's what I heard one of the weather people saying, on the TV."

"In Puerto Rico, hurricane come and destroy everything. Homes of people lifted up and gone."

"Yeah, you mean that one last year? Hurricane Maria, right?"

"Maria, *si*."

"Were you there for that, Diego?"

"No, I don't go to Puerto Rico for ten years."

"But you have family?"

"Me? No, no *familia*."

Floyd nodded. The man was a puzzle, no doubt about it.

Floyd slowed the car as they approached an alleyway near Sawyer's apartment. He pulled up alongside it and kept the engine running.

The silence grew louder.

"We meet Eddie here?" Diego said.

"Eddie, yeah. He be here in a minute."

Floyd glanced at the storage compartment in the door next to his leg, his Sig Sauer inside it in case things went south.

"So, Diego, you ever robbed a bank before?"

"No. But I kill many people. Even U.S.A. senator. Nobody see me." He was more alert now, sitting tense in the seat as he peered out the windshield and shot glances in the rear-view.

"You're stone cold, Diego, talking about killing like that. So you do more than just get rid of people then, huh? You robbing banks now."

"I don't steal from bank. I drive car, then I kill Eddie."

Fair point. Diego reminded Floyd of somebody. But who . . .

Sawyer rounded the corner ahead of them and nodded a greeting.

Floyd glanced at Diego, the man about to have the back of his head blown open.

"Who this guy?" Diego said, the "guy" sounding funny coming from him.

"That's Eddie."

Diego frowned for a second before his expression went back to blank.

Sawyer opened the door. "Afternoon ladies." He got into the seat behind Diego.

A startling flash of movement and Diego had his hand under Floyd's chin. Floyd felt a sharp pain in his neck.

"Drop the gun or I cut him open," Diego said.

"I can shoot you faster'n you can cut him," Sawyer said.

Something warm ran down Floyd's chest. It took him a second to realize it was blood.

"Drop the fucking gun, Sawyer, I'm bleeding up in here," Floyd said.

"Okay okay, I'm dropping it."

Floyd heard the gun hit the floor. Diego darted toward the door on his right, threw it open, and was gone. Floyd spun his head and saw Diego sprinting down the street. Sawyer dove for the gun and fumbled at the door next to him. He got it open as Diego rounded the corner and raced after him.

Floyd put a hand to his neck. When he lifted it away it was wet with blood, but he hadn't felt any surging of the stuff, which was good. He leaned over the passenger side and opened the glove compartment and took out the cloth he'd brought to wipe away the Puerto Rican's blood after Sawyer shot him. He tied it around his neck. The irony was not lost on him.

The Samurai. That's who Diego reminded him of. Deacon 'The Samurai' Jones. Been a long time since he'd thought of that crazy fool.

Floyd sat in the oppressive silence of the car for a couple minutes until Sawyer returned and collapsed into the seat beside him, panting.

"He's a fast little fucker, I couldn't catch him."

"Shit."

"How'd he know I'm not Eddie?"

"Must have seen a picture of him. The man's a pro. I figured he might know what Eddie look like but I didn't expect him to pull a blade."

"What we gonna do?"

"Keep going. We can't be late, job has to be done at one."

"We're still doing it?" Sawyer said.

"You damn right we still doing it. Two million bucks."

"What if he tells Saul?"

"It don't matter now. Come one ten, we outta here."

Sawyer clapped a hand on Floyd's shoulder, grinning. "I like how you think. You tell your wife anything?"

"Not a thing. She think I'm coming home tonight."

"That's cold," Sawyer said.

"Nah, she fuckin' hates me. Bitch probably celebrate."

"Where we gonna go?"

"Anywhere."

"I always wanted to go to Europe."

"Works for me."

"Italy?" Sawyer said.

"Why not."

Sawyer smiled and brought his face close to Floyd's.

Floyd pulled away. "Woah woah, easy. I'm not a faggot, okay? I just—"

"You just like filling your mouth with my cock." Sawyer smirked, blue eyes playful.

Floyd hesitated, a little shocked at hearing it out loud. He felt a smirk forming on his face, despite himself.

"Guess I do. Maybe I'd like to fill your ass with mine."

"Anytime, big man," Sawyer said, and brought his face toward Floyd's again, slowly.

Floyd didn't fight it this time. He closed his eyes and let Sawyer's lips press against his own. A heat filled him, his body vibrating. He kissed Sawyer back, tasting cigarettes. The kiss was at once less profound and more comfortable than he'd expected. It felt different than any kiss he'd shared with a woman, including his wife. It felt right.

The kiss ended and Sawyer pulled away. He raised an eyebrow, looking smug.

"Well hallelujah," he said. "Let's rob a bank."

"Amen," Floyd said, and accelerated onto the street, his hands trembling on the steering wheel.

The quiet of the apartment wasn't doing anything to soothe Eddie's nerves. He paced around the living room in circles, stopping every few steps to gaze out the window at the street below.

Dakota's beautiful face kept coming to him—the expression it had held when they were lying in bed together. But then her peaceful expression would morph into one of shock followed by horror as she learned of her sister's murder over and over again in his mind. He could never take back what he had done, but he could stop it from happening to Dakota. He'd never be able to live with himself if he didn't try.

Eddie peered out the window again as a car pulled up outside the building. To his surprise, Floyd got out of the car, then Sawyer. They entered through the first gate that was always left unlocked and sauntered up the path. The buzzer rang and Eddie unlocked the second gate, then unlocked his front door and waited in the living room.

Floyd appeared first. "Eddie, my man. Together again at last."

Sawyer followed him into the room, a black sports bag in his hand. "Eddie."

"Thought you were dead," Eddie said to Floyd.

"I wonder why you thought that. Maybe it's 'cause you left me alone and unconscious with a psychotic Jesus-freak cowboy killer, huh?"

"When you point a gun at somebody, be prepared to get hurt," Eddie said.

"It was just to make you listen. I wasn't gonna shoot yo' ass."

"I didn't wanna listen, or go with you. I know where that road leads."

"No, you led us to this moment right here instead."

Floyd went into the kitchen and unwrapped a bloody cloth from his neck. He tossed it in the bin and went over to the sink, splashed water on himself.

"I wasn't expecting you two," Eddie said.

Floyd said, "Who else could it be? The three of us, we the dream team." He returned to the living room, drying his neck with a kitchen towel.

"It's like the good old days," Sawyer said, "but instead of stealing ice we're stealing from a bank."

Eddie said, "This is crazy, even for Saul. A year ago he never would have even considered something like this.

Who's he trying to be, Don Corleone?"

"Is what it is," Floyd said. To Sawyer: "Am I bleeding?"

"Nah, you're good."

"What happened?" Eddie said.

Floyd said, "We running out of time. Let's go over the plan. Sit down."

Eddie sat on the sofa and Floyd sat beside him. Sawyer dropped the bag and dragged over a chair from the kitchen. He faced it away from them and sat in it backwards, his arms crossed over the back of it.

Floyd pulled a sheet of paper out of his pocket and unfolded it on the coffee table, smoothing out the creases: a blueprint of the bank.

Eddie said, "Doing this in the middle of the day downtown is the worst idea in the world. Didn't we learn anything from San Diego?"

"Job has to be done at one," Floyd said. "Our contact says the Federal Reserve is loading the bank with the two mil' at twelve forty-five. The vault is time-locked and only opens between twelve thirty and one thirty. Our contact cuts the silent alarms at twelve fifty-five."

"What if they don't?"

"Don't load the bank or don't cut the alarm?"

"Either."

"Then we fucked." Floyd grinned. "Saul says his contact is good for it, ex-army tech specialist been trying to get Saul in on a bank job for years. Calls himself Edward Bunker but you can be sure that ain't his real name. No stranger to this kind of job. You hear about the bank robbery in Oklahoma City last year? They got away with almost a million? That was his."

Floyd pointed to a small room at the top left of the map. "See here, that's the vault. Only one man in the bank has the key, the manager. Name of Marvin Reeves. We need his fingerprints to open the first door and his key to open the second. The cash will fit in two bags—one each for me and you. We go into the bank with big fuck-you rifles. We ain't gonna use them, point is they make everybody shit themselves. Pistols won't do it these days, people seen too many movies. And this is America—everybody and their babysitter got a pistol. You go into a bank with an assault rifle and, motherfucker, you mean business."

"Loaded?" Eddie said.

"Shit yeah loaded. If I need to put a motherfucker down, I'mma put a motherfucker down. We taking extra clips, too, and bulletproof vests."

"This is madness."

"Ain't nothing gonna happen," Sawyer said. "But you gotta plan for every eventuality."

"Exactly," Floyd said, "I mean, in the unlikely event we get shot at, I wanna know it ain't gonna hurt. But, listen, this ain't hard. We walk in shouting, guns pointing at everybody. Get everyone on the ground, scare them, be loud and aggressive. On the inside we stay calm and composed but on the outside we crazy and ready to kill a motherfucker. I get to Marvin, make him open the vault while you watch the crowd. Tell them anybody move they all get shot. Hit somebody with the gun if you need to. When Marvin opens the vault we switch. You go in, grab the cash, put it in the bags while I keep everybody quiet. This part you gotta be fast. You fill up one bag you slide it to me and you fill the next. When you done that you put the bag over your shoulder and walk straight out the bank into the car. I be right behind you. We put our masks on and take them off right before we enter and exit the bank. The guns we hold inside our suit jackets—that's another thing, we all wearing suits. We doin' this shit like they did in *Heat*."

"Heat?" Eddie said.

"The movie, with Bobby De Niro."

"That ended in a fucking shootout in the street for Christ sake."

"It had to happen like that 'cause it's a movie."

Eddie shook his head. "Stop talking about goddamn movies. What about the guards?"

"No guards. Banks don't use guards no more. They too expensive, and them being there increases the likelihood of violence by three hundred percent, so banks don't use 'em."

Sawyer slipped a cigarette out of his shirt pocket and lit it. "Sounds easy to me."

"Did I say you could smoke in here?" Eddie said.

"You didn't say I couldn't." Sawyer exhaled a cloud and sucked another drag.

Floyd said, "It is easy. Like stealing ice like we used to. We just gotta be discreet going in, keep our cool inside, and be discreet coming back out. Then we drive to a certain location, switch the car, and we home free, baby."

"Oh yeah? And what are you two getting out of this?" Eddie said. "I assume Saul's taking almost all of it."

"Don't worry 'bout us, Eddie, we got a sweet deal," Sawyer said. "You'd do best to worry 'bout your girl—get the job done and get the hell out of Dodge."

"Anything happens to her I'll kill the both of you."

Floyd closed the map. "Hey now, we all friends here. The dream team back in business." He stood up and pointed at the sports bag. "Give me that."

Sawyer kicked it over and Floyd bent down and zipped it open. Christ—he was pulling out an assault rifle.

"See these?" Floyd said, pointing at a dial above the grip of one of the rifles, three markings jutting out of it: "S," "A," and "R." "'S' means safety. 'A' means automatic, which means long as you have that trigger pulled bullets will fly. 'R' means semi-automatic, which means one trigger-pull shoots one bullet. I'm switching it to semi right now, which means the safety is off, and the guns are loaded and cocked, so don't pull that trigger 'less you tryna hit a motherfucker." He touched a lever on top of the gun. "This where you rack the slide after you reload. You pull out the empty magazine down here and slot the new one inside till you hear it click into place, then you pull this lever back and you good to go. If you have to shoot, aim carefully, take a breath, tense your body so the recoil don't knock you back, and squeeze the trigger. Then repeat."

Eddie rested his palm on his neck. "You ever shoot one of these things before?"

"Shit yeah."

Eddie looked at Sawyer. "What about you?"

"Yeah, I fired 'em, and a lot more besides."

"Where?"

"Iraq."

"Iraq? Fuck were you doing in Iraq?"

"Killing Muslims."

"You were in the army?"

"Not for long. Went A.W.O.L. soon as they shipped me home. But I was the best shot in my squad."

Eddie shook his head. "This just keeps getting weird-er."

"Just the way we like it," Floyd said, tossing the gun into the bag. "Get your suit on."

Eddie followed Floyd to the car—which, for some reason, was a Honda Civic—Sawyer behind him. The bulletproof vest felt tight beneath the shirt, the suit a little too big. He felt like he was back in Catholic school in his broth-er's hand-me-down suit, about to receive his First Holy Communion.

Floyd opened the trunk of the car and tossed the

sports bags inside.

"We made it to the big leagues, huh?" he said.

"You've lost your mind, Floyd. You—" he nodded at Sawyer—"him, and Saul. Kidnapping, bank robbery, those fuckin' military-grade weapons in there—this is way beyond slingin' some dope."

Floyd shut the trunk. "Don't tell me that in all those hotel rooms and jewelry stores you never once wondered what it would feel like to do it like the pros do it, the real pros who walk into a bank with *real* guns and leave with *real* money. None of this small-time hustling bullshit, running errands for that fat fuck Saul, but doing a real job for just once in our piece-of-shit lives. Don't tell me you never wondered what that would be like."

"Like Robert De Niro in *Heat*."

Floyd nodded. "Exactly."

"Except Robert De Niro wasn't running back to Saul Benedict with the money. Why you doing a job this big for him? He must be offering you something good."

Sawyer brushed past Eddie's shoulder heading toward the driver's side of the car. Floyd glanced at him.

"Like Sawyer said, don't worry 'bout us, Eddie. Worry 'bout that little Indian all tied up waiting for you to rescue her." He turned away and went toward the passenger door as Sawyer got into the driver's seat. "Get in."

The car got hot, fast. Eddie tugged at the collar of the suit.

"Can we get another window down in this thing? I can barely breathe here."

Floyd's window came down halfway.

"Tell me something," Floyd said. "Back in the club, and then the motel, why you go so outta your way not to come with us? I mean, I get it, Saul's a piece of shit, but what you think, he was gonna kill you?"

"Floyd, I once saw Saul shoot some poor bastard in the kneecap for being five minutes late to a meeting. Shit, you were there, you saw it yourself."

Floyd barked a laugh. "I remember that. Man screamed like a bitch. I don't blame him though, shot in the kneecap of all places. You got a point, sure, but one thing you don't know is that the man Saul shot disrespected him couple days before that in front of some Mexicans. Said something like, 'If you was smart, Mr. Benedict, you'd take this deal and stop losing money like a chump.' I knew right then nigga was gonna pay for that. That's the thing with Saul—motherfucker cold but he know how to play people. He shoots the man's kneecap and everybody thinks, 'Shit, this one bad motherfucker, I best not cross any lines with him, best not be a single second late to a meeting or nothin',' but really that fool got shot the second he opened his mouth front of the Mexicans, he was just waiting for the bullet to arrive. Saul's gone and lost his shit, don't get me wrong. Man's head grown too big for his body, gonna burst one day. But he knows how to play people, make situations . . . align. Even when you think you know how something goin' down, the man finds a way to surprise you."

Eddie gazed out the window at the streets zooming by and thought about it.

"All right, you're right," he said. "I'll tell you why I didn't wanna go with you. Because who the fuck does Saul think he is? He calls me up on my night off. I'm putting my feet up about to watch some TV with some Chinese food. 'Eddie, Floyd's picking you up in thirty' he says. So you and me, we go to this guy's condo, threaten him to pay Saul, a guy you tell me always pays so what's the point anyway? Seems like an exercise in being a cruel mother-fucker you ask me. Next thing, the guy runs at me. And I don't mean he got up and came toward me, I mean the fucker jumped to his feet and charged me like a bull. My finger slips on the trigger; what you expect? I'm not happy about it, I'm there on my night off trying to make Saul's deep pockets a little deeper. Instead of gratitude, what do I get? 'Eddie, come see me. Don't make me have to find you,' when I been nothing but a star employee for two fuckin' years? Nah, fuck that, and fuck him. I was done with his fat ass the second I pulled that trigger."

A few seconds of silence.

"You know what, man?" Sawyer said, looking at Eddie in the rear-view. "I woulda done the same thing."

"Thank you."

"You made one mistake though."

"Yeah, what's that?"

"Not leaving town the minute you got home after we buried those bodies. Running around with the girl like that—that was stupid, Eddie, no matter what way you look at it."

Eddie agreed with him so he said nothing.

"You really like that girl, huh?" Floyd said.

"Yeah, I do. She's different, man. Way different. But, there's something about her . . . man, you wouldn't believe me if I told you."

"Bet I would," Floyd said.

"You know that girl we killed?"

"That girl *you* killed, Eddie."

"Yeah, well, that's her sister. Her fuckin' sister, can you believe it?"

Floyd and Sawyer glanced at each other.

"Her sister, huh?" Floyd said.

"Her fucking sister. Jesus Christ. Don't say anything about it though, when we go drop off the money. Okay? She doesn't know I had anything to do with it. I don't want her to look at me like that."

"Like what?" Floyd said.

"Like how she'd look at me if she knew I'm the one who shot her little sister."

"I get you. I can promise you this, brother—she won't ever hear a word from me."

15 | Heat

Sawyer stopped the car fifty yards from the bank on the same side of the street.

"Your mask," Floyd said and tossed something at Eddie. Eddie caught it: the face of an eyeless white-haired man stared up at him.

"The fuck? Is this Einstein?"

"You got it," Floyd said.

"What, were they out of Stephen Hawking?"

"They was on sale."

Sawyer snorted a laugh.

Eddie said, "You cheap fuck, Floyd. We're about to steal two million bucks and you buy three-dollar masks 'cause they're a dollar off."

"I'm deeply sorry you ain't dressed up as your favorite superhero, Eddie. Now let's do this thing."

Floyd got out of the car and shut the door.

"Break a leg," Sawyer said. "And don't fuck it up."

Eddie exited the car and looked around. The street was far busier than he'd have liked, people in suits hurrying in every direction. On the sidewalk opposite a woman pushed a pram.

Floyd opened the trunk of the Civic.

"You got those extra mags in your pocket still?" he said.

Eddie nodded, his intestines doing somersaults.

"Take one of them rifles and hold it vertical inside your suit. Just before we go inside, put your mask on. The second we get through those doors point that gun at every man, woman and child looks your way. Got it?"

Eddie nodded and bent into the trunk and picked up one of the guns. It was less heavy than he'd anticipated, the metal cold as death. He glanced behind and pulled it out of the trunk quickly and slipped it inside his suit jacket. The barrel pointed out beneath the jacket, terminating at his knee cap.

"Here." Floyd tossed a black sports bag at him and Eddie put the strap over his head. Floyd did the same with the other bag.

Floyd opened the rear door of the car, grabbed one of the rifles out of the trunk, tossed it onto the back seat for Sawyer, and shut the door. He grabbed the third rifle and slipped it inside his suit. He nodded at Eddie, his face hardened by determination, and made for the bank.

Eddie went after him onto the wide rectangle of open concrete paved outside the bank. A man talking into a cell phone almost bumped into him, glancing at Eddie's face as he passed. The barrel of the rifle brushed against the inside of Eddie's thigh.

Beneath one of the tall gray columns that supported the building and created a lavish entrance, Floyd stopped and pulled his mask over his head. Eddie did the same. At once his vision narrowed.

Floyd threw open the bank doors and burst inside.

"Get down on the fucking ground!" Floyd roared as Eddie entered behind him swinging the rifle horizontal, his hands already wet. Cold air conditioning blasted his neck.

The crowd of about twenty people stood frozen on the shiny floor like a photograph.

"I said down!" Floyd smashed the butt of his rifle into the face of a nearby woman. She hit the floor, squealing. At once the crowd dropped to its knees.

Floyd glanced behind and Eddie saw a vacant Albert Einstein looking back at him with hard eyes. Floyd raised two fingers and pointed at the crowd, signaling to Eddie to watch over them.

"Ladies and Gents, this is a robbery," Floyd said. "Your money is insured, you won't lose a dime. Nobody move, nobody get hurt."

He marched toward the tellers, his shoes clicking loudly against the hard floor. "Into the middle, now. You too, Lionel Richie, let's go."

The tellers hurried toward the rest of the crowd, the man with the afro he'd called "Lionel Richie" tripping on himself.

Floyd marched into the manager's office, its door open. "Marvin Reeves," he yelled. "Get out here, Marvin."

He entered the office and came back out shoving a man wearing glasses and a gray suit into the center of the bank. "I said out, Marvin. Give me the key."

"What key?" Marvin said.

Floyd punched him and Marvin clutched at his face with a cry. Floyd grabbed a keychain from around Marvin's neck and tore it free.

"To the vault. Now," Floyd said, nudging Marvin with the rifle. Marvin shuffled toward the vault, one hand on his nose.

Eddie watched the crowd. A woman probably in her sixties sat with her back leaned against the wall, breathing heavily. Another woman held a young boy into her chest, looking up at Eddie with wet, fearful eyes. Just beyond her, a man lying on his belly moved a hand toward his waist.

"Don't fuckin' move," Eddie said. "One of you moves a fucking inch and I shoot everybody." His voice boomed inside the mask, his breath filling it with sticky heat. He kept the gun trained on the crowd, aiming at anyone who so much as shivered. At the far left corner of the room, Floyd had managed to open the first door of the vault with Marvin's fingerprints.

Eddie heard the door open behind him and spun. A young man stood frozen as the door swung shut behind him.

"You, get in here," Eddie said, and darted for him. The man lunged for the door. Eddie grabbed his arm and whacked him with the rifle. The man dropped to his knee. "In there, move," Eddie said, shoving the man toward the crowd. He couldn't be sure but some people seemed to have shuffled around.

"I said nobody move or I'll shoot all of you. Don't fucking move!"

The woman holding her child squealed and shuddered and Eddie hated himself. Threatening a mother and her child—what the fuck kind of life was he living?

Floyd returned to Eddie and pointed his rifle at the crowd. "You're on," he said.

Eddie jogged toward the vault and tossed the bag off his shoulder. He entered the vault and nearly fainted: he'd never seen so many bills in his life. A mad urge to take it all for himself and run surged through him, a life of possibility opening up, before an image of Dakota's face resting on his naked chest returned to him. He set the rifle on the little table beside the wall of the vault and grabbed the bag, zipped it open. He tossed bundles of cash inside until the bag was full and picked the bag up, heavy now, and slid it out of the vault.

He started on the second bag. A few seconds later Floyd appeared outside the vault and picked up the first and heaved it onto his shoulder.

"Stay down, motherfucker," Floyd yelled at somebody, moving out of sight.

Eddie worked faster, tossing four bundles into the bag at a time. Soon this bag was full, too. Some bundles remained in the vault but that would have to do.

He lifted the bag onto his shoulder, grabbed the rifle, and hurried out of the vault toward the bank doors, the strap putting pressure on his skin.

Floyd kept his gun pointed at the crowd as Eddie passed.

"Ladies and Gents, it's been a pleasure," Floyd said behind him. "But stay on the fuckin' floor."

Eddie slipped the rifle vertical inside his jacket and pushed open the doors and walked out into the heat. The street looked normal, no army of cops kneeling behind a barricade with guns in their hands. He pulled his mask off and gulped at the fresh air, sweat rolling over his right eyebrow. Excitement flickered inside his belly as his nerves began to calm. They might actually pull this off.

He glanced behind as Floyd exited the bank and peeled off Einstein's face. Floyd's gaze lingered on something beyond them, concern swarming into his expression. Eddie followed his gaze: a police car was parked across the street outside a café. The car was empty, the cops obviously inside the place.

"Be cool," Floyd said, continuing toward him.

Eddie kept his gaze fixed on the Civic, hoping he wouldn't drop the rifle now slippery with sweat. Sawyer watched them with alert eyes from behind the wheel.

Fifteen yards from the car, Sawyer tensed in the seat, a look of alarm on his face. Eddie heard a loud pop from behind, followed quickly by another. Sawyer threw open the door of the car, assault rifle in his hands, as another pop sounded. Something slammed into the back of Eddie's thigh, throwing him onto the ground. His palms scraped against the pavement as the rifle clattered onto it, the bag of cash slipping off his shoulder. A burst of gunfire exploded from the Civic. Eddie raised his head to see Sawyer firing at the bank, the rifle pressed into his shoulder. A woman screamed. Tires screeched against the street.

Eddie looked behind, becoming aware now of a burning pain in his left leg. A man lay facedown and unmoving on the concrete outside the bank, a pistol five yards from his outstretched hand. He was the man who'd moved his hand toward his waist inside the bank.

Eddie flattened his slashed palms against the pavement and pulled himself to his feet. Agony exploded in the back of his left thigh. Beside him Floyd said, "Move," and raised his rifle. Eddie grabbed the strap of the bag in one hand and his rifle in the other as Floyd fired at the café across the street, the cops hurrying out of it now, alerted by the gunfire.

Eddie dashed toward the Civic, ignoring the pain. He opened the back door and tossed the bag inside and took cover behind the door. Floyd sidestepped toward him while shooting at the café.

Floyd's firing ceased. "Cover me," he yelled, and sprinted toward the Civic. A cop stuck his head above the police car as Sawyer fired a burst.

Floyd slid toward Eddie and dropped the bag of cash. He leaned his back against the car.

"What happened?" Eddie said when Sawyer stopped pulling the trigger.

"Motherfucker came out of the bank after us and started shooting. Off-duty cop maybe, or someone wanna be a hero."

The car window opposite Eddie smashed as a pop sounded. He ducked. Sawyer resumed shooting. Floyd tore the magazine out of the rifle and tossed it onto the street. He pulled a fresh magazine out of his jacket, slid it into the rifle, and racked the slide.

"I got hit in the leg," Eddie said.

"You lucky it ain't your ass," Floyd said. He nodded at the street. "Watch our back. Police station's three minutes from here." Only now did Eddie register the sound of sirens screaming nearby. Fuck.

Eddie aimed the rifle in the direction of the sirens. They sounded as if they were coming from far down the street ahead, but it was possible that some cops could appear from the corner just ahead, too.

Beside him Floyd lunged upwards and riddled the café and police car with bullets, nearly blowing Eddie's eardrum. Christ, how many bystanders had been hit by now? The cops would no longer even pretend to try to make arrests. It was kill or be killed.

A police car raced down the street ahead, followed closely by another, the sirens screaming louder. Eddie aimed for the windshield of the car closest and squeezed the trigger. The gun shuddered in his hands and knocked his shoulder back. Recoil—he'd forgotten about that. The car kept coming. He hadn't released the trigger but the gun had only fired a single shot. Shit, the dial on the side. Eddie switched it to "A" and tried again. The rifle spat out a burst of bullets, rattling the teeth in his skull, but he kept his grip firm, the butt pressed firmly into his shoulder until the magazine had been emptied. A couple bullets found their mark, shattering the windshield. The car swerved violently and smashed into a fire hydrant where a white column of water erupted as if from a geyser.

The police car behind the first slammed on the brakes, tires screeching, and came to a halt sideways. Two cops slipped out the passenger door at the far side of the car and opened fire. Eddie dove behind the Civic.

"Cops at the café are down," Sawyer said, and crouched behind the trunk of the car.

Eddie and Floyd shuffled toward him on their

hunkers. "We need to get the fuck outta here," Floyd said. "If they come from behind they can pin us down."

"Get in the car," Sawyer said. "I'll cover you, then cover me out the window while I get in the front and get us outta here. Don't let them hit me, I'm a sitting duck in there."

Floyd said, "All right." To Eddie: "Ready?"

"Wait, I need to reload this thing," Eddie said.

He popped the magazine out, tossed it onto the ground, and retrieved a fresh magazine from his jacket pocket. He slotted it into the body and pulled back the lever.

"Okay, ready."

"On three," Floyd said. "One . . . two . . . three!"

Eddie darted toward the open rear door of the car as Sawyer unleashed a spray of bullets. But his shooting stopped abruptly.

"Sawyer's hit!" Floyd said.

A cluster of cops emerged from around the corner ahead. A bullet tore through the windshield as Eddie peered out from behind the door.

"Forget the car," Floyd said. "Grab the bags."

Eddie lunged for the bag he'd left inside the Civic as a bullet punctured the back seat less than half a foot from his head. He heaved the bag out and tossed it behind the car. Sawyer lay flat on his back on the street, the rifle beside him, Floyd dragging him toward the rear of the vehicle.

Eddie grabbed Floyd's bag from the ground and dived behind the car as a bullet ripped a hole through the open door.

Sawyer lay slumped against the license plate. He pulled his shirt and bulletproof vest up, exposing reddened, but unpunctured, skin. "Didn't go through," he said, "but it hurts like hell."

"We need to push them back," Floyd said to Eddie. He fired over the car. Eddie leaned out behind the trunk and fired a burst. The cops retreated toward the corner.

"Can you walk?" Floyd said to Sawyer.

"Yeah."

"Grab a bag," Floyd said to Eddie while heaving one onto his shoulder.

Eddie swung the remaining bag over his neck.

"We can cut through the alley next to the bank," Floyd said.

Floyd shot at the cops who had retreated around the corner now, peering out from behind it. He hurried toward the bank. Sawyer ran after him while Eddie emptied another magazine at the cops. More sirens wailed nearby.

Eddie darted after Sawyer, half-hopping, each step shooting pain up through his leg and into his teeth. The million dollars was heavy on his shoulder. Ahead, Floyd and Sawyer disappeared behind the bank's entrance columns. Eddie kept running but the pain was intensifying and slowing him down. The chorus of sirens grew louder as his hope began to fade. What had he been thinking?

He'd seen enough news reports to know how this ends.

A bullet broke off a chunk of the column in front of Eddie as Floyd and Sawyer disappeared into the alley beside the bank. He dived behind the column and stayed there in its shade, gasping at the air, the pain impossible to ignore now. He reloaded the rifle with his last magazine and shut his eyes. He couldn't run any more. This was it— the last stand. What a miserable fucking life he'd lived. But he wouldn't let them arrest him, throw him on the pavement like a piece of meat and lock him up for twenty years in six feet of nothingness. Fuck that. And now another innocent young woman would die by his hand, and he could never live with that. That left only one option.

He opened his eyes, the city around him appearing at once more vivid and less tangible. The sirens were close now. A dozen cops would no doubt be creeping their way toward him from the street. He breathed in deeply, bracing himself for what he was about to do.

Goddamnit, Dakota, I would have loved you. Maybe I already do.

An engine roared in the alley beside the bank, becoming louder now, sounding like it belonged to something fast, and a bright red sports car shot out onto the street and screeched to a stop twelve yards from Eddie. The rear door flew open and Floyd waved an arm at him from the back seat.

"Get in."

The nigger had left the restaurant with a little spic and they took off in a car. He had a funny look about him, the spic, sort of goofy but unaware of it. Rufus almost followed them out of curiosity, but Saul Benedict had remained inside the restaurant with only the one man Rufus had watched go inside with him early this morning. Maybe it was time to pay Benedict a visit, no more waiting for Eddie and the blond to show. Benedict could tell him where to find them—before he got his tongue torn right out his mouth.

Rufus gripped the door handle as an S.U.V. pulled up outside the restaurant. Three men got out—no, four— at least two of them ex-cons; he could tell by how they looked all the way around themselves, a sharpness to their eyes. The men entered the restaurant. Rufus released the door handle.

Things were heating up.

Rufus relaxed into the seat and turned the music up. Willie Nelson sang about a bloody blade on "Highwayman." He'd always had a way of capturing the mood just right, Nelson.

Rufus rolled the window down, the heat in the car stifling. He'd wait a little longer, and if Eddie didn't show, he'd go inside that restaurant and kill every one of them. He was a highwayman, after all.

Sawyer gunned the engine and swung the car screeching around a corner, throwing Eddie and Floyd across the back seats. A man in a suit crossing the street dived out of the way barely in time as Sawyer floored it through a red light, a chorus of horns wailing from either side.

"Where the fuck you find the ride?" Eddie said, gripping the handle above the door tightly.

"We jacked it from some rich asshole on Los Angeles Street, behind the bank," Floyd said. "Ain't you lucky. You was finished back there; what the fuck you thinking?"

"My leg. I couldn't keep up."

"So you was going to prison if we didn't save your ass, huh?"

"No, I was going somewhere else."

Floyd frowned. "What you saying?"

"They might kill me, but they won't ever lock me up."

Floyd clapped a hand on Eddie's back. "My nigga."

Sawyer slammed on the brakes. Eddie was thrown forward, his forehead thumping into the handbrake.

"I nearly went through the windshield," he said, holding his face.

"Cops ahead," Sawyer shouted back. "Hold on, this is gonna get bumpy."

Eddie heard the sirens ahead of them now, and from behind. And, was that—

"You hear that?" Floyd said to Eddie.

"Helicopter," Eddie said, hearing more clearly now the sound of the blade cutting through the air like a train chugging in the distance.

"What you say?" Sawyer shouted back as he swerved left onto a one-way street.

"Helicopter," Floyd said. "It's San Diego all over again."

"Fuck," Sawyer said, and dodged an oncoming station wagon with a staring family inside, their mouths like Cheerios. He reached into his pocket and took something out, tossed it over his shoulder. It landed on the seat beside Eddie: Sawyer's cell phone.

"Connect to Bluetooth, open Spotify and play some Pantera," Sawyer said.

Eddie couldn't believe his ears. "You serious?"

"He serious," Floyd said. "Trust me."

Eddie shook his head. He knew Sawyer had a thing for playing this shit while driving, but this was something else.

"*Cowboys from Hell*," Sawyer said, skidding around an oncoming cab and weaving right onto the perpendicular street. They were heading in the same direction as the other vehicles now, at least.

"What?" Eddie said.

"The song he wants you to put on," Floyd said, looking unsurprised.

Eddie connected to Bluetooth and found the song—fuck it, if they were going to die, let the man have his music. Chugging guitars exploded out of the speakers. Sawyer turned it up until it was so loud Eddie couldn't think, then started banging his head, his blond hair flapping around him.

"That's more like it," he roared. Eddie felt the wheel picking up speed. The helicopter was close now, he could hear it even over the music. Shit, it must be right above them. They raced through a crossroads and Eddie spotted a squad of speeding cop cars level with them on the road parallel. Another had almost reached them from behind, twenty feet away and closing.

"Cops on the right," Eddie said.

"I see 'em," Sawyer said. "Hold on."

He glanced in the rear-view and slammed on the brakes. The police car behind them shot ahead before braking hard and sliding into a parked van. Sawyer threw the gearstick into reverse and turned around in his seat. The crashed cop car ahead shrank as they zoomed backwards, Sawyer expertly avoiding the oncoming traffic. Eddie felt sick. He trusted Sawyer's driving skills, but, fuck, they were moving backwards *fast*, and the blaring music was starting to sound like a demented choir from hell.

Sawyer faced ahead and jerked the handbrake, spinning the steering wheel like the captain of a ship. The car—Eddie saw by the logo on the wheel that it was a Porsche—did a one eighty, shuddering almost to a stop before Sawyer flung it into drive. White smoke from the burning rubber clouded around them as they screeched forward. A multitude of flashing lights approached ahead. Eddie looked at Sawyer, who had gritted his teeth and slapped both his hands onto the wheel, staring straight ahead. Christ—he was going to meet the cops head-on.

"Put your seatbelt on," Eddie said to Floyd as he scrambled to put on his own.

Floyd snatched at the belt.

Sawyer dodged a cab, the driver brandishing his middle finger at them, and accelerated toward the police cars rushing at them. The Porsche was moving fast now, impossibly fast, the buildings on either side little more than blurs.

Eddie looked at Floyd, who looked back at him, wide-eyed.

The four police cars were thirty feet away now, spread across the street like the points of a star.

"Hold onto your hats," Sawyer shouted back at them, grinning madly in the rear-view, and turned up a screaming guitar solo until it was so loud it hurt.

Eddie squeezed his fists and shut his eyes.

16 | The L.A. River

Alison returned from Indio in time to collect Charlie from school. She parked across the street and listened to the radio. A news reporter described an ongoing high-speed pursuit downtown following the armed robbery of Union Bank. Five people had lost their lives so far, the criminals giving no indication of surrender.

"Never a dull moment," she muttered. She switched off the radio and waited until it was time to line up with the other parents in anticipation of the screaming horde of children that would soon rush the gates.

Five minutes later she stood behind the crowd of parents, hoping to go unnoticed by the few she recognized.

The school was a giant gray brick. She almost smiled at the thought of all the children sprinting out toward their parents, ecstatic at being free for the day, until she wondered how many of those kids would grow up to become addicts and rapists and murderers, and hated herself for thinking it.

"Alison, nice to see you. It's been a while."

A parent of one of Charlie's classmates approached her, a pleasant-looking man in a short-sleeve shirt. He was a single parent, she remembered that, but what was his name?

"Oh, hey there," she said. "Sure has."

Short-sleeves reached her and smiled broadly. "How have you been? We've missed you around here." He waved an arm at the crowd of parents, not one of them looking their way.

"Yeah, been busy with work, you know. Murderers never rest, unfortunately."

His smile faltered. "No, I imagine they don't . . ." He seemed to recollect his thoughts. "How's Charlie doing? Peter's always talking about him—Charlie this, Charlie that. He keeps pestering me for a sleepover."

Peter Walsh was his kid. That would make him—

"Tom!"

He tilted his head. "Yes?"

Shit, she'd said it aloud. "It's . . . good to see you. A sleepover for the boys would be nice. How about this weekend?"

He nodded. "Sure. Your place or mine?"

She thought about it. There was no guarantee she'd be there to supervise.

"Yours would be better, in case I get called away."

"Those pesky murderers, hey?"

She wasn't sure she'd heard him right until he grinned.

She grinned back at him. It felt wrong on her face. "Pesky. Exactly."

He chuckled. "Here they come."

For a moment she thought he was referring to the murderers, until she heard the screams. Children poured out of the front doors in a sea of tiny faces and brightly colored backpacks. She peered over the parents, looking for Charlie. Half the kids had left the schoolyard before she spotted him coming out of the doors with Peter. He looked so tiny from this distance. Her heart softened in her chest.

"Always the last to leave," Tom said and rolled his eyes. "I always tell Peter if he likes it so much in there he's welcome to stay. Never goes down well."

Charlie was in deep conversation with Peter, looking altogether more mature than every other kid. Alison stepped out in front of the remaining parents to give him a better view of her. Some moments later, he looked up toward her. She waved, smiling to herself. Even from this distance she saw his eyes widen. He hopped with excitement and waved backed and sprinted toward her, his backpack thrashing side to side.

"I wish Peter was that excited to see me," Tom said behind her.

Alison squatted on her heels and opened her arms wide. Charlie ran into her, almost knocking her over. She closed her arms around him and squeezed his little body. His hair smelled of chalk and Play-Doh.

He broke the hug and looked at her. "You're here, Mommy."

"Sure am."

Charlie's expression grew concerned. "Are you going to work now?"

"No, sweetie, I'm bringing you home and then we're going to a movie."

Charlie's mouth fell open. "A movie?"

"Yep. I promised we'd see a movie after school, remember?"

"What are we going to see?"

"Anything you want. You can choose a movie when we get there."

"Okay!" He hopped on his toes and Alison stifled a giggle.

"Let's go." She stood up. "I'll see you soon, Tom."

Tom stepped toward her. "I don't believe I have your details. Should we exchange numbers?"

The surprise must have showed on her face because Tom scratched his stubble and said, "For the sleepover this weekend, I mean."

Heat spread across her cheeks. "Right, yes, of course.

I'll put it into your cell."

Tom pulled out his cell phone, unlocked it, and handed it to her. She inputted her number, called it, and pressed "Cancel."

"It's the last dialed number. Speak to you soon."

"Yes, definitely. Enjoy your movie, you two." He winked at Charlie, becoming suddenly quite handsome.

Alison smiled and glanced away quickly. She gripped Charlie's hand and together they made for her car, Alison cursing her lack of charisma. She could say what she wanted about the dead, but they never made her feel self-conscious. Then again, they never made her feel anything at all.

He'd never felt so alive. How could he have forgotten this feeling? It was better than anything—sex, drugs, maybe even love. That last one stopped him for a second.

Sawyer had managed to dodge the wave of oncoming police a couple minutes previous, causing most of the cops to smash into one another and the rest to smash into something else. Now he'd brought the Porsche onto I-10 and drove at the speed of light. The hot sun glared through the windscreen, blinding Eddie for a moment. He remembered a line from one of the *Matrix* movies: *The freeway means suicide.* Something like that.

"We need to lose that heli before more cars arrive,"

Sawyer shouted over the heavy metal.

"We gotta switch the car," Eddie said. "Where's the parking garage?"

"No garage. We got something better," Floyd said. "You gonna like this."

They zoomed along the freeway, the helicopter hovering above them like a spirit. They were moving so fast Eddie thought the Porsche might take off into the cerulean sky, its engine roaring over the music. Every slight movement of Sawyer's hands on the wheel was like pulling the reigns on a horse.

Sawyer slowed as they crossed the Los Angeles River—and it was actually there, the river, thick and flowing from all the strange rain this summer, instead of summer's usual river of concrete.

Sawyer took an exit onto two-lane I-5 and turned down the music. "This is the spot, Floyd."

Floyd nodded and twisted in the seat to look up at the sky. "I don't see the heli. Must be right above us."

"Perfect," Sawyer said, and slowed further as they approached a wide overpass that blotted out the sun.

"The spot for what?" Eddie said.

"Switching the car," Floyd said. "We planned for this case it turned out to be San Diego all over again. Good thing we did, huh?"

"I don't see the car . . ." Eddie said, but then he understood.

Sawyer stopped the Porsche in the shade of the

overpass. The traffic had been light on the freeway but thirty seconds of this would be enough to cause mayhem.

Floyd exited the car and Eddie got out after him, wincing when his foot hit the pavement, as Floyd raised his rifle at the vehicle behind: a beat-up and rusted old Ford pickup, the cargo bed covered with blue tarp and an old man in dungarees and a flat cap behind the wheel.

Floyd stepped toward the pickup, gun raised. The old man pounded on the horn in response.

"Get out the way 'fore I run you over," the old man yelled out of the window in a hick accent.

A second vehicle approached behind the pickup. Floyd fired a shot into the tarmac. The vehicle behind the pickup screeched into acceleration, pulling out from behind the pickup and racing past Floyd. Eddie almost had to dive out of the way to avoid it.

The old man got out of the pickup with his hands raised. "All right, you win, you no-good sons of bitches."

The helicopter's whirring moved beyond them and to the right as it attempted to circle around. A third vehicle drove by them, the parents and two kids inside staring open-mouthed at Eddie and Floyd as it passed.

"Move, old man," Floyd said, shouldering him. The old man stumbled and fell onto his ass.

"Damn sons of bitches," he said. "In my day I woulda took those rifles outta your hands and beat you with 'em."

Eddie limped past him toward the pickup.

"Think you're tough with that big gun, don't you boy?"

the old man said. "In Nam I killed gooks with my bare hands."

"Congratulations."

Floyd pulled back the tarp, tossed the bag and rifle onto the cargo bed, and slid them inside.

"Hurry," he said.

Sawyer reached the pickup before Eddie and got into the driver's seat.

"Your gun," Eddie said to him.

Sawyer shook his head. "I'm keeping it." He shut the door.

Floyd grabbed the bag off Eddie's shoulder and threw it onto the cargo bed. Eddie handed Floyd his rifle and went around to the passenger side and got into the middle seat. Floyd came in after him and shut the door. The helicopter was somewhere on their right, sounding closer than before, probably descending.

"Nicely done, boys," Sawyer said. He handed the rifle to Floyd and got the wheels of the pickup turning.

The old man had clambered to his feet. He watched them with defiant fury as they rolled by. "Sons of bitches," he yelled, raising a fist.

"Man, that's one angry cracker," Floyd said.

"There any other kind?" Eddie said.

They drove out of the underpass slowly. The sun hit them like a searchlight, hot and dazzling. Eddie shielded his eyes while they adjusted. The dark blur of the helicopter came into view high above on the right. By now a few more vehicles had driven out of the overpass before them. There was no way the helicopter could know which to pursue, but Eddie held his breath anyway. He was sure it would spot them packed tightly into the front seat, but as they picked up speed and cruised away, the helicopter did not follow; instead it shrank in the wing mirror's reflection until it was just a buzzing insect.

"Holy crap, we did it," he said, breathing at last. "We fucking did it."

"It ain't done till it's done," Sawyer said. He switched the radio on.

A news reporter started speaking: " . . . but when pressed about the possibility of migrant children suffering lifelong trauma from being separated from their families and, quote, 'kept in cages,' the president rejected accusations of systemic racism at the border, claiming that the government is acting in the best interests of the children. In Los Angeles, the search continues for the killers of William Kane and Kaya White. L.A.P.D. discovered the victims buried in Angeles National Forest Wednesday morning after a group of teenagers spotted suspicious activity the night before—"

Sawyer slapped the radio off and Eddie felt his mood sour, black thoughts of murder returning like a haunting. Dakota's sister. Jesus Christ.

"How many people you think we killed today?" he said.

"Just cops. No real people," Floyd said.

"How do you know?"

"I was just shooting at cops. I assume you was just shooting at cops, too."

"Yeah, but—"

"Sawyer, what 'bout you? You just shoot at cops today?"

"Yup."

"See? Just cops. No real people. Don't ask questions like that; what's done is done."

Eddie kept his mouth shut, dreading the news report that would tell him exactly how many more lives he'd taken through his bad decisions—through his own hands.

Sawyer took them to a secluded parking lot beside the river in East Compton. He killed the engine and the three of them sat in silence.

"Well, we're officially bank robbers," he said.

Floyd slapped the dash. "We badass motherfuckers is what we are. Shit, I want that stamped on my wallet."

Eddie smirked, feeling high as a kite from the rush of it all. "Like De Niro. You were right."

"Hell yeah I was right. But I'm Bobby. You the blond with the ponytail."

"You mean Val Kilmer," Eddie said. "Nah, that's Sawyer."

They all laughed.

Eddie looked around the parking lot. It was empty except for two dumpsters graffitied with gang signs and a black S.U.V. A fence at the back of the lot separated it from the river.

"You left that here?" he said. "I'm surprised it wasn't stolen."

"This my hood, niggas know better. Besides, it's not so bad round here no more. Not like when I was a kid."

"So we torch the pickup, take the money to Saul in the S.U.V., and Dakota goes free. Right?"

Their hesitation told him everything.

"It ain't that simple," Floyd said.

"You're keeping the money," Eddie said.

Floyd and Sawyer glanced at each other.

"How'd you know?" Floyd said.

"Two million bucks . . . a fuckin' bank . . . all for that fat fuck? Come on, Floyd, I might be an idiot but I'm not stupid."

Floyd nodded slowly. "So you okay with it?"

"Of course I'm not okay with it. He's gonna kill her, man! Don't you care about that?"

"No, I don't. That's the difference between you and me, Eddie. That's why I will always win."

Eddie looked at Sawyer.

Floyd said, "He don't care neither. The way it is, Eddie—accept it. You never should have got that girl mixed up in your shit. We giving you a way out."

Eddie clenched his jaw, concentrating hard. If he

could snatch the rifle out of Floyd's hands . . .

Floyd read his mind: "Before you do something stupid, there's something you should know. Saul wanted you dead. He hired a guy to do you after the bank and wanted me to make sure it happened and bring him the money. Me and Sawyer made sure that didn't happen. You should be dead, Eddie. We saved your life."

"That slimy piece of shit. I figured he'd want me dead, but I thought he'd do it at the meet."

"You're welcome," Floyd said.

"Fuck you!"

Floyd pressed the rifle against Eddie's forehead.

"Don't make me have to take the life I just saved," he said. "This what gonna happen: We all gonna step out this truck together. Sawyer sets it on fire, and me and him get in that S.U.V. with these bags so we can give them to my nigga who gonna deposit them into an offshore account while we get the fuck outta this country of racists and rich assholes. I don't care what you do or where you go, but my advice, from one friend to another—leave California soon as you get out this truck and never return, 'cause sure as the pope shits in the woods Saul will kill you soon as he lay eyes on you. Forget the girl; she was dead the second you dragged her into this."

Floyd opened the door and stepped out of the pickup, the rifle pointed at Eddie's chest. "C'mon."

Fuck, there was no way out of this. Eddie opened the door and stepped out of the truck. He stared into Floyd's eyes. That money was his only chance at saving Dakota and there was no way these two were going to walk away with it while he was breathing. Behind him he heard Sawyer exit the vehicle and shut the door. If he moved fast enough, maybe he could knock Floyd's gun out of the way in time, hit Floyd hard, and get ready for Sawyer coming at him. It was the only option.

Floyd narrowed his eyes, the rifle pressed against his shoulder.

"I don't like that look you giving me," he said. "Don't make me put you down, Eddie. In my mind we still friends and I want it to stay that way."

Eddie squeezed his fists. On three he'd lunge. One . . . two . . .

A loud crack boomed across the parking lot and Floyd's face went blank. Eddie had just enough time to register the dark hole on Floyd's forehead before Floyd slumped to the ground, the rifle clattering against the pavement.

Eddie spun to see Sawyer staring open-mouthed. Sawyer met Eddie's gaze.

Eddie ducked behind the pickup as Sawyer dived over the hood. The window next to Eddie's head shattered as another gunshot rang out.

"Where the fuck's it coming from?" Eddie said.

Sawyer crawled toward Floyd and shook the dead man's shoulders. "Get up! Floyd! Get up!"

Eddie grabbed Sawyer and shoved him against the

truck as another shot ricocheted off the pavement.

"Sawyer! What's going on?"

Sawyer searched Eddie's face like an amnesiac. His vacant expression scared Eddie as much as the shooter.

"Snap out of it," Eddie said, shoving him against the vehicle again. "Listen to me: Somebody is shooting at us. Floyd is dead. If we don't so something quick, we're gonna be dead too."

Sawyer stared at him blankly for a moment until his eyes focused and Eddie felt the presence of the man return.

A burst of rapid gunfire rattled across the truck, blowing out all the windows. The shooter had switched to what sounded like an uzi. Eddie peeked out behind the pickup. A short man in a white shirt was approaching them from the dumpsters, a submachine gun in his hands.

Eddie pulled his head out of sight right as the man pulled the trigger and a spray of bullets blew holes in the pavement at Eddie's feet.

"We need that gun," he said, looking at the rifle beside Floyd's corpse. He stretched out a foot in an attempt to drag it back with his heel. Another spray of bullets and he jerked his foot back.

Eddie heard the shooter reach the other side of the pickup. He'd have to dive for the gun or die here in a parking lot in East Compton—the worthless-loser end he'd always feared. He swallowed hard and tensed, about to lunge, and heard the shooter lift the tarp on the back of the pickup. The sound of a bag scraping against the cargo bed, then another.

The money.

Eddie lunged for the rifle, scraping his palms on the concrete. He spun, bringing up the gun. The shooter was ready for him: he had one bag over his shoulder and the other at his feet, the submachine gun waiting patiently for a target. Eddie felt the bullets before he heard them—like powerful fists pounding on his ribs. He fell onto his back, hot pain roaring through his chest, the wind knocked out of it. His wounded leg burned with fresh agony.

He squinted through the red haze of pain and saw the shooter—a Latino with a ponytail and blank face— reloading the submachine gun. Eddie rolled out of sight as a blast of bullets riddled the truck. Sawyer ducked his head, almost toppling onto the ground. Through the underside of the truck, Eddie saw the Latino's ankles and feet approaching, the man about to come around the back and finish them off.

Eddie aimed at the Latino's left leg and held his breath. He squeezed the trigger. A bullet tore through the man's calf muscle, exposing glinting bone. The leg buckled and the Latino let out a high-pitched wail. He hopped behind the bag of cash, which he began to drag backwards, his legs shielded by it.

Eddie scrambled to his feet and raised the rifle over the truck's roof. The Latino was ready for him: a hail of bullets slammed into the truck. Eddie ducked. When the shooting ceased, he peered through the glassless windows. The Latino was heading for the fence that led to the river. He fired again and Eddie ducked again, squeezing his eyes shut. When he opened them the Latino had hopped the fence and disappeared down the slope to the water, both bags of cash over his shoulders, the man stronger than he looked.

Eddie raced after him despite the pain and wheezing breaths, hoping the bulletproof vest had lived up to its name. But his leg slowed him down; the Latino, despite a bullet to the ankle, was gaining distance.

Eddie tossed the rifle over the fence and jumped, his cut palms stinging as he gripped the metal. He yelled as he swung his wounded leg over the top, and again when he landed on the grass below. The Latino had jumped onto a small, flat motorboat on the river. Eddie scrambled for the rifle as the boat's engine came to life.

The boat was skipping down the river by the time Eddie fired. At first, the front of the boat lifted up out of the water as it propelled forward, like a motorcycle doing a wheelie, but gradually it settled down as it got further away, skimming the water like a stone. Eddie emptied the magazine as the boat got smaller, but hit nothing. With one hand on the motor, the Latino had turned his head to watch Eddie as he raced away. Eddie couldn't make out his face but he'd bet his last lottery ticket the fucker was smiling.

Sawyer pulled up in the S.U.V. as Eddie hopped

back over the fence. The driver-side window came down. Sawyer looked even more pissed than usual.

"Get in. We're going after him."

Eddie climbed into the S.U.V., the rifle in his hand.

Sawyer chucked a fresh magazine to him. "Reload it." He reversed at speed and pulled the handbrake while spinning the steering wheel with his palm. The S.U.V. swung around to face the exit of the parking lot and Sawyer accelerated toward it.

Eddie switched the magazines. "Who the fuck was that?"

"Name's Diego. He's the hitman supposed to kill you." Sawyer shook his head, forehead in a crease. "We should have killed him. Then Floyd wouldn't be . . ."

"You met him before?"

Sawyer raced out of the parking lot onto a street flanked either side by white bungalows with iron bars over the windows.

"I pretended to be you," he said. "I wasn't supposed to be on this job; Saul didn't want me on it, and he don't know I'm on it now. So I pretended to be you at the meet with Diego, but he knew right away I ain't you and took off."

"So, what, this guy is fucking Saul over too? Is Saul really that out of touch?"

"Maybe he ain't fucking Saul over," Sawyer said, skidding onto Alondra Boulevard. "I got some questions for Diego when we catch him."

Eddie gripped the handle above the door as Sawyer overtook a Toyota. "And how are we gonna do that? He sailed away on a fucking boat."

"He's headed for the ocean, but a small jon boat like that can only go so fast. We can get ahead of him on the seven ten. Runs parallel to the river all the way to the Pacific. We take it the whole way, then turn onto the bridge on Ocean Boulevard toward Long Beach, just before the river opens up. We wait for him on that bridge. We'll see him coming right for us."

"Then what?"

"Then I'll shoot him."

Eddie wiped his brow, wet as a washboard. The plan might work—if Sawyer drove like the devil.

Seven breathless minutes later they reached an exit near Ocean Boulevard—a narrow road bordered by concrete barriers. A hatchback ahead slowed them for thirty seconds until they passed beneath the bridge and the barriers on the left side of the road were replaced by a stretch of dirt that led up to the bridge. Sawyer hit the brakes hard, the S.U.V. veering so suddenly onto the dirt that for a moment it seemed it would topple onto its side and send them hurtling into the cages of electrical generators clustered beside it, the river behind them. The S.U.V. was too wide to make it up the dirt track; they'd have to go on foot. They had spotted Diego only once, a few hundred yards ahead of them in Los Cerritos, since he'd taken off in the boat, but Sawyer had seemed certain that they'd passed him at some point after that.

"How do you know?" Eddie had asked him a couple minutes previous.

"The speed the boat was movin' when we saw him—fast for a jon boat, but we've been faster."

"Why you so sure he's going to the ocean? He could be keeping the cash for himself and disappearing anywhere."

"Nah. Either he's taking the boat to Venice Beach and it's a short trip from there to Beverly Hills and Saul, or he's screwing Saul and taking the money to Mexico. Either way he's going to the ocean, which means he has to pass under that bridge. Must have planned this from the beginning. The stories I'd heard about him were always extravagant. I figured they were just rumors, until now . . ."

Eddie wasn't so sure, but what was the alternative?

When the S.U.V. came to a stop in the dirt, Sawyer snatched the rifle from Eddie, threw open the door, and sprinted up the slope toward the bridge, small clouds of dust swirling up behind him. Eddie had never seen anyone move so fast; Sawyer had even left the door of the S.U.V. open. Eddie pushed it shut as he hurried after him as quickly as his pulsating leg would allow, which was not very quickly at all. Could the boat even make it to the Pacific from the river? Wouldn't dams block the boat along the way? Ordinarily maybe, but the river was surging from all the recent rain and the boat was flat and narrow. You wouldn't be able to take a boat very far, however small, from the ocean into the river, but, in these conditions, the other way around wasn't unthinkable. Diego—Sawyer had told Eddie he was a true pro—had obviously planned this whole thing out in advance; he wasn't about to get stuck in a dam with two million bucks. Right?

When Eddie reached the bridge, Sawyer was halfway across it pointing at the river.

"It's him!"

Eddie followed Sawyer's finger. The black speck of the boat was hopping toward them. But the bridge was close to the water; Diego would surely spot them.

Eddie reached Sawyer, panting. "I can't believe it."

"Told you we could do it."

"Now you have to hit him. And hope the cops don't show." Eddie glanced at the rifle in Sawyer's hands, conscious of the many vehicles passing them in both directions.

"I was the best shot in my squad in Iraq. I'll hit him."

Sawyer crouched before the knee-height barrier and aimed at the approaching Diego, the rifle pressed securely into his shoulder. Eddie crouched beside him and watched Diego's face come slowly into view. Even from this distance Eddie saw the guy had a strange look about him—one of a man who doesn't belong anywhere.

"You can do it," Eddie said to Sawyer, not sure he

believed it himself. Diego was moving fast, and in less than thirty seconds he'd pass beneath them toward open water, and be gone.

Sawyer sucked in a deep breath and exhaled slowly. "This is for you, Floyd," he said quietly. For a moment, time seemed to slow almost to a stop and Eddie sensed the beauty of the world that thrummed around him: the river became an opal under the gleam of the sun and the soft breath of the warm wind tickled his ears and the sounds of everything vanished until there was only the surging of the water and the squawk of a bird, and Eddie appreciated his home—his life—in a way he had never allowed himself to. How carelessly he had gambled it all.

Then Sawyer pulled the trigger.

The pop of the rifle made Eddie flinch.

Diego swung the boat to the left, noticing them now, unharmed.

"Shit," Sawyer said and aimed at him again. Diego swung right, then left again, careening the boat in zig-zags up the river. In a matter of seconds he would pass under the bridge.

"We're gonna lose him," Eddie said.

"No we won't." Sawyer closed an eye and looked down the barrel.

"Get down!" Eddie grabbed Sawyer's shoulder and pulled as Diego raised his gun in one hand. They fell onto the road, almost getting flattened by a garbage truck that had to swerve to avoid them. Bullets thumped against the side of the bridge. The boat buzzed beneath the bridge as they got to their feet.

Sawyer darted across the road without even looking at the oncoming vehicles, almost causing a collision. Eddie waited for an opening and went after him. Standing upright, Sawyer aimed the rifle at Diego's back. The boat was still careening side to side. It would be a hard shot to make, and in a few seconds would become impossible.

Sawyer followed the movements of the boat with the gun, waiting for the right shot. But he was waiting too long.

"Sawyer—"

"Shh."

Sawyer continued following Diego's movements, one eye shut and the other staring down the sights.

He squeezed.

Diego's body jerked, then slumped backwards, his hand still on the motor. The boat swerved violently to the right and Eddie had a horrible image of the bags of cash sliding into the river. But the boat stayed upright, speeding now toward the electrical generators on the bank.

The narrow, flat boat shot up the slope of the bank and into the sky like an arrowhead, heading for the generators. It plowed through the metal cages and into the generators in an explosion of white electricity and disappeared behind them.

"Christ," Eddie said. "If the bullet didn't kill him, that sure as shit did."

Sawyer blew the tip of the rifle as if he was a gunslinger and it his six-shooter. "Told you I'd hit him."

"Nice shot. The cops are gonna be here any minute, we gotta hurry."

They jogged down the dirt path and found to their amusement that the boat had come to a stop beside the S.U.V. Diego lay sprawled on his back at the rear, one of his arms bent at an unnatural angle. One of the bags of cash was still on the boat, the other lay in the dirt a few yards away. Eddie glanced at Sawyer. Two problems were out of the way in Floyd and Diego, but Sawyer was a third. Maybe if Eddie "checked" to see if Diego was dead, he could swipe the uzi and turn it on Sawyer before Sawyer could shoot him first. But what if it was empty?

Eddie stepped toward Diego and stood over him, gazing at his mangled body. His arm was definitely broken, maybe one of his legs, his body sliced all over and smeared in blood.

Diego opened his eyes with a gasp and Eddie nearly had a stroke.

"Jesus, he's alive," Eddie said.

"What?" Sawyer hurried over. "Goddamn."

Diego stretched out a bloody arm and grasped Sawyer's jeans weakly, gasping, his eyes searching for something. Sawyer stepped out of the man's reach. He crouched onto his hunkers and gazed down into Diego's face.

"Why did you kill Floyd and take the money?" he said.

Diego appeared confused by the question, probably hallucinating, maybe seeing another dimension of the universe.

Sawyer said, "Diego, listen to me: You are going to die. That's for sure. But you're in a lot of pain right now, and your death may take some time. And if the cops get here, they won't make it any easier for you. If you answer my question, I'll put a bullet clean into your head. There won't be no pain, and you'll die the death you've earned as a man of the gun."

Diego focused on Sawyer's face and seemed to nod almost imperceptibly.

"Now get ready, Diego, 'cause here it comes: Did Saul tell you to kill Floyd along with Eddie, and take the money?"

Diego narrowed his eyes slightly and let out a moan. They clouded over as he writhed in agony.

Sirens screamed in the distance.

"Sawyer, I hear the cops."

Sawyer grabbed Diego's face in both hands. "Diego, listen to me. Did Saul want you to kill Floyd and take the money?"

Diego nodded, his eyes half-shut.

"Is that a yes, Diego? I need to be sure. Say it. Say yes."

"*Sí*," Diego said, nodding clearly now, his teeth gritting through the pain.

"Thank you. Rest in peace." Sawyer pointed the gun at Diego's face and the man seemed to smile, looking content, as if this was how he'd always dreamed his death. Sawyer shot him in the forehead and, at last, Diego was dead.

They stared at the corpse as the sirens wailed nearby.

"I know what you're thinking," Sawyer said.

"Yeah, what's that?"

"You're thinking what's to stop me from killing you and taking that money for myself."

"You're right, that is what I'm thinking."

"I don't wanna kill you, man. I never did. All I wanted was . . . me and Floyd, we were gonna . . ."

Sawyer looked at Eddie and Eddie was surprised to see a tear sliding down the man's cheek. "Saul's gonna pay for this. I'll help you get that girl out of there, and together we'll kill Saul."

Eddie couldn't believe it. "You're saying . . ."

"I'm saying I'll help you rescue your girl if you help me kill that piece of shit. Then we split the cash and go our separate ways."

Eddie nodded, his head spinning as a surge of hope swelled inside him.

"How do we do it?" he said.

"Saul got no idea that I'm here right now, unless Diego told him when he saw me pretending to be you, but I'm betting he didn't. Saul's gonna call me in any minute now once he realizes his money ain't coming. I'll show up and play dumb. You call him once you get the cash somewhere safe and tell him you got his money and want to arrange a meet to trade it for the girl. With Floyd missing, he'll want me there at that meet, and when it goes down, I'll turn on him and whoever else he got with him, and together we grab the cash and get the fuck outta this place forever."

Eddie nodded. They could pull this off.

"You don't mind me keeping the money?" he said. "How you know I won't bail?"

"You would have bailed long before now if you were gonna bail. And besides, you're a decent person. You ain't like the rest of us."

Eddie remembered Dakota's sister screaming beneath the duct tape, and wasn't so sure.

17 | A Tale of Two Southerners

The blond showed up at the restaurant right as Rufus had decided he'd waited long enough. So he decided to wait twenty more minutes. If no one else arrived, and if the blond did not come out of the restaurant by then, he'd pay them all a visit.

But whatever meeting the blond had in there was a quick one: he left the restaurant ten minutes after going inside. Rufus had a dilemma: follow the blond, or wait for Eddie—if Eddie was going to show at all. But he was tired of waiting, and the blond could tell him what he wanted to know. And it would be nice to punish the man for interrupting his fun with the nigger.

Rufus turned the keys and woke the engine of his Impala. By now the sun had passed its peak and was drifting northwest across the clear blue sky, and the stifling heat had mellowed slightly. The blond got in the S.U.V. he'd arrived in and took off down the street. Rufus gave it ten seconds, then hit the accelerator and cruised after him.

He hit play on the car's tape player and Johnny Cash picked the intro to "Solitary Man." Rufus tapped his fingers on the steering wheel to the beat, enjoying the sense of impending destiny flowing through him. Soon he would sit down with Mr. Blond and peer inside the man.

The blond drove thirty minutes to a small apartment block in Boyle Heights. He parked on the curb and went inside. Rufus parked across the street and followed him. There was no lock on the doors, or anything else stopping a non-resident from strolling in. The blond disappeared up the stairs and Rufus went up after him. He caught sight of the blond again going down a hallway on the second floor, and reached the hallway as a door twenty feet ahead on the right side closed.

Rufus stood outside the door now, letting some seconds pass. He tried the handle: the door was unlocked. He pushed it open slowly and looked around. The place was a dump, dirty plates and pizza boxes and bottles of beer discarded everywhere. It stank worse than it looked.

Rufus stepped inside the apartment, one hand fingering the knife in the left holster. Even walking softly his boots were loud on the hardwood floor, but the blond hadn't noticed: a tap turned on in the kitchen, just ahead on the right. Three more steps and Rufus saw him. The blond was facing the sink, his back to Rufus, filling a glass with water. He raised the glass to his lips and tipped his head back.

In two large strides Rufus grabbed the blond's hair and tugged it hard. The man cried out, both hands grasping at Rufus's fist as the glass smashed onto the floor. Rufus raised his other fist and swung it toward the blond's face like a hammer. It crashed into his nose with a crunch. The blond screamed, his hands rushing to his face. Rufus released the blond's hair and the man hit the floor, writhing like a serpent, blood sliding down his neck and pooling behind it.

"That's a nasty wound you got there," Rufus said. "We'd better clean it up. Don't want it to get infected." He threw open a couple cupboards and found what he was looking for: a bottle of hard liquor—tequila in this case. He twisted off the cap and took a swig. "Mexican piss," he muttered, and turned the bottle upside down above the blond's head.

The man wailed and shielded his eyes. He tried to roll onto his side. Rufus kicked him in the stomach.

"You ain't goin' nowhere, boy."

The blond clutched at his belly, gasping silently.

Rufus said, "You got a smoke? I could use one." He searched the man's pockets. He took the blond's wallet out of his front pocket and slipped it into his own, and found a box of cigarettes in the man's back pocket. He withdrew a smoke and closed his lips around it. The gas burners on the stove would do for a lighter (since he'd lost his, which he was still pissed about). He got one burning and bent forward and set the cigarette on fire.

"Now that," he said, exhaling silky smoke, "feels good." He fished the man's wallet out of his pocket and flipped it open. "Sawyer Harris. This a Texas driver's license, Sawyer. And that's one mighty fine Southern name you got. This address here . . . Austin. Well, would you look at that. I'm from San Antonio. We're practically neighbors."

Rufus sucked deeply on the cigarette and enjoyed the rush of seven thousand chemicals whirling through his veins. "This changes things, Sawyer. I don't want to hurt a fellow Texan more'n I have to. Answer my questions and we might even have a good time here, what d'ya say?" He stepped toward Sawyer. "Come on, get up." He grabbed the man's shirt in one hand and pulled him to his feet.

Sawyer reflexively bent forward, still sucking at the air.

"Stand up straight, fella, you're closin' your lungs like that," Rufus said. He straightened Sawyer's spine for him and held him there, fixing the man's shirt collar with his free hand.

"Here," Rufus said, grabbing a dish towel from a

hanger in the wall and handing it to Sawyer. "Hold it against your nose."

Sawyer did as he was told.

Rufus pulled a chair out from the table. "Sit."

Sawyer collapsed into the chair.

Rufus stood by the doorway and observed him.

"Sawyer, I need to know a few things and you're gonna tell me. You saw what I did to your nigger friend, so I don't need to tell you what happens when folks don't answer my questions. You hearing me, boy?"

Sawyer nodded, the towel against his face.

"For this to work, you're gonna have to speak at some point."

"When you gonna quote scripture at me?" Sawyer said, his voice muffled behind the cloth.

Rufus almost smiled. "You a Christian?"

"No, sir, I most certainly ain't."

"Why'd you come to Los Angeles? The center of the universe."

"I went A.W.O.L. from the military. That ruled out pretty much any career worth having 'cept one. L.A.'s as good a city as any to be after that. Better than most, even."

"I can't argue with that. There's always been too many spics 'n' niggers here for me. But I guess you don't care about that, do you, boy?"

Sawyer held the cloth away from his face and looked at it. The bleeding had slowed now, the man's chin caked with dried blood.

"Really I came to L.A. to be away from men like you," Sawyer said.

Rufus nodded. "And we're glad to see men like you leave. Well, Sawyer, to respond to your question, I only quote scripture to men I'm 'bout to kill."

"I'm sure God appreciates that."

"I don't give two shits 'bout what God appreciates or don't. I'll let you in on a li'l secret. But first I need another one them smokes."

Rufus took the box out of his pocket and tossed a smoke between his lips. He headed for the stove to light it. As soon as he passed Sawyer the man made a run for it. But Rufus had expected it. Already inside his jacket, his quick fingers flung a knife at the fleeing man. The blade penetrated Sawyer's Achilles tendon and Sawyer hit the floor screaming, one hand stretched out in front of him fingering the threshold of the doorway.

Rufus lit the cigarette and sat in the chair Sawyer had vacated. Sometimes it's just too goddamn easy.

"What was I saying?" he said. "Oh yeah, a li'l secret I'm gonna make you privy to: I ain't a Christian. It's not that I don't believe in God. I do believe; I have heard His voice on the wind and witnessed His hand skimming a field of corn. It's that I know I'm goin' straight to hell. I don't care. Heaven's too dull for a man like me. I quote scripture because I enjoy reminding that dictator up there that I'm in charge of my destiny down here. Maybe He can punish me when I'm dead, but while I'm alive, I'm calling the shots."

Rufus rose from the seat and stood over Sawyer as the man crawled slowly toward the doorway. "While I'm alive on this planet, *I'm* the one taking lives and punishing those who defy me. I got a picture of Jesus behind my bed, not so I have to look at Him, but so He has to look at *me*. While I'm alive, *I am God*."

Sawyer moaned as he slithered toward the doorway. Rufus tugged the knife out of his leg and Sawyer screamed, the man's body spasming.

"You gonna do something or just lie there and bleed?" Rufus said. "No, I didn't think so. Now listen to me, boy—there's a lot more places I can put this knife. You're gonna answer my questions with nothing but truth, and you're gonna do it without my having to ask twice."

Rufus ran the blade gently along Sawyer's unharmed leg and felt him shudder.

"Where is Eddie?"

His leg hurt less now that he'd bandaged it up, swallowed a handful of painkillers, and washed them down with vodka, but Eddie felt nervous now that he was alone. What was to stop Sawyer from bailing? (Except the prospect of losing a million bucks, of course, which was admittedly a pretty big one.) And even if Sawyer showed, could they pull it off or would they get themselves and Dakota killed?

And with the police on the search for Kaya's killers, it was only a matter of time until the cops came sniffing for him . . . Shit, all this because a rich asshole charged him and his finger slipped on the trigger. All this from one bullet, just like the bullet that started the Great War; he remembered that from history class, amazed back then by how so many people had lost their lives because one dumbass had moved his finger an inch.

Eddie took a cab to LAX and told the driver to wait, he'd only be a few minutes. He carried both of the bags of cash inside despite only needing one for this task, not trusting the cab driver with the other. The hair on his arms stood on end as he passed the airport police and sniffer dogs near the entrance. For all he knew the cops had connected him to the murders already and plastered his face all over the news. These airport cops were trained to spot the guilty; he'd have to be fast and keep his cool.

He headed straight for the lockers, then thought better of it. It would look less suspicious if he pretended to check his flight time first. He stood before the screens and gazed up at them, half-wishing he was on one of those myriad planes out of here, zooming toward freedom. A cute woman in a short polka dot dress smiled at him, gazing up at the screens herself.

"Where are you headed to?" he asked her in an attempt at appearing normal, glancing at the cop near the entrance.

"Prague. To see my family," she said in a sexy European accent. "Long time since."

"What a coincidence—so am I. I'll see you on the plane." He winked and made for the lockers.

Eddie reached the lockers and bit his tongue. Shit. Of course—they accepted only credit cards. The police could be tracking his card, and even if they weren't they could be soon. Then they'd simply wait for him to collect the cash later and grab him (he saw it in a movie once—shit, probably more than once—but it seemed likely). He'd have to swipe someone else's. He looked at the European, standing there all pretty in that dress. She looked like she could use a drink . . .

Eddie strolled over to her. "Hey, listen, we still have a while before the flight. You wanna grab a drink? I'm buying." He flashed his most charming smile, a million bucks over each shoulder.

She didn't seem at all surprised. Girl like her probably scratches her head when she *doesn't* get asked if she'd like a drink

"Sure, I like to drink," she said.

"We have that in common then. This bar right here will do just fine." Eddie led her to a couple stools at the bar—one of those sleek but charmless three-hundred-and-sixty-degree airport bars that serve overpriced, underpoured cocktails and spirits. He stacked the bags on top of each other at his feet, making sure to keep his leg against them.

They ordered a couple cocktails and Eddie eyed her

handbag, which she'd set on the bar beside her.

"Why you go to Prague?" she asked him while they waited for the drinks.

He tried to conjure an answer. What country was Prague in again? Slovenia? Slovakia? One of those "Slov" countries around that area, he was pretty sure.

"You want to know the truth?" he said. "Nothing brings me there except my finger and one of those model globes of the earth."

"I no understand," she said, frowning in that expressive way Europeans have with their faces.

"It's true—I spun a globe of the earth, closed my eyes, and stopped it with my finger, and wherever it landed was where I was gonna go. That place was Prague."

Her manicured eyebrows crawled up her forehead. "You Americans, you are all so dramatic. Everything is like movie with you."

"You know, that's probably the truest statement I've ever heard."

"What if your finger found the middle of the sea?"

"Then I would've found a boat."

She giggled, one hand over her mouth as if laughter was a criminal offense.

The cocktails arrived. Eddie's was pink, just like the cocktail Dakota had brought him in the Pink Room a lifetime ago. His stomach sank, and he missed Dakota sorely.

"You know nothing of Prague?" the European said.

"Not a thing. I barely know what country it's in." He grinned and she laughed, her hand curling down to slap the air in front of him in a feminine gesture.

"You are funny," she said. "You American men try very hard to be funny but I am thinking you are the real deal, maybe."

"Honey, I'm as real as they come. Your turn—what brings you to L.A.?"

"I am model. L.A. has many opportunity."

"Do you like it?"

She gazed beyond him for a moment, considering the question. "Yes, but, it is not like movie. I come here thinking it would be more like movie, but really it is just a city, like any other city. But I do like it very much. It is maybe a little more . . . dull than I imagined. But more fun than Prague, and more opportunity for me."

"Lady, if you think it's dull here, you've been hanging with the wrong crowd."

It was time to swipe the card. Eddie stood up.

"I'm gonna pay a visit to the little boy's room but I'll be right back," he said. He pulled out his chair and faked a stumble, knocking her cocktail and handbag onto the floor.

"Oh crap, I'm so sorry," he said, aware of the cop nearby watching now. "Let me get that."

He bent down to pick up her bag and glimpsed her purse. He was in luck—it had a flap opening rather than a zipper. He slipped his fingers inside and grabbed what he hoped was a credit card. He pocketed the card as he turned to face her with the bag in hand.

The barman arrived looking irritated.

"Sincere apologies, my man," Eddie said. "I can clean that up for you."

"No, it's not allowed," the barman said, stepping through an opening in the bar.

"Oh, well, okay. Hey, can I get the lady a fresh drink when you're ready?"

The barman nodded joylessly.

The European was smiling coyly at him.

Eddie said, "Sorry again. At least you didn't get wet; that makes me feel better. I'm gonna drop these bags into a locker, visit the little boy's room, and be back before you know it. When I get back, I wanna know your name."

He made for the lockers, hoping the "accident" hadn't aroused any suspicions. The airport was thrumming with people of every creed and color. It took a minute to weave through them all. He paid for one of the big lockers on the bottom and squeezed one of the bags inside—leverage in case the meet with Saul went south. The other he'd be bringing with him.

Nobody approached him as he walked away. He thought about leaving the airport right then and tossing the European's credit card in the bin, but if she noticed the card was missing before she got on the plane, things could get messy. He'd finish his drink, slip the card inside her handbag, and tell her that he'd meet her on the flight.

But first, it was time to call Saul.

Another night, another murder. Alison received a call from the station informing her that one more person had been killed in a manner that resembled the murders of the Texan, lawyer, and gas station victims. She rushed to the location, an apartment in Boyle Heights. After the movie earlier that day, Charlie had fallen asleep as soon as they got home, and, left with no leads to follow, Alison had opened the laptop and researched newspaper reports through the years while Charlie slept on her lap. She'd been looking for unsolved murders that matched the M.O. of those she was investigating. And she found them. A whole lot of them. Her search had proved even more fruitful when she widened it to include all of California, and then neighboring states. There had been a whole string of murders dating from 1987 to 2009 spread out across various cities of a band of western states from Oregon to Arizona. Then the trail went cold. As far as she could tell, nobody had yet connected the seemingly disparate murders, but connected they surely were. The details were too similar and specific to be coincidence, and all of the victims had been involved in the criminal underworld in some way. Alison was sure that the man she was hunting was some kind of assassin who'd retired only to be pulled back into the game after William Kane's murder. And now he'd killed again.

She entered the apartment, glad to be at the scene before forensics, and nodded a greeting at the officers inside. The apartment stank, and not just of death. She had to step over filth on her way to the body. And there it was: a man in his thirties with long blond hair and a sliced throat. The man's shirt was drenched in blood, some of it still wet by the look of it. She noticed the wound in his sternum. There was no doubt about it: this was the work of her killer.

"What do we know about the victim?" she said to anyone within earshot.

"Nothing yet," said a young male officer, stepping closer. "The old lady next door called it in after hearing a disturbance, but she knows nothing about him, and we can't get a hold of the landlord just yet. I didn't want to touch anything, but maybe he has some ID in his pocket."

"You did good. There's nothing I hate more than a spoiled crime scene. Go tell the neighbor I'll need to speak with her in a minute."

Alison took gloves out of her back pocket and stretched them onto her hands and searched the dead man's pockets. Nothing. What did this man have to do with the Texan and the lawyer? Maybe he'd worked for one of them. Maybe he'd been one of the three men who'd pulled the trigger on Kaya White and William Kane and buried them in the forest. If that was indeed the case, that left two of those men alive—but not for long. She'd talk to the neighbor and let forensics do their thing. Hopefully they'd find a fingerprint they could use, though she doubted it.

The neighbor was an old Russian lady with severe white hair and a voice ravaged by cigarettes, one of which she held in her hand currently, puffing at it every few seconds. The woman probably smoked in her sleep.

"I tell the police already—I hear loud banging, men shouting, screaming. I call the police, the police come. What more you want from me."

Alison couldn't help looking at the Russian dolls arranged in a line on a bookshelf. A doll inside a doll inside a doll . . . the sensation was familiar.

Alison said, "Sorry to bother you again, but I'm hoping you might have seen or heard something that can help us. Maybe a name was mentioned?"

The woman waved her hand briskly, dropping ash on the carpet. "No no, only screams. I see nothing, I hear nothing. I would like to be on my own now."

Alison glanced away and rolled her eyes. People could be so selfish in this city.

"All right, I wouldn't expect an old Russian like you to be any help anyway," she said with calculated risk, and turned away.

She had a hand on the door handle when the woman said, "Wait. There was something."

Alison faced her. "Yes?"

"A car, outside. After I hear the shouting, everything go quiet. I call the police and open the window to let some fresh air in before the police come. Then I see a car outside drive away. I remember because it was a beautiful car. Very old, but it looked like new. Maybe this car had nothing to do with it, I don't know, but that's all I saw."

"A car?" Alison stepped closer, excitement building inside her as she remembered something. "Was this car teal-colored with a cream roof?"

"Teal? What color is this?"

"Green, with a hint of blue."

"Now that you mention it, yes . . . the car was the same color as a beautiful lagoon on a tropical island."

Alison dug her phone out of her pocket and searched Google for images of a 1966 teal and cream Chevrolet Impala—the same car the old man in the liquor store in Indio had described that morning.

"Is this the vehicle?" she said, holding her phone in front of the woman's face.

The woman squinted into it, and met Alison's gaze. "That's exactly it."

18 | The Good, the Bad & the Ugly

Outside the apartment block, a red sun was slowly dropping away from the earth. Thick warm air wrapped its arms around Alison. She unlocked her unmarked police car and got into the driver's seat, leaving the door open.

She grabbed the radio. "This is Detective Alison Lockley issuing an urgent request to all units: Be on the lookout for a lone white male driving a teal and cream 1966 Chevrolet Impala. The suspect is wanted for multiple murders and likely armed and dangerous. Radio immediately upon sight of a vehicle matching this description but do not attempt to engage the suspect. That's a teal and cream 1966 Chevrolet Impala."

The officer she'd spoken to in the apartment exited the building as two more arrived. He exchanged some words with the other two.

Alison waved him over.

"Yes, Detective?"

"You're coming with me."

"I am?"

"You are."

"Where we going?"

"I don't know yet but I'll need the back-up. Hop in."

He glanced down the street. "What about my patrol car?"

Alison whistled at the two officers outside the apartment block. They looked over.

"Can one of you get that squad car back to the station, please? Officer . . ." She looked at the officer next to her window. "What's your name?"

"Bukowski."

"Me and Officer Bukowski here have somewhere to be."

"Who's asking?" said one of the officers, stepping toward Alison's car.

"Detective Alison Lockley. And I'm not asking."

The officer nodded reluctantly.

To Bukowski: "Get in."

Bukowski got into the seat beside her. "What's this all about, Detective?"

"I put a B.O.L.O. out for a vehicle, a teal and cream

sixty-six Impala. Soon as someone spots it we'll be racing to the location. The suspect will be armed and won't go down easy, and I might not have time to wait for back-up."

Bukowski nodded, his forehead creased in an extremely serious manner that made her want to chuckle. Up close like this she saw that he was even younger than she'd thought. Probably a rookie.

"What's he suspected of, Detective?" Bukowski said.

"Murder. And a lot of it." It did nothing to relax his expression. "You ever pull your gun on someone, Bukowski?"

"Yeah . . . once."

Christ, he *was* a rookie. "Good. All you'll have to do is point your weapon at the suspect and I'll do the rest. If the situation looks bad you'll cuff him and I'll drop him if he tries anything."

He nodded. "I can do that. So now what?"

"Now we drive around and look for the car while we wait."

"You mind if I smoke in here, Detective?"

"Yeah, but I'll let you this time since I'm dragging you around."

Bukowski put a smoke between his lips and patted his leg. He patted the other leg. Now he was groping at his shirt.

"Jesus, here," Alison said, and held out the golden Zippo she'd found under the lawyer's desk. She'd kept forgetting to take it out of her jacket and was quickly getting used to having it there.

"Thanks," Bukowski said after exhaling a plume. "The fuck, is that made of gold?"

"Long story. You hungry? 'Cause I'm starving."

"There's a decent burger joint around the corner."

"They got anything vegan?"

Bukowski frowned. "I dunno."

"Let's find out."

Alison turned the keys and pulled out onto the street. In the distance, the giant globe of the sun had almost vanished behind the twinkling skyscrapers, the sky above them pink like a wound.

Eddie approached the restaurant with a pistol in his waist and a knot in his stomach. The million-dollar bag was over his shoulder, heavy as ever. The sun had set over Los Angeles and the freaks and losers would soon come out to play. Not that anyone would much notice in Beverly Hills. The restaurant was painted white and a massive neon sign ran along the length of it spelling out "The Long Goodbye" in an '80s, *Miami Vice* kind of script, the tail of the "y" in "Goodbye" curling beneath the final "e" and trailing behind to underline the entire title. It looked good: minimal and cool.

Eddie hesitated before he opened the restaurant doors. It occurred to him suddenly that this might be the last doorway he'd ever pass through alive.

Fuck it, everybody dies eventually. He pushed open the heavy door and crossed the threshold into the entrance foyer. Instantly two men were upon him.

"Woah, take it easy," he said.

One of them took the bag from his shoulder while another pushed him against the wall and spread his legs. Shit, they were gonna take the gun; he'd been hoping Sawyer would be the one to search him. He tried to peer inside the restaurant but the man searching him held him in place.

"You didn't really think you were gonna get this inside, did you?" the man said, holding the pistol by the barrel next to Eddie's face.

"No, but stranger things have happened. I know a guy who survived a bullet to the head and the very next day slipped on a wet tile coming out of the shower and broke his neck. Died instantly. So, me keeping that gun wasn't out of the question."

"It was rhedorical," the man said.

"Rhedorical?"

"A question not s'posed to be answered."

"You mean rhetorical."

"No I don't. Keep your mouth shut and follow me."

The man stepped in front of Eddie and walked deeper into the restaurant. He was broad-shouldered and stocky with a blotchy tattoo of something indistinguishable on his neck. Eddie followed him, the other man carrying the bag of cash behind them.

Eddie passed through the foyer into the large oval-shaped dining area. Jeweled chandeliers sparkled all over the ceiling; a hundred bottles glistened behind a white marble bar to the left; small round tables circled the room, longer rectangular tables in the center, each covered in white cloth; a giant mirror ran along the circumference of the room, creating a sensation of infinity. A space had been cleared in the center of the room where three men stood beside a small round table. The chubby man sitting at the table picked up a cup and sipped.

"Eddie. Glad you made it," Saul said, setting the cup down on a saucer. "And with my money, I presume."

The man behind Eddie went to Saul and dropped the bag on the table.

"Where's Dakota?" Eddie said. And where the hell was Sawyer?

"I killed her and ate her heart," Saul said.

Eddie stared at him.

Saul smirked. "I kid, I kid. She's alive and well." He waved a hand and one of the men standing beside him disappeared into the kitchen area. He waved again and another lifted the bag of cash onto a nearby table and began taking out the bundles and stacking them.

"Cup of tea, Eddie?" Saul said.

"Give me a real drink, for fuck sake."

Saul smiled, but it didn't reach his eyes. His smiles never did. "You've earned that much." He wagged a finger and his waiter, who Eddie remembered was named Marcel, seemed to materialize out of the wall.

"The Springbank," Saul said.

Marcel nodded and hovered silently away. He passed through the kitchen doors as the man who'd gone into the kitchen area a minute before returned, Dakota shuffling along before him with her hands tied and duct tape over her mouth. Her gaze found Eddie but did not linger. She looked . . . distant, and her eyes and cheeks were red, from crying, probably. But she was unharmed. Relief surged through Eddie, and with it a new sense of urgency. Only now did he become fully aware of the thought that had been scratching the back of his mind since the night before—the thought that had said Dakota was already dead.

The man counting the cash finished the task. He placed the bundles back into the bag and zipped it shut and said something into Saul's ear. Saul nodded, never taking his gaze off Eddie.

"Have a seat, Eddie," Saul said, gesturing toward the empty seat opposite him.

"I'll stand."

"I wasn't asking."

Saul's men were staring at Eddie, looking like they'd love nothing more than to bruise their knuckles.

Eddie sat in the seat. This close to Saul, he could see the small pearls of sweat permanently on the man's fleshy face, smell the man's musty cologne.

"It all comes down to this, doesn't it, Eddie?"

"What's that?"

"The meet. The money for the girl. The last-ditch attempt to save your skin. We've all seen this a thousand times."

The guy thought he was in a fuckin' movie. "Well, it's certainly a first for me," Eddie said.

"What do you think I'm going to say next?"

Playing games, as usual. "I don't know, Saul."

"Oh come on, you do. I'm going to tell you that half the money is missing."

Eddie waited.

"And what are you going to say next?"

Eddie waited some more.

"You're going to say that if I let the girl go, you'll tell me where the rest of my money is."

"You got it, Saul. You should have had this meeting by yourself."

Marcel appeared at the table with a half-empty bottle of amber liquid and two glasses. Saul watched Marcel pour the stuff into the glasses. A smell of oak and peat wafted up from them.

Marcel faded into the background somewhere behind Eddie.

Saul said, "You see, Eddie, you don't have as much leverage as you think. I hold your life in my hands. Hers too. And you're gonna make *me* do something?"

Eddie glanced at Dakota. She was staring at the floor, vacant.

"Why don't you just let her go?" Eddie said. "Let her walk out the door and I'll tell you where your money is. She's got nothing to do with this."

"Didn't I tell you you'd say that? But she does have something to do with this. And before you start complaining, remember that *you're* the one who didn't live up to your side of the bargain. I told you to bring me two million."

"I'll get your two mil', just—"

Saul raised a hand. "Enough. Tell me what you think of that scotch."

Eddie blinked, his mind reeling.

"Taste it," Saul said. "Then I'm going to tell you something."

Eddie picked up the glass, submitting fully to the man holding all the cards, and tasted the whiskey. It was like drinking silk, warm and spicy. He felt it descending his chest.

"What do you think?" Saul said.

"It's the best whiskey I've ever tasted."

"Do you know how I got in this business?"

"No."

Saul picked up his glass and circled it beneath his wide nostrils. He sighed with pleasure, and swallowed some of the scotch. He set the glass down.

"I was sitting where you're sitting right now. One man had a pistol aimed at my face, the other had a contract spread out in front of him. 'You see this pistol,' the man with the contract said—the one holding the gun didn't say a thing the whole time—'This pistol can come for you anytime. It can come into your home when your family are sleeping.' They told me to sign the contract, which would make their employer, Jemeka Johnson, the 'Coke Queen of L.A.'—maybe you've heard of her—this restaurant's primary distributor of fresh produce. I signed it. And they did deliver produce, top quality stuff. But they also delivered cocaine. They were laundering their money through the restaurant and using it as a base to conduct deals, and paying me well for it. They look for businesses they can get involved in, look for business owners they think are more likely to reap the rewards than tell the cops."

Saul sipped the whiskey and straightened his cuffs. "Business was good. I was making more money than I could have made in ten years of only owning a restaurant. But I never forgot what that fuck said to me that night, here, at this very table. One year later almost to the day I brought a pistol of my own to his home while his family were sleeping. I shot his wife and two little girls while they slept, but not him. I made him look at their bodies, see how it was his fault for ever putting me in that position, for disrespecting me. Then I killed him. As for the Coke Queen . . . let's just say that nobody will ever find her."

Eddie's mouth felt dry as a corpse.

"Take a good look at your girl here, Eddie. Make it count."

Eddie lunged forward. "No Saul, wait, Jesus—"

A thick hand grabbed Eddie's neck and slammed his forehead against the table. The pain was at once vivid and far away.

Saul rose from the chair and stood over Dakota, who did nothing but continue to stare at the floor as if unaware of what was happening around her, or simply not caring.

The hand remained on Eddie's neck, holding him in the chair. One of the men handed Saul a pistol. Saul cocked it and pressed it against Dakota's temple.

"Wait! Wait! Saul, please! Wait!" Eddie struggled in the chair. A fist thumped his jaw and sent him sprawling onto the floor. Two men grabbed him and pulled him to his feet. One of them punched him in the gut and he dropped to his knees, gasping. The men held him by the shoulders. Dakota lifted her head and looked at him. Her eyes held no fear in them, or sympathy. Nothing.

Saul said, "You're a stupid fuck, Eddie. All you had to do was show up here when you were told after that shit with Bill. I would have given you a slap on the wrist and sent you on your way. It was only ever about respect, and you were set on giving me none. Now look what happens."

"Saul, wait, I'll get your money, all of it, just don't hurt her."

"You're the one hurting her, Eddie," Saul said, and turned his head away as if to avoid the spatter of blood.

They cruised around downtown Los Angeles in aimless circles looking for a classic teal and cream Chevrolet Impala. It was proving fruitless. They'd only seen one car that could be described as classic, but it certainly wasn't a Chevy and the driver looked too old to walk up the stairs, let alone murder dozens of men in cold blood.

Alison chatted with Bukowski while she drove, a little disappointed at her hunger for contact with another adult.

"I have to say, you've got good taste in music, Detective," Bukowski said while they waited at a red light. She'd played one of her Spotify playlists while they cruised; currently Patti Smith's "Because the Night" grooved out of the speakers.

"Yeah, thanks. Makes the shifts go by a bit easier."

The lights turned green and Alison leaned on the accelerator.

"You married, Bukowski?"

"Why, you interested?"

"Just curious."

"No, I'm not married. But I am expecting a child soon."

"Oh, congratulations. Your first?"

"Yeah."

Alison smiled. "I have one myself, an eight-year-old."

"Boy or girl?"

"Boy."

"I don't know what mine is yet. A boy would be nice. Or a girl."

Alison took a left at an intersection, not bothering to check where they were. "How long until?"

"Just two months now," Bukowski said.

"Nervous?"

"Oh yeah."

Alison chuckled. "Yeah, I bet."

"Any advice? You know, for when the baby's born."

Alison glanced at him, his expression as serious as ever. She couldn't help feeling a kinship with this man about to embark on the most terrifyingly beautiful experience there is.

"Put your child first, always. Fuck this job. I gave it too much of myself for too long, and now there's not much left. Your relationship with your child is everything."

Bukowski nodded, his forehead creased with earnestness.

Alison glanced around. They were on Alameda, outside Chinatown. She took a left onto Alpine. Ahead, a yellow sign with red kanji letters beneath "JEWELRY" glowed on a street corner like a lava lamp.

"I could use some noodles right about now," Alison said.

"After that burger and fries? Bullshit."

Before Alison could respond the radio came to life.

"Detective Lockley, this is Officer Davies," said a crackly voice. "I may have spotted your suspect vehicle."

Alison lunged for the receiver. "This is Lockley. What's your location?"

For a few long seconds there was no response. Alison almost asked again before Davies said, "Third and Highland. Suspect is heading west."

"What car is the suspect driving?" Alison said, needing confirmation.

"It's a classic Impala, that's for sure, and looks like a sixty-six from the picture I got here."

Alison's pulse galloped. "The color?"

"Teal and cream, like you said."

"That's him, that's him," Alison said to Bukowski, adrenaline beginning to rush through her. Into the radio: "Tail the suspect from a distance and do not intercept. I'm on my way."

She pressed her foot to the floor and made sure her seatbelt was fastened.

She looked at Bukowski. "Hold on."

It was dark when Rufus reached the restaurant. He preferred it that way. After the blond, Sawyer, had told him that Eddie would be showing up at the restaurant soon, and with two million dollars, Rufus finished Sawyer off and drove straight to a gun store and got himself a 12-gauge Remington 870 and a couple boxes of shells. He enjoyed the irony of the purchase: before he'd watched the life leave Sawyer's eyes, the man had asked him through bloodied teeth what kind of cowboy don't carry a gun.

Rufus had answered by saying that guns were for cowards, which he believed still, but only a dumbass would walk into a room full of guns with nothing but a pair of daggers. Plus, a shotgun inspires fear. Point that long, hungry barrel at somebody and they'll do anything to stay off the menu.

He parked across the street from the restaurant and killed the engine. He fed the shotgun some shells and shoved the rest into his pockets.

Outside the car, the warm night air tickled his skin. A sharp sickle moon cut into the black velvet sky.

Two million dollars. Not only would he make them suffer for what they did to Bill, he'd get rich in the process. He'd buy a ranch with the money, like he should have done before he squandered his retirement fund after leaving this goddamn city a decade ago. He'd buy a ranch and have Bill's body brought there and bury him under an oak tree out the front, his brother home at last. The thought brought a smile to his face. He gripped the cold steel of the shotgun from the passenger seat, shut the door of the Chevy, and crossed the street toward The Long Goodbye.

"Well well, looks like I missed the party," said a gruff voice behind Eddie. It took him a second to remember where he'd heard it before: the motel. It was the fucking cowboy.

Saul gazed past Eddie, his pistol still at Dakota's temple.

"I was wondering when you'd show up," Saul said. "But you've caught me at a bad time."

"So you've been expecting me," the cowboy said.

Eddie watched the cowboy in the mirror behind Saul. He'd forgotten how large the man was; with the hat and those boots he appeared over seven feet. A leather jacket came down to his knees, black as oblivion. In his right hand he held a shotgun.

Saul lowered the pistol. "If you had any sense you would have left L.A. soon as you caught wind of my name. But if you had any sense you wouldn't have come to L.A. looking for trouble in the first place. So yes, I've been expecting you."

"Then you got no excuse."

"Excuse?"

"For not running as far away from me as your li'l legs could carry you," the cowboy said, coming to a halt halfway between Eddie and the entrance foyer.

Saul wheezed a humorless laugh. "This guy," he said, glancing at the men around him. "One of my men didn't show tonight. I suppose you know something about that?"

"If you mean the blond, you might like to know that his last act in this life was to piss himself while he begged me to spare him. Right after he told me everything about this meet, and his plans for you."

The cowboy smirked. "Look at you. Ain't got a clue. Ignorant fool."

"Enlighten me."

"Sawyer did your bank job with him—" nodding toward Eddie—"and the nigger. Sawyer and the nigger was goin' leave the country with the money but your hitman disrupted things. That's the problem with lazy pieces of shit like you—you get too many people involved in your business and never do nothin' yourself. You think I'd get a man to do *my* killin' for *me*? Eddie here probably told you the hitman killed your nigger outta double-crossing them, but that ain't the truth. Your hitman killed the nigger 'cause *they* crossed *him*. Your hitman was bringin' the money to you when they killed him. Eddie and Sawyer knew you wanted Eddie and the nigger dead soon as that job was done. They was planning on killin' you here tonight. But there you stand, dumb as a fuckin' post. You ain't got a clue what's goin' on round you. All y'all behind each other's backs like a bunch of schoolgirls. Ain't a single one of you knows 'bout loyalty. I always hated this city, but loyalty used to mean something here."

Saul glanced at Eddie, looking smug. "Looks like you did me a favor then," he said to the cowboy.

"I couldn't have the blond killing you. I came a long way for the privilege."

Saul's eyes narrowed, the man getting tired of the back-and-forth.

"You're guilty of ignorance yourself," he said. "Bill

Kane. He was your brother? The reason for all these theatrics? Eddie there killed your brother, and not because I told him to, but because he's an imbecile and his finger slipped on the trigger. And that's it, that's the whole reason. Your brother was a pathetic man, and he died a pathetic death. And so will you."

Saul glanced at his men. "Someone shoot this fucking guy already."

19 | A Long Goodbye

They spotted the Chevy right as the driver—a monstrously tall man dressed up like Lee Van Cleef—stepped out of it and marched toward a restaurant across the street with a shotgun in his hand. Parked in front of Officer Davies in his patrol car, Alison had to think fast about what to do. She signaled to Davies to remain inside the car and watched as the Texan entered the restaurant, a swanky place lit up by neon.

"What are we waiting for?" Bukowski said.

"I don't want to risk a gunfight on the street when we can surprise him behind closed doors. Plus, a shotgun isn't this guy's style. I think something big's about to go down.

I'm gonna go speak with Davies. Confirm back-up's en route and follow me."

She exited the car and went to Davies.

"Looks like it's your guy," Davies said through the half-open window. "What now?"

"Now we go in. I don't know what we're walking into but we don't have time to wait."

"And here I thought I was gonna have a quiet night."

"In this city?"

"No shit. What's this guy wanted for?"

"Multiple murders. He's a homicidal maniac. I've linked him to a bunch of murders on the West Coast since eighty-seven."

Davies nodded. "Then let's get the bastard."

He got out of the car and checked his pistol. Bukowski exited Alison's car and jogged over to them. He nodded a greeting at Davies.

"You ready to go in there, Bukowski?" Alison said.

"Ready as I'll ever be, Detective."

"You got your weapon ready?"

Bukowski took his Glock 22 out of its holster and racked the slide.

Alison said, "I don't know what we'll find in there. Keep your gun pointed at threats and if someone shoots at you, shoot them back. Got it?"

Bukowski nodded vigorously.

Alison grabbed her own pistol from its holster. "Let's go."

They crossed the street, which was quiet now that the stores were closed, and, passing under palm trees, approached the restaurant in silence. Alison felt the tension in her muscles and a sharpening of her senses as she peered into the darkness outside the restaurant doors.

A red sign on the frosted glass of the doors indicated that the restaurant was closed. Davies took the left side, Alison the right, Bukowski behind her.

Davies nodded at her. She nodded back and took a breath, held it in. Whatever awaited them in there wasn't going to be pretty. On the exhale she stepped in front of the door and pushed it open with her shoulder, both hands gripping the pistol tightly.

The opened doorway revealed a small foyer with a leather sofa and hollow window area behind which a maître d' would presumably deal with arriving customers during business hours.

A man was speaking somewhere inside: "Bill Kane. He was your brother, right? The reason for all these theatrics?"

Alison stuck her head outside the foyer and glimpsed the dining area. There was the Texan, standing with his back to her, the shotgun pointed at the floor in his right hand. Ahead of him, two men in suits held a man on his knees by the arms. Three other men, also in suits, stood nearby, one of them—a short, chubby man—holding a pistol next to a young woman also on her knees. Mirrors along each wall gave it all an eerie, spaceless sensation.

The chubby man continued speaking: "Eddie there killed your brother, and not because I told him to, but because he's an imbecile and his finger slipped on the trigger. And that's it, that's the whole reason. Your brother was a pathetic man, and he died a pathetic death. And so will you."

So the Texan was Kane's brother, lusting for vengeance. And the man on the floor was one of Kane's, and Kaya's, killers.

The woman on her knees—with dark skin, an Indian look about her—lifted her gaze from the floor and met Alison's. For a second Alison thought she saw surprise on the woman's face, but then the woman looked at the floor again.

Indian . . . that would make her Dakota. Those eyes— Alison had seen eyes just like them before . . .

The chubby man glanced at some of the men around him. "Someone shoot this fucking guy already," he said.

Fuck. There was no other choice but to make a move.

Alison lunged out of the foyer. "L.A.P.D.! Drop your weapons!"

Never in his life had Eddie ever thought he'd be glad to hear someone scream "L.A.P.D.!" He almost pissed himself out of sheer surprise when he heard the woman's voice, and he could see the same shock on Saul's face now as Saul and his men pointed five guns over Eddie's head. Dakota seemed to have perked up at the sound; she watched the source of the scream intently, her eyes alert. Eddie tried to make eye contact with her but he may as well have been in Belize. He spun his neck to look. A woman in a gray suit held a pistol in that unmistakable, tight, two-handed police-grip, her eyes darting to the left and right in an attempt to watch all of the men at once. Behind her two men in police uniform aimed pistols of their own at Saul and his men, the younger-looking cop appearing much less comfortable than the older. The cowboy stood in the middle facing Eddie, cool as a desert breeze.

"Drop the weapons!" said the woman in the suit, probably a detective. "The building is surrounded, you have no other choice."

Saul said, "The building's surrounded and they brought you three in? Sounds about as likely as my wife growing a dick."

The detective said, "The way it is, either you're going to drop your weapons, or we are, otherwise we'll all be killed. If we drop ours you'll kill us anyway. But you know we won't shoot if you drop yours. You don't have a choice."

Eddie glanced at the cops behind her. The older one appeared still and composed, his gaze slowly scanning the room. The younger one, though—he looked tight as a coil, his back foot trembling and his eyeballs darting all over the place.

"Did someone hand out invitations?" Saul said. "Who

told you about this meeting?"

"Nobody," the detective said. "We're here for him." She nodded toward the cowboy. "But I can't leave without those hostages."

The cowboy smirked when the detective referred to him, watching the cops in the mirror. The smirk turned into a wicked grin exposing a mouth of yellowed teeth, a chunk of them missing. Now he was laughing audibly, a deep, slow bellow, the sound echoing through the restaurant.

Everybody watched him.

"Do you know how many pigs've come lookin' for me, girl?" the cowboy said at last.

The detective licked her lips and straightened her fingers before tightening them around the pistol again. "Drop the shotgun or I'll drop you. Something tells me these men wouldn't give a shit about that, and I'd like to put you in the ground."

The cowboy grinned that horrible grin. "As you wish." The shotgun clattered to the floor.

"Raise your hands and step back toward me. Slowly."

The cowboy met Eddie's gaze, his grin morphing into something more menacing. He raised his hands above his head and stepped backwards.

The detective gestured to the younger cop. The guy looked shocked. The detective nodded, and the cop nodded in return, his eyes wide. He fumbled his pistol into its holster and pulled a pair of handcuffs out of his ass.

"Slowly," the detective said as the cowboy approached her. "Nobody else try anything. We're all better off with him in cuffs." She kept her gun trained on Saul while the cop behind her kept his on Saul's men. That cop hadn't moved a muscle. Shit, he might not have even blinked.

The cowboy came to a halt three feet from the detective. She nodded at the cop with the handcuffs and he stepped carefully toward the cowboy.

The cowboy looked at Eddie again, not smiling now. Absolute darkness lived behind his eyes, Eddie could feel it, as if the cowboy was the grim reaper himself. Maybe he was. A chill shivered through Eddie's bones.

The cop reached out to grab the cowboy's wrist and the cowboy spun so fast Eddie almost couldn't see him, the cowboy's hand slipping inside his jacket. A blur of movement and flash of silver later and the cop was holding his throat with one hand while the other reached out toward something ethereal, the fingers tragically stroking the air. By the time the blood had begun to squirt out of the cop's neck the cowboy had grabbed the man's pistol from its holster and was sprinting toward the bar at the side of the room.

Eddie wasn't sure who'd squeezed the trigger, but after that first shot the place became a warzone. A cacophony of bullets zoomed over his head in both directions. He launched himself onto the floor and hit it hard, pain stinging his palms and swelling inside his kneecaps. He squeezed his eyes shut as glass shattered around him, bracing himself for a bullet.

Dakota. She was right in the line of fire with her hands tied together.

He lifted his head. One of Saul's men lay unmoving on the floor, and Saul and the other three men had dispersed across the restaurant, shooting now at the cops from behind tables and chairs.

But Dakota was gone.

Alison couldn't remember diving behind the wall in the foyer but here she was. The pistol trembled in her hand, which was drenched in blood, as was her arm, neck, and face. She tasted the hot metal of it in her mouth. It wasn't her blood. The man it had belonged to—been a part of— lay pale and lifeless on the floor a few feet from her, his hand stretched out toward her like an accusation. Officer Bukowski, the rookie, the soon-to-be-father, who she had delivered to his death. She didn't even know his name.

The Texan will die for that.

Davies was crouched on her right firing shots through the hollow in the wall that separated the foyer from the restaurant. The Texan had sprinted toward the bar.

Alison peeked out from behind the wall. The other men were scattered across the back of the restaurant, squatting behind tables. One of the hostages—the male— was lying flat on his stomach; she couldn't tell if he'd been shot or not. There was no sign of the woman. In the space in the center of the room, a black sports bag sat on top of a round table. Either drugs or cash were inside that bag; whichever the case, The Texan wouldn't leave without it, Alison was sure of it.

She couldn't lose sight of that bag.

A bullet tore through the wall an inch from her face.

How long until back-up arrived? It couldn't be much longer. Keep them busy so they can't escape out the back.

She aimed at one of the men crouched behind a table on the right side of the room. The man's head came up like a Whac-A-Mole. She squeezed. He dropped.

Killing the pig had been easy, but getting out of here alive with the cash would be a challenge. And Saul and Eddie had to die. That was more important than anything.

Rufus squatted beneath the bar while bottles smashed around him, soaking him in pungent alcohol. He examined the gun he'd swiped from the dying cop. A full clip. He could do some damage with that.

He peered over the bar. One of the men lay dead in the center of the room, another lay dead on the right, and the waiter lay unmoving at the far wall. Eddie lay on his front, his head up and moving. Still alive. Good. A bullet was too merciful for him. That left Saul and two of his men, and the two pigs.

Time to thin the herd.

Rufus scanned the room for one of the two remaining thugs. Gotcha. The man, a broad-shouldered grunt with a face like a bulldog's, was reloading behind a group of chairs he'd fortified himself with. The pigs had his full attention. Rufus aimed the pistol and closed his left eye. The man finished reloading and peered over the chairs, exposing half of his body to Rufus. Three shots and the man was down.

Hallelujah.

Next.

Rufus scanned the room for the remaining thug, feeling how a shark must feel when it cruises the vast darkness of the ocean. Killing was easy work, and he missed being a working man. Maybe after this was all over he'd put out the word and take some contracts again. Why go down a legend when you can go down a god.

He spotted the final thug beside Saul, a skinny jumpy-looking fool who looked fresh out of San Quentin. The thug was firing at the cops from behind a large rectangular table flipped onto its side. Rufus could see only the man's head each time the man raised his weapons to fire, Saul's head peeking out intermittently beside him.

Saul glanced his way and met Rufus's gaze. Saul's eyes widened. Rufus smiled. Saul's eyes widened further. He ducked behind the table. A moment later the thug's head surfaced and the man looked straight over at Rufus. The head descended. The thug would soon be creeping toward

Rufus on Saul's orders.

Rufus slid to the end of the bar that was closest to Saul, where the thug would arrive from, and tucked his body tightly beneath it. He removed one of his daggers from his jacket and gripped the cool handle in his fist. The blade was hungry for blood and he would feed it. Gunshots continued to go off, but they were fewer now, and further between. The pigs would soon realize that most of the men were down, if they hadn't already, and would sweep the room.

Thirty seconds later, a shiny gun barrel appeared above Rufus's head as the man holding it no doubt wondered where its would-be victim had vanished to. Rufus lunged upwards like a Great White, the dagger coming up with him. He roared as the blade found the man's chin and went up through it all the way to the hilt. Rufus had put such force into the movement that he stood now holding the man high above his head with one hand, the dagger jammed in his skull and Rufus roaring still. He felt powerful, more powerful than he'd ever felt. He could kill a hundred men like this. They were beneath him. He was something else, something better, something more—

A gunshot bellowed and Rufus was thrown forward. He dropped behind the bar and grasped for the pistol he'd left on the floor. He snatched it and rose.

The male cop was out of the foyer and approaching the bar, gun raised. Something smashed into Rufus's chest and twisted his body backwards before he registered the flash of the pig's gun. But Rufus had squeezed the trigger as he'd been hit. Rufus saw the cop's head snap backwards as he crashed into the bottles behind the bar, more alcohol drenching him.

The cop hit the floor and lay still. Pain exploded inside Rufus's chest, but pain was of little concern right now. More pressing was Saul, Eddie, and the cash.

Looking for the latter, Rufus saw Eddie grab the bag from the table, throw it over his neck, and dart toward the kitchen, the shotgun in his hands.

Not today, Eddie.

Rufus lunged over the bar in a single bound and chased after him.

"No!" Alison had screamed when Davies went down, and now she screamed it again kneeling over him. It was all going to shit, and it was her fault.

She pulled herself together. There was plenty of time to feel guilty. Right now she had to get the Texan.

She grabbed her Glock and sprinted for the doorway the Texan had disappeared through and crashed through it, feeling no fear now but a focused calm.

The Texan was at the end of the kitchen, about to turn a corner. She aimed and fired. The man crashed into an oven, buckling its steel door. He vanished beneath the island of countertops and appliances that ran the along the center of the kitchen.

Alison moved toward him, pistol raised. The floor behind the countertops came into view as she neared the back of the room, but the Texan wasn't there.

She sensed him before she saw him. Something gleamed at the edge of her vision. Then a sudden burning heat in her side.

The shotgun was heavier than he'd expected, and the bag of cash on his back wasn't making things easier. Nor was his leg, still sore from the wound the day before despite being treated by a nurse who had owed him a favor.

Eddie swept the kitchen with the barrel, looking for Saul. He'd seen him flee through here only moments ago. Shiny steel glinted at Eddie from every side. He took a left into a large pantry. Saul was waiting for him, holding a pistol to Dakota's head, who had at some point managed to get her hands untied and removed the gag.

Saul said, "Your bitch thought she could sneak out the back door. Drop the gun and give me the bag and I'll let you both live."

"Hurt her and I'll blow you away."

A gunshot went off nearby, possibly as near as the kitchen. Saul flinched, the gun drifting a few inches from Dakota's head. Dakota snatched at the opportunity by raising her arm and driving something into Saul's shiny shoe. Saul screamed like his skin was being peeled as Dakota rolled away from him.

Eddie pulled the trigger. The shotgun almost jumped out of his hands, winding him and sending shockwaves through his wrist. Saul's head popped like a grape, painting the room red and pink with blood and brain.

Eddie gazed open-mouthed at Dakota. She was spattered with blood, fleshy red pieces caught in her hair.

Dakota grabbed the pistol Saul had dropped and slipped it into her jeans.

"Lose the shotgun," she said. "It's too conspicuous out there."

Eddie nodded, relieved to hear her speak, and dropped the weapon.

Dakota ran for the back door. Eddie took one final glance at the headless Saul sprawled on his back, a steak knife sticking up through his snakeskin loafer.

The man's head had always been too big.

The Texan had sliced her with the dagger, but she'd seen him coming and twisted her body out of the way just enough to avoid the worst of it. It hurt like hell. And she'd dropped the Glock.

Alison ducked as the blade came around again, but didn't see the fist that followed until it collided with her jaw and sent her reeling onto the tile.

"You like that, bitch?"

Alison crawled backwards as the Texan stepped toward her, desperately scanning her surroundings for something to defend herself with.

"Only thing I hate more'n a pig is a woman," the Texan said. "But pigs and women have something in common: they both end up in the kitchen." The man had been shot twice, at least, but, except for the dark, wet patches on his jacket, you wouldn't know it.

"What the hell are you?" Alison said.

"The devil." He bared yellow teeth and stepped forward until he was standing over her, the dagger dripping blood in his right hand. She caught an overwhelming stench of alcohol and saw that his jacket was soaked with more than just blood. He'd been hiding behind the bar. All those bottles . . .

Alison shoved a hand into her pocket and fished out the golden Zippo and flipped it open. She thumbed the wheel and a flame leapt out of its mouth.

"Lose something?" she said, and tossed it at the Texan.

His jacket ignited immediately. Shock swarmed across his face, followed by terror.

Alison kicked him in the crotch and scuttled backwards. The Texan buckled onto his knees, wailing as the flames spread across his shoulders, hands grasping at his jacket.

Alison rolled the two yards to her pistol and snatched it from the floor. She pointed it at the Texan's head.

He was screaming now, the flames on his legs, in his hair, devouring his face, and looking right at her, into her eyes, as if begging her to pull the trigger.

She lowered the gun a few inches and shot him in the shoulder. He collapsed onto the floor on his back, silent, as the flames consumed him.

His screaming resumed.

Alison leaned a hand on the countertop and pulled herself to her feet.

The Texan writhed in agony. The flames had eaten most of his hair now, the leather jacket coming apart, exposing scarlet skin. The acrid stench of burning flesh made her want to puke.

She watched him scream, and when he looked about to pass out, she put a bullet in his skull.

His hairless, sizzling head was shiny and pink. Like a pig.

Alison spat on his corpse.

They burst through the restaurant's back doors into a narrow alleyway washed in the glow of the moon. The night was warm and filled with promise. A lone piece of graffiti in an ugly black scrawl marked the otherwise untouched brick wall: "FUCK THE NRA."

Halfway down the alley, Dakota stopped jogging and Eddie caught up with her.

"I'm so glad you're okay," he said. "I was so fucking worried. Man, was I worried. I missed you."

"Is the money in there?" Dakota said, her blank expression impossible to read.

"What? Yeah yeah, the money. Well, half of it. Are you okay?"

"What do you mean 'half of it'?"

"The other mil' is in a locker in the airport. It was the only leverage I had."

"You got the key?"

Eddie looked at her curiously. "Yeah, I got the key. What's with the questions?"

Dakota's eyes narrowed, the moonlight bathing her face in silver. Her hand reached behind her back and returned with Saul's pistol. She pressed the cold muzzle against Eddie's forehead.

"Give me the key," she said.

Eddie's breath seeped out of him like air from a blown tire. "What are you—"

Dakota fired a round behind him. Pain exploded inside Eddie's ear, followed quickly by a piercing ringing. He dropped onto one knee, a hand against his head, and heard someone yelling, then realized it was him.

The gun kissed his forehead again.

"I said give me the key."

Eddie reached inside his pocket, hoping to Christ the key was still there. How could she do this to him after everything they'd just been through?

His fingers found the key.

"Here," he said, extending his hand.

Dakota snatched it from his fingers, the gun never breaking contact with his skull. "Take the bag off."

Eddie lifted the bag over his neck and dropped it at her feet. The ease with which Dakota pulled it onto her shoulder surprised him.

"Did she cry when you murdered her?" Dakota said.

Eddie looked up at her, his heart deflating in his chest. Silver tears streamed down her face like drops from the moon. That was it, then—she knew.

"Dakota—"

"Answer me!"

Eddie flinched. "Yeah, she cried. But—"

"You bastard. You fucking bastard."

"Dakota, I didn't—"

"How could you do something like that?" She was crying audibly now, her body shuddering. "How could you do it? My sister. My baby sister."

Eddie opened his mouth to speak, but what answer could he give? He had no idea how he could do something like that.

"Tell me it isn't true," Dakota said, wiping her eyes with her free hand. "Tell me that bastard was lying."

Eddie met her gaze and held it. "I don't know what to tell you, but Saul wasn't lying."

Dakota screamed at the sky so violently it must have shredded her throat.

"My sister's name. What is it?" Her voice raspy. She pressed the gun hard into Eddie's skull, almost knocking him over.

"Dakota, wait—"

"Say her name!"

"Kaya."

"Kaya what?"

"Kaya White."

"Say it again!"

"Kaya White."

"Say it again!"

"Kaya White! Kaya White! Please, Dakota, I didn't mean to, don't fucking shoot, Jesus Christ."

Dakota stared at him. "Goodbye, Eddie."

Eddie swallowed. "I love you, Dakota."

Dakota's expression softened momentarily.

"I hate you," she said.

Eddie closed his eyes, accepting what was about to happen. No more running. It was what he deserved, and he doubted he could live with himself much longer anyway.

A feeling of peace descended over him.

The sound of the restaurant's doors crashing open behind.

"Drop the gun," came a woman's voice. The detective. Eddie wasn't sure if he felt disappointed or relieved. But he wouldn't let her arrest Dakota.

Dakota said, "Stay out of this. He murdered my—"

"Your sister. Kaya. I know."

Confusion settled across Dakota's face. "How do you—"

"You're Indian, right?" The detective's voice was louder, closer, her footfalls approaching. "I'm the homicide detective investigating your sister's murder. We know from D.N.A. tests that Kaya had a Native American parent, and we know that a young Native American woman was asking around for Kaya at the club she used to work at. It didn't take me long to connect the dots."

"Then you understand why I have to do this."

"I understand it," the detective said, right behind Eddie now. "But it's too easy a way out for him. What's death next to a life behind bars? Having to live with your mistakes day after day, forever. That's hell. Killing him is mercy."

Dakota swallowed, her face tight with concentration.

"You can keep that bag," the detective said, "I never saw it. And I never saw you. No one knows you were here. No one will come looking for you. Just let me arrest this man. It's the only way I can let you go and forget you were ever here."

Eddie said, "It's a good deal, Dakota. Live your life and be free."

"You shut up!" Dakota roared, pressing the cold metal further into his skin.

"You don't want to become a killer, Dakota," the detective said. "Death will follow you home."

Dakota's face contorted with rage and the gun trembled in her hand. Eddie shut his eyes, sure a bullet would come, but instead the gun broke contact with his skin.

He opened his eyes. Dakota was crying, the gun at her side. She let it clatter to the ground.

"I hate you, Eddie," she said, looking into his eyes. "Never forget what you did. Because I won't."

She spun on her heels and jogged down the alley, a million dollars over her shoulder. The moonlight faded into shadow near the mouth of the alley, swallowing Dakota as she passed through it onto the street.

She didn't look back.

"Hands behind your head," the detective said.

Eddie's heart sank deep down inside him like an anchor to the lightless ocean floor.

Cold steel clamped around his wrists.

Sirens sounded in the distance.

The sky was black and eternal.

Epilogue

Charlie stared out the open window in the passenger seat, the wind tossing his hair back, mesmerized by all the bison, hundreds of them, maybe thousands, roaming the green and yellow fields of South Dakota's seventy-one-thousand-acre Custer State Park. Taking the highway through the park was a slightly longer route to their destination but Alison had taken it for exactly this reason. At eleven years old, Charlie was moving out of his animal-obsessed phase, and it would only be so long before his child's sense of awe and wonder became replaced by teenage apathy. It made her smile to see him so enthralled, and she was quite enthralled herself: the infinite beauty of this part of the country was beyond anything she had imagined when they packed up the car and left Los Angeles. And the air—so pure. It smelled of freedom. And, at the moment, manure.

"This is cool, huh buddy?" she said.

"This. Is. Awesome!"

Charlie tapped at her phone from its holder on the dashboard and selected another song from her '80s playlist, the subject of his latest fascination (they hadn't left the decade yet since leaving L.A.). A bass synth and drum machine introduced "Out of Touch" by Hall & Oates. Alison turned it up and accelerated, enjoying the sensation of the hot sun washing over her face as the wind blew back her hair.

It felt good to feel good.

One hour later they arrived at the northwest corner of Pine Ridge Reservation and shortly after that a large building of pretty orange and brown brick. The building looked new, because it was. Less than three years old, in fact.

Alison switched the engine off. "Okay buddy, five minutes in here and then we're back on the road to Rapid City where we can get a room for the night."

"What's this place?" Charlie said.

Alison pointed at the sign. "'The Kaya White Women's Center for Trauma Recovery.'"

"What's that mean?"

"It means that this place helps women who've had bad experiences to live happy lives. Come on."

They exited the car, Alison startled again by the silent serenity of this vast state. They reached the front doors of the Center and went inside.

An Indian woman at reception smiled at them, looking a little puzzled.

"Hello there," she said. "Are you lost?"

"We're here to see somebody."

"A patient?" the woman said, looking confused.

"Ms. White, actually."

"Ah. Do you have an appointment?"

"No, but it will only take a moment, and we've come a long way."

"Can I get your name?"

"Alison Lockley."

The woman picked up a phone and relayed the details.

"Ms. White will be with you in a moment," she said, and clicked at her computer.

Alison took Charlie by the hand and wandered around the reception area. Photographs of women smiling in clusters, most of them dark-skinned but not all, hung on the walls. A few of the women exuded the professional confidence of doctors. A doctor—that's what she should have been. Saving lives rather than avenging them.

"What's that?" Charlie said, pointing at a scarlet banner over the entrance doorway. In the center of the banner eight white triangles pointed outward in a circle like the rays of a sun. A thick blue band bordered the banner.

"That's the flag of the Oglala Tribe, on whose land you now stand," said a woman's voice behind them.

Alison turned to see Dakota standing beside the reception desk.

"The red symbolizes the blood shed by my people in defense of this land. The circle of eight tepees represents the eight districts of the reservation. And the blue represents the United States, which borders us and which we are part of. Hello Alison. And who is this?"

"This is Charlie, my son."

"Hello, Charlie. He's a handsome one, isn't he?"

Charlie's cheeks turned red as the flag. He hadn't yet managed to take his gaze off Dakota, probably falling in love with her.

"Let's talk in my office," Dakota said. "Piama here will take good care of Charlie."

Dakota's office was pretty, and unlike any other. It had all the usuals—desk, chair, computer, phone—but potted plants hung from the ceiling, the plants growing down out of the pots and reaching for the window, and Hollywood movie posters dotted the walls: *Pulp Fiction*; *Kill Bill: Volume 1*; *L.A. Confidential*; *Jaws*; *The Shining*; *Chinatown*; *The Good, the Bad and the Ugly*; *Thelma & Louise*; *Seven*;

True Romance.

"You like movies," Alison said.

"I live for them. Please, sit." Dakota gestured toward the chair opposite the desk as she dropped into her own.

Alison sat into the seat. "I'm not here on police business, if that's what you're thinking. Actually, I'm not a cop anymore."

Dakota said nothing.

"I'm not here on any business. We're moving to New York State, Charlie and I, to build a new life, start fresh. This place was on the way, kind of, so I thought I'd swing by."

A question came to her. "Which is the fake name, Dakota or Ramona?"

"Does it matter?"

"Not really, but it would be nice to know your real name."

"Ramona is my birth name. People here have only ever known me by that name."

Alison nodded. "It's nice what you've done with the money. I guess some good came from all of that, in the end."

"Yes, our anonymous donor was very generous," Dakota said, a smirk at the corner of her lips. "I'm happy. It feels good helping people in need."

"What do you do here, exactly?"

"We help young Native American women fleeing from sexual and other abuse in their homes, or elsewhere.

Not just Native American women, we don't turn away anyone here, but mostly. Many of them are addicted to substances, and we help them with that too. Most of the women come from the reservation, but, as word has spread of our existence, some women from cities across the country have arrived, seeking shelter and counseling. We give them therapy, but we also educate and train them to help them reintegrate into society, and find—and hold onto—jobs more easily. We teach them how to be independent and resilient in the face of discrimination and everything else they will face outside those doors.

"Some of the stories those women have told me would break your heart, but watching them grow as individuals while they're in here, seeing them finally walk out those doors as confident, strong women, optimistic and ready to face society head-on—that's the best feeling in the world."

"I have to say, I'm impressed," Alison said. "I thought you'd be living in a villa in the Mediterranean. But then, about a year ago, I read about this place, and knew you were involved even before I saw that 'Ramona White' was the name of its director."

Dakota smiled. "Well, some of our anonymous donor's money helped to repair the community and improve living conditions, but otherwise every cent went toward the Center. I live in the same home I always have. I might have a pretty big TV to watch movies on, but that's all." She winked.

Alison chuckled. "I think you've earned that." She

stood up. "Well, I just wanted to say hi and see this place for myself. I best get Charlie some food before he gets moody."

Alison hesitated. "I'm proud of what you've done here."

Dakota had remained seated and looked up now at Alison with glistening eyes. "Thank you . . . for doing what you did."

Alison smiled. "Don't mention it."

She tossed Dakota a wave and left the room to find her son and the open road and the promise of a better life.

Eddie stared at himself in the mirror. The wig (to mask his buzz cut) looked ridiculous, and would distract from the credibility of his performance. But the knee-length white tunic and purple cloak over one shoulder looked good, authentic. So did the sandals. Ordinarily the stark white walls of this hellish place were anything but inspiring, but, today, wearing his costume before the first dress rehearsal, they helped Eddie get into character.

He watched himself recite some of his lines: "'Nay, an I tell you that, I'll ne'er look you i' the face again: but those that understood him smiled at one another and shook their heads; but, for mine own part, it was Greek to me.'"

Eddie saw the door open behind his shoulder and Skinny Pete slunk into the room—the man slunk everywhere he went, looking out the sides of his eyes like a serpent—carrying his own costume. They'd arranged to practice their lines together before the dress rehearsal. Some of the other inmates—the ones not involved in this production of *Julius Caesar* for Shakespeare at San Quentin—would be watching the rehearsal, and, since they were going to be laughed at anyway, Eddie and Skinny Pete had figured they may as well not maximize that laughter by totally messing up their lines.

"Eddie," Skinny Pete said, shutting the door behind him.

"Skinny," Eddie said. He'd had to give the guard a pack of cigarettes for the privilege of the man waiting outside the door rather than inside the room, but it was worth it. Few things are more off-putting while reciting Shakespeare than a prison guard staring at you, smirking.

"You nervous?" Skinny said, dropping his costume onto a table and quickly undressing. A tattoo across his flat belly screamed "LIVE FREE."

"Not really," Eddie said, which was true, more or less. He couldn't give a shit about what the other inmates thought of him. He already didn't get along with most of them, largely because he kept to himself and signed up for every course and extracurricular activity available. But he was nervous about what Ms. Summers, the young theater director at the helm of Arts in Corrections and Shakespeare at San Quentin, thought of his performance. Maybe it was just a fantasy from serving three long, womanless years of a thirty-year sentence, but he thought he saw a spark in her eye whenever she looked at him. Even if he was wrong, she was a nice lady, kind and non-judgmental, and he wanted to do her proud. They all did.

"Yeah, me neither," Skinny said, scratching his fore-arm anxiously. He pulled his tunic over his head.

"Yo, can I ask you something?" Skinny said.

Eddie turned to face him.

"Is it true you represented yourself in your trial before you got here?"

"Who told you that?"

"I heard some of the blacks talking 'bout you in the yard. They call you 'Saint Eddie,' you know that?"

"I heard it was 'Eddie the Martyr.'"

"Either way they think you're up your own ass. Yo, I'm just tellin' you 'cause you need to watch your back in here. For real, bro, they don't like your style."

"Too bad for them."

"Is it true?"

"What?"

"That you represented yourself and plead guilty."

"That's correct, Skinny." But it's not like he'd had much choice. The police had extracted his D.N.A. from a hair on his belt that he'd tied Kaya's hands with and stupidly forgotten to remove before burying her, and two witness-es had identified him: the concierge of the condominium building, and the kid who'd looked him in the eye when he, Floyd and Sawyer had stumbled out of the bushes after burying the bodies. Not to mention the testimony of the detective who'd arrested him. (She hadn't said a word about Dakota, and claimed instead that she'd overheard Eddie admit to the murders before the shit hit the fan in Saul's restaurant.) But, regardless of all that, it was true that Eddie hadn't wanted to deny anything.

Skinny grabbed his own head in both hands. "You crazy, bro. Who does that? You're fuckin' *nuts*."

"Maybe, but I'm also at peace with myself and the decisions I made."

"Why you'd do it? I gotta know."

Eddie sighed and faced the mirror. "It was the only way I could show the person I loved that I was truly sorry." He watched himself speak, hating how little words meant, in the end.

"They forgive you?"

"I doubt it."

Skinny shook his head, grinning stupidly. "Yo, you the only guilty person in here. We all s'posed to fight the system together."

"We've been fighting the system our whole lives and look where it got us."

Skinny was out of responses, it seemed.

"What is it you're innocent of, Skinny?"

"Armed robbery. But it wasn't me, bro. Cops pinned it on me. Racial profiling and all that shit."

"You're white as fuckin' snow, Skinny."

"Yeah, and the cops who arrested me were spics."

Eddie shook his head. Some people would blame the starving kids in Africa before they'd blame themselves.

"'Nay, an I tell you that, I'll ne'er look you i' the face again: but those that understood him smiled at one another and shook their heads; but, for mine own part, it was Greek to me . . .'"

Acknowledgements

Writing a novel has been a dream of mine for as long as I can remember, literally—I attempted to write my first crime thriller at ten years old. In those early days I never got much further than eight pages. Sixteen years later, I've finally managed to finish one. If it wasn't for the support of my parents, who, over the course of my life, always encouraged and supported my artistic endeavors, I could not have reached this point in my career which has allowed me to scrape together enough ability and dedication to write, and finish, a novel. Thank you, Mam and Dad.

This novel could not exist without the unwavering support of my wonderful wife, Alex, who often during the process of writing this novel was the primary source of our income, working difficult serving shifts late into the nights and early mornings. Thank you, Alex, for never once complaining about us having to live extremely frugally while I typed word after word about a bunch of people who don't exist.

Thanks to my brother, Patrick, for being the best sibling and friend, and for being a truly good person and the kind of younger brother I often look up to and could turn to for anything.

Thanks to my good friend Heath Brougher for his limitless support and kindness since the day we met, and for the infinite passion he has for Into the Void, as well as the stellar job he does there as poetry editor. Thanks also to Amanda Gaines and Laura Halpin for being the best nonfiction and flash fiction editors respectively that Into the Void could have. Heath, Amanda and Laura have been with Into the Void virtually since the beginning, and I'm so proud of what we have accomplished thus far.

Thanks to both my dad and punk rock for teaching me the value and importance of working hard and doing things myself, on my own terms. For teaching me how to believe in myself.

As an homage of sorts to film, books and music, *Nobody Move* couldn't exist without the art that inspired it. To that end I thank every daydreamer who created something out of nothing and helped make our planet a less lonely and more interesting and fun place.

Finally, I thank you, good reader, for splashing your hard-earned cash and taking a chance on this book.

Note from the Publisher

Thank you so much for purchasing this book and supporting small press publishing and the arts. We truly appreciate it.

You may have noticed the frequent references to music throughout the book. You can check out those songs, along with a selection of other songs not mentioned, on the official *Nobody Move* soundtrack on Spotify, curated by the author.

We hope you enjoyed reading *Nobody Move*. We'd love to know how you found it. Please consider posting an honest review of the book on its Amazon and Goodreads pages, and/or anywhere else you wish. Aside from purchasing a book, reviews are the most effective way to support a writer. The quantity of reviews (positive or negative) of a book increases how many people discover that book, even if the reviews are just once sentence long.

Stay tuned for...

Coming September 2020

It's the year 2000 and 78-year-old Mickey O'Rourke has been a Los Angeles P.I. for a very long time. He'd thought he'd seen it all until the disappearance of porn star Jeffrey Strokes sends him from the sex-filled studios of Porn Valley to the desperate ghettos of Compton and the crossfires of a strange and sadistic drug dealer who calls himself "The Samurai," where Mickey's final case becomes his biggest test. Flash back to 1999 and struggling hair salon employee Jemeka Johnson, suspecting boyfriend Ray-Ray of infidelity, follows him one night from their East Compton home to what turns out to be a drug deal gone sour. Saving Ray-Ray's life with her battered Ford Tempo, Jemeka finds herself tossed onto a dark and dangerous path—one that offers huge reward for someone bold enough to seize it. Meanwhile, tired of robbing small-town diners and sleeping in filthy motel rooms (and with a rapidly escalating dope addiction to feed), newlyweds Richie and Alabama return to L.A. in search of the perfect score. Paths cross and past meets present as terrible actions hurtle toward terrible consequences—and no one will ever be the same again.